The Antique Hunter's

Guide to Murder

THE ANTIQUE HUNTER'S Guide to Murder

❧ A NOVEL ❧

C. L. Miller

ATRIA BOOKS

NEW YORK ❦ LONDON ❦ TORONTO ❦ SYDNEY ❦ NEW DELHI

ATRIA
BOOKS

An Imprint of Simon & Schuster, LLC
1230 Avenue of the Americas
New York, NY 10020

First Atria Books hardcover edition February 2024

ATRIA BOOKS and colophon are trademarks of Simon & Schuster, LLC

Simon & Schuster: Celebrating 100 Years of Publishing in 2024

For information about special discounts for bulk purchases, please contact Simon & Schuster Special Sales at 1-866-506-1949 or business@simonandschuster.com.

The Simon & Schuster Speakers Bureau can bring authors to your live event. For more information or to book an event, contact the Simon & Schuster Speakers Bureau at 1-866-248-3049 or visit our website at www.simonspeakers.com.

Interior design by Yvonne Taylor

Manufactured in the United States of America

1   3   5   7   9   10   8   6   4   2

Library of Congress Cataloging-in-Publication Data

Names: Miller, C. L. (Cara L.) author.
Title: The antique hunter's guide to murder : a novel / C. L. Miller.
Description: New York : Atria Books, 2024. | Series: The antique hunter's guide to murder
Identifiers: LCCN 2023038063 (print) | LCCN 2023038064 (ebook) |
ISBN 9781668032008 (hardcover) | ISBN 9781668032015 (paperback) |
ISBN 9781668032022 (ebook)
Subjects: LCGFT: Detective and mystery fiction. | Novels.
Classification: LCC PR6113.I5562 A84 2024 (print) | LCC PR6113.I5562 (ebook) |
DDC 823/.92--dc23/eng/20230920

LC record available at https://lccn.loc.gov/2023038063
LC ebook record available at https://lccn.loc.gov/2023038064

ISBN 978-1-6680-3200-8
ISBN 978-1-6680-3202-2 (ebook)

For my mother,
Judith Miller
and my father,
Martin Miller.

"'Know thyself' was written over the portal of the antique world. Over the portal of the new world 'Be thyself' shall be written."

—Oscar Wilde

This book was written in consultation with international antiques expert, Judith Miller (1951–2023), a regular specialist on BBC *Antiques Roadshow*. Judith was also the co-founder of the bestselling annual *Miller's Antiques Price Guide*, started in 1979. She went on to write more than 120 books on antiques and interiors.

PROLOGUE

If Arthur Crockleford had been a normal antiques dealer, then perhaps this night would never have arrived.

Arthur hunched over his desk making his final preparations. He had just finished gluing the last photograph into his journal when he heard the rumble of tires on the cobbles behind his antiques shop. He checked the time on his Georgian longcase clock—he adored that clock; it was one of the first antiques he'd ever bought, from a dealer on Portobello Road—the brass hands showed twenty-eight minutes past one in the morning.

A rush of icy night air swept through the back door as it opened and down the long corridor to enter the shop, which was lit by the table lamp on Arthur's desk. The gust pricked the hairs on the back of his neck.

They're here.

He shivered, and his fountain pen marked the final full stop in his journal. The clock chimed the half hour.

Time is up.

Arthur rose and hurried to the stairs leading to his apartment above the shop. He knew each noisy step and had to climb over a couple to avoid detection.

His old knee injury clicked.

At the top of the stairs he stopped, scanning the shadows below him, wondering which one of them had come. All the lights in the apartment were off and he was surrounded by thick black night.

A sweep of the rooms reassured him that everything was in order.

The tap of someone's footsteps on the medieval floorboards below made Arthur shudder.

For decades, he had loved every second of his secret life. Until Cairo. If he'd made different choices, left this underground world behind, then maybe tonight could have been avoided. But what was done, was done, wasn't it? He could only hope Freya would one day understand. And that it wasn't too late to make things right.

Arthur walked back down the stairs, this time intending to be heard.

In the dim lighting, he scanned the antiques around him. Each was priced to sell, but it didn't mean he wanted to part with them. Seeing all the treasures he loved ignited a fury in him, but he knew this was one fight he, at last, would not be able to win. Arthur ran his hand through his shaggy gray hair, readjusting his cravat with the other. If this was to be the end, at least Carole would be proud he'd made such an effort to die stylishly.

"Hello? Is anyone there?" he called, hoping the neighbors would hear him. It would give a more accurate time of death if that was needed.

He positioned himself beside a mahogany tilt-top table, which held a couple of his favorite vases.

Maybe he should've tried to set off the alarm. Maybe he should've screamed out. Maybe he should've raced for the phone to call the police. But the darker side of the antiquities world was finally catching up with him and he conceded that he probably couldn't outrun it forever. He was too old for running.

It's over to you now, Freya.

Out of the coal-black corridor a figure emerged. Arthur strained his eyes. Shadows hung over the intruder's face, but Arthur could just make out what they were doing: they were tugging at their gloves—checking they were on.

They stepped into the shop and into the light.

"You weren't who I was expecting," Arthur said.

1

"All hunts begin with something that has been lost . . . or taken."
—Arthur Crockleford

Freya

Outside the Victoria and Albert Museum in London I brushed my fingertips over a shrapnel dent in the building's wall. It had seen a lot, that wall, and had survived whatever had been thrown at it since being built in 1909. No war or hurricane had taken it down. I wished I were as strong.

Early that morning I'd left my house before the real estate agent arrived and fought the commuter's hustle, bus after bus, to get to South Kensington. I'd waited in a café nearby until the museum opened. The V&A was the place I always escaped to, my very own safe haven.

A smiling man opened the museum's main entrance. I was one of the first inside—the tourists were probably still having their buffet breakfast.

The familiar smell of polish hit me, then the echo of my boots tapping on the tiles in the cavernous hall. I smiled. It was almost enough to make me forget the "For Sale" sign being nailed to my gate.

Ever since my ex-husband, James, moved out almost nine years ago he had insisted the house be sold. Apparently, a large Victorian house in an expensive suburb was wasted on me. James had finally agreed I could live

3

in the house until our daughter, Jade, was eighteen, and now that she had left for university in America there was little I could do to stop the sale. I couldn't afford the mortgage alone when the child support stopped— Jade wasn't a child any longer.

I was almost on autopilot when I reached the beginning of the British Galleries on the first floor. I passed the Great Bed of Ware, an enormous bed so large it could sleep two families and so famous it was mentioned in Shakespeare's *Twelfth Night*. Farther along on my right was a free-standing bookcase like the one Samuel Pepys once owned. Eventually I reached the stone stairway to the third floor and the Chippendale furniture. I hadn't been part of the antiques world for over twenty years, but I still adored a finely crafted chair or a beautifully gilded mirror.

I knew each item in the Chippendale furniture section by heart, and something about the Chippendale Garrick Bed (named after the once-famed actor David Garrick) looked wrong. I leaned as close as I dared and studied every inch of the ornate fabric. A couple of moments later I saw it. A very slight indent on the cover. A visitor had decided to check the comfort level of the mattress and left their mark.

Annoyance bubbled inside me and I looked around for a gallery assistant.

My phone rang with Aunt Carole's ringtone. Jade had put that jingly ringtone on before she left for LA and I'd never gotten around to changing it. I pulled out my phone and silenced it. I desperately wanted to hear my aunt's voice, but now wasn't the time. I scanned the empty gallery and walked back toward the stairs in the hope of finding a member of staff when my phone rang again, vibrating insistently in my pocket. I should've known Carole was not to be ignored. She would only keep calling until I answered.

"Carole," I whispered. "I'm sorry, I—"

"Freya, darling," Carole interrupted dramatically. "Is it today?"

"Yes, they're putting a sign up this morning," I replied.

"What a rotter James is." She was trying to sound annoyed, but there was something strange in Carole's tone; it was the voice she used when she was acting. "Might be time to let go? Find a new path, a new adventure somewhere—"

"I won't move." I tried to keep my voice steady. "I won't give him the satisfaction."

"Of course." Carole sniffed. "But, darling . . . I may need you to come home for a bit."

"Why?" It wasn't like Carole to ask such a thing; I hadn't set foot in Little Meddington for decades. "What's wrong?"

"Well . . ."

"Carole?" My gut twisted and my pulse picked up. It was unusual for Carole to be unsure of her words. "Are you all right?"

She took a deep breath. "Something terrible happened . . . to Arthur . . . it's so . . ."

"Arthur?" The calm I had momentarily found was shattered. What on earth was Carole doing bringing up *that* man when she knew what he'd put me through all those years ago in Cairo? She knew I hated to hear his very name, let alone discuss whatever trouble he was in. I headed for the stairs—this conversation was probably not one for a museum.

"It's just . . . they're saying he fell down those old stairs in the dark and had a heart attack, but there has to be more to it. I'd gone to check on him because he phoned me on Saturday afternoon and sounded strange. When I got there . . ." Carole's voice cracked.

"Carole?" I froze on the museum staircase. "Is he . . . ?" I couldn't say the word "dead" out loud, but I knew in my heart that was what Carole meant.

Is he gone?

My first reaction was an unexpected wave of relief. But it was immediately chased by a sharp pang of guilt about my initial response. Arthur was the person I liked least in the world, but he was Carole's closest friend—Arthur was family to her. And once, long ago, he'd been like a grandfather to me.

"I wasn't going to call you with everything going on today, but when I was standing outside the shop that new solicitor slicked his way over and told me he needs to see me *and* you right away."

I could hear the tremor in Carole's voice, but I couldn't take in her words.

"I'm so sorry, Carole," I managed to say. She blew her nose, and I could imagine the tears tracking down her cheeks. I wondered if Carole was fixated on this solicitor because the thought of losing Arthur was just too much to process. It was a quick, easy decision. "Of course I'll come up and help you out with the solicitor."

"Oh, how wonderful." Carole brightened instantly, and I knew she'd been angling for that all along. "I know you and Arthur didn't see eye to eye ever since . . ." She hesitated. "Well, we won't go into that, will we? Not the time. But I know he wanted you here."

I knew he wouldn't have, but Carole needed me and that was what mattered. "I'll pack a bag and get to Colchester station this afternoon—I'll stay for as long as you need me. We'll take on the solicitor together."

"Excellent. I'll pick you up if you text me when you're on your way."

"No. It's quite all right. I'll catch a taxi," I said quickly. Carole was the worst driver in East Anglia and her ancient convertible Mercedes was highly impractical for small country lanes. Carole believed she could handle any speed. We'd never agreed on the topic.

"Absolutely not! It's spring sunshine and roof down weather!"

How could I say no after what had just happened? "Well, if you're absolutely sure you're up to driving?" I would need to pack appropriately: weatherproof jacket, scarves for my hair, and a copy of my life insurance.

"I'm absolutely fine to drive. See you soon."

After I hung up, unwanted memories of Arthur began to surface. I tried to quash them by focusing on the merits of splurging on a taxi to get home from the V&A and pack quickly, but they wouldn't be silenced.

I'd been a twelve-year-old orphan with a badly burned right palm—

after unsuccessfully trying to open my parents' flaming bedroom door—when Carole first took me in. The children at my new school stared at my hand and didn't want to befriend the odd girl. I couldn't answer all the prying questions of my inquisitive peers. Everyone wanted to know how I'd survived a fire, but they didn't seem to want to know the girl behind the bandage. All I knew back then was that I was broken and different. Soon, I'd stopped talking altogether.

When Carole first introduced me to Arthur Crockleford, her best friend, he was standing in his antiques shop polishing a silver candlestick. He was about fifty, of average height, with salt-and-pepper hair immaculately swept to one side, and wore a bright blue suit. Arthur's smile was warm and his eyes kind. ""It's lovely to meet you," he'd said. "Carole tells me you have an eye for detail." He held the candlestick up to the light and I saw the unpolished side his cloth had missed. I walked over and pointed it out.

Arthur had tutted and kept polishing. He asked about my father's job in the British Museum and my mother's talent as an art restorer—he was never perturbed by my lack of response; he would keep chatting while I absorbed the warmth of his presence. Arthur helped me focus on their lives, not their deaths. I loved him for it almost instantly.

Carole was worried about my silence, but Arthur had a plan.

Six months after my parents' death, Arthur invited Carole and me to his shop one Saturday afternoon to show me an antique porcelain plate that had been repaired with kintsugi—the Japanese art of putting broken pottery back together with gold. I traced my finger along the shimmering lines. Words I'd shut away began to form on my tongue and in my breath. "It's . . . beautiful." My voice was rusty and weak, but Carole had bear-hugged me when she heard it.

"This plate is different than before, but it's still precious," said Arthur. "Most of us have been broken in one way or another. We don't need to hide the scars, for they make us who we are. This break was mended with real gold."

In that shop, holding on to the kintsugi plate, I felt something loosen in my chest.

"Who broke the plate?" I asked. "Why?" But Arthur had shrugged and put the plate back in the cabinet.

"I must know how it was broken," I demanded.

"That isn't the important part of the story," he replied.

"It is to me. I need to know."

Arthur smiled. "Very well. Long ago it belonged to a family who lived by the sea, until one night a tsunami crashed into their house. Only one son survived. When he returned to the land where his home once stood, all he found was that broken plate." Arthur tapped the glass cabinet that held the plate on its stand. "He mended it, placed it in his bag, and set sail across the seas for new adventures."

I had pressed my nose to the glass. I understood how broken that boy must have felt, and I admired how he'd mended the plate and set out for a new life. Arthur had given me hope, showing me that pieces like the plate could glitter with mystery and exploration. It was the day when I began to understand that each item held a story waiting to be unlocked.

Years later, when I started working in the shop, I would sometimes pick up the plate and smile. I no longer believed Arthur's tall tale, but he had made me see that starting again was possible and given me the hope I needed.

By letting one memory in, others followed: The image of Arthur with his brightly colored handkerchiefs neatly placed in his jacket pocket, sitting behind his grand mahogany desk, flicking through auction catalogues, his pen always clenched between his teeth, ready to circle an item he wanted to bid on. An aristocratic collector or a drinking partner calling him on the shop phone. Arthur was well-known for his outrageous turns of phrase and his long chats with anyone who walked into the shop so that they always felt obligated to buy something before leaving. Everyone loved him.

Maybe if I'd focused on learning how to identify a "big profit" art or antique to sell on, I wouldn't be in my current predicament. Although antiques dealing wasn't in fact Arthur's main passion, he still kept an eye out for a "sleeper"—an undiscovered or unidentified antique—at auctions or fairs that would give his shop a good payday. I had no interest in being a traditional antiques dealer. I had therefore concentrated all my efforts on following Arthur into his somewhat covert second business of hunting down something that had been stolen and returning it to its rightful home. But years later that career had been taken from me and I couldn't get it back.

The sun dipped behind a cloud and the world darkened. I sighed, knowing I might have to accept there was nothing I could do to keep my home, but there was something I could do for Carole. I could try and help her in her unimaginable grief just as she had helped me with mine when I had lost my parents over thirty years ago.

I searched for a black cab and waved at the first one I saw. I no longer cared about the expense. There was somewhere I needed to be.

2

"Listen, Freya, always listen."

—Arthur Crockleford

L ater that afternoon, I sank into the passenger seat of Carole's nautical-blue convertible Mercedes and held on for dear life as Carole sped around the narrow Dedham Vale lanes, driving and waving—simultaneously—at any dog walkers or cyclists she passed. The vehicle swept by so fast that faint cries of terror trailed behind us, and I wondered if this would be the drive that finally killed me.

"If you gasp again," Carole called over the wind thundering in my ears, "I shall increase my speed and then we'll really see where all your gumption went."

A gust whipped my hair and made my eyes stream. I retrieved one of my beloved vintage Hermès scarves, tying it around my wind-beaten curls, and demanded we stop and put the roof back on to give us some added protection in a crash.

Carole rolled her eyes. "You must stop being scared of everything. You can't spend your life in museums and antiques fairs *looking* at things. You need to *do* things—get the wind in your hair. And anyway, I have expert collision avoidance techniques. It's taken years to master this skill."

"Skill!" I gritted my teeth. I had a feeling Carole was looking for a fight, anything to help her ignore the grief that must have been threatening to

10

overwhelm her, but the criticism of my love of museums and antique fairs stung. Over the years it had become my only connection to a world I so adored. "To be clear, I am *doing* something when I'm in the British Museum or the V&A or the Winter Art and Antiques Fair at Olympia. I'm *studying* the craftsmanship and exquisite quality of the best antiques in the country." After leaving the antiques world, I knew the only way to keep my skills sharp was to continually study the finest antiques I could find.

Carole shook her head and was about to respond when a top-of-the-range Land Rover came hurtling toward us. I held my breath, closed my eyes, and waited for impact—wondering who to pray to when I entered churches only for births, marriages, and deaths. Carole's car swerved and came to a shuddering halt at an angle, branches brushing my cheek. My eyes snapped open, my hands still gripping the seat.

We'd stopped on one of those passing points cut into a hedge.

Carole was waving erratically, her turquoise bangles jangling together, as a large tractor came trundling around the blind bend.

"Morning, Simon! How are those prize cows?" She beamed.

Simon touched his fraying baseball cap. "All well." His Suffolk accent was broad and soft. "Got guests, then, Carole?" The engine of his shiny new tractor hummed.

"This is my niece over from London," said Carole, throwing me a pitying look. "She needs a bit of fresh air."

Simon nodded knowingly, as though the very mention of London might give him breathing difficulties.

"And, well." She paused, in the time-honored tradition of giving bad news space to settle. "We're arranging Arthur's funeral."

"Terrible thing, him passing so suddenly. I'm sorry for you." Simon touched his cap again.

"Thank you." Carole put the car in gear and got ready to leave. "We will see you there?"

"More than likely." He turned and heaved at the brake. "Go well, then," he called back, in the local way.

Carole slammed her foot down on the accelerator. "Simon Craven is a lovely man and his wife, Agatha. She took over the Teapot Tearooms from her mother *and* she's on the Parish Council." She took her eyes from the road and gave me a knowing look. I didn't understand what Agatha Craven and the Parish Council had to do with anything.

"And?" I asked.

"She knows everything before everyone else. We'll pop in and see her at the Tearooms and get the local news."

In a village like Little Meddington, knowledge was the highest form of currency. Carole wasn't normally one to entertain gossip, and I began to wonder what she was up to. I'd thought she was going to be a crumpled mess of emotions when I arrived.

The scented air of spring drummed my face as Carole spun the convertible around another corner.

"Seat belt," I cried in vain, pointing to Carole's shoulder.

"You used to be one of the most go-getter girls around here. All those traveling adventures you had when you were hunting stolen art and such—" Carole stopped herself, knowing not to speak of what happened back then. She changed the subject. "I curse that obnoxious James. He was always putting you down and making you believe you couldn't have your own career."

"Our marriage was good at first . . ." I hesitated, before the lie became too great.

The annoyance at the memory increased Carole's pressure on the accelerator, and at rocket speed we shot down our lane, passing the sign for the footpath to the pub. It was the route I'd stumbled down after a few too many when on break from my history degree at Newnham College, Cambridge. I remembered always being able to look up and see Aunt Carole watching from her bedroom window to check I was back safely.

Within seconds my childhood home came into sight.

The Old Forge was a Grade II listed house that sat next to a little lane with high banks that looped around the outskirts of Little Meddington. The house's pointed, thatched roof and wonky walls overlooked rolling farmland. One of John Constable's favorite churches to paint—St. Mary's, built in the late fifteenth century—could be seen standing tall and proud in the distance. There was good reason the area was often referred to as Constable Country. I allowed myself a reluctant smile. It was good to be home again after so long, and I hoped being there would help Carole. If I was honest, I was also grateful to be far away from the stream of prospective buyers walking around my home over the next couple of days. I anxiously visualized them opening every cupboard and rummaging through my things before they'd even made an offer, like snooping was a necessary part of house hunting.

The car came to a brisk halt and I clambered out, feeling unsteady. The house windows were wide open. "You did lock the front door, didn't you?" I asked.

"Who's going to come thieving down these lanes?"

"It's exactly where they would come stealing because there's no one around to see them. I've investigated enough thefts to know," I replied.

Carole laughed dismissively. "No one's breaking in with Harley in there."

Harley, named after a Harley Davidson motorcycle that Carole once owned, was my aunt's ancient chocolate labradoodle. She took him swimming every Sunday in the Stour to keep his joints moving, but mostly Harley slept by the Aga or on the sofa.

"You've been in the city too long. I promise to lock up while you're here and I've had all the fire alarms checked last month like you insisted."

"I'm making sure you're safe." My right hand clenched over the burn scar on my palm.

Carole reached out and unfolded my fingers, entwining our hands together—the way she always did when she noticed me withdrawing—and gave a strong squeeze. "I'm not going anywhere." She pulled me into a hug. "Welcome home. Let us get some tea on. We need a chat."

I inhaled deeply and lifted my face to the sky, letting the sun warm my cheeks. I hadn't allowed the pain of my home going on the market and the muddled feeling I held over Arthur's death to reach me on the journey to Suffolk. As I watched Carole open the back door and walk into the house, I realized her comforting smile and big hugs were the way she always tried to protect me from any worry. After the fire, I'd lost my parents and Carole had lost her older brother. I used to wake in the night, screaming out for my mom, and Carole was always there to soothe me—we had clung on to each other back then, and I was glad I was home and could be there for her when the shock of losing Arthur sank in.

Beams of spring sunshine stretched through the leaded windows of the farmhouse-like kitchen, and dust motes danced over the large, oak kitchen table. Even on a spring day, the Aga still pumped out heat. I ran my hand along the wooden countertop and reached for the kettle. It felt like I'd never left.

As I waited for the water to boil, I gazed out the window and down the cottage garden filled with daffodils, wild poppies, and apple blossoms. The lands beyond the garden could be walked for miles and there was always a nice country pub somewhere close by to stop for a large glass of wine. It reminded me how wonderful Suffolk could be in the sunshine.

"Your garden's just beautiful," I said, reaching for the cookie tin behind the sugar.

"It's the best time of year. Arthur was meant to mow the lawn for me tomorrow and after we were to go for breakfast at Agatha's." The memory seemed to catch Carole by surprise, and she coughed down the pain that wrinkled her forehead. I gave her shoulder a brief squeeze. She was thinner than I remembered.

Carole tapped my hand to let me know she was grateful. "Now you're here, we need to talk about Arthur." Perhaps I rolled my eyes, as she added, "I *do* want to hear everything about Jade and her exciting new life in California, of course I do. But, darling, first we must talk about Arthur, and I won't stop until you hear me out. No matter how mad you get."

I sighed and nodded.

"Good, because when I looked through the shop window this morning I saw the wrong vases on the table. It got me thinking, but I didn't want to talk about it over the phone." Carole paused and lowered her voice, as if we might be overheard. "I've got that 'deep-in-my-bones knowing,' as my mother used to say. There's something fishy going on."

Harley sauntered over and put his head on my lap—waiting for a biscuit. I stroked his head.

"Are you sure?" My aunt had a wild imagination; it was a hangover from her glory days as an actor, surrounded by eccentric creative types.

"I am," replied Carole. "And I need you to do a little bit of your digging."

I opened my mouth to object.

"And don't say you can't." Carole wiggled a finger at me like I was a child. "I've seen the files in your house. I know you sit late into the night on your computer, trying to search for all those missing old things from the safety of your bedroom."

"Those 'old things' are *stolen antiquities*, taken from their original country and kept in private, black-market collections, away from their rightful place in a museum." I was trying to keep calm.

"Oh, absolutely, darling." Carole retrieved the milk from the fridge. "And if you could just use that snooping instinct, we'll get to the bottom of what happened to Arthur." Carole gave the briefest nod to herself—in the way she always did when she was satisfied.

I found I couldn't let what she had said drop. "What do you think happened?"

"The week before Arthur died he called me from the car after visiting some lord—I forget his surname—and said something about being 'fit as a fiddle and not having any accidents any time soon.' Now, after what happened, it seems like a very bizarre thing to say." She straightened. "And then he called again on the Saturday before he passed, and on that call we were reminiscing over the past, all our trips, you and your trouble with the house, how he would love to help you. It makes me believe that on both phone calls he knew something was about to happen."

The teakettle whistled. I was more than a little shocked that Arthur had been talking about me. I played mother with the teapot, placing a cup of tea in front of Carole's favorite chair at the kitchen table. "Maybe he was sick?"

"No, that's not it at all. I think he disturbed a burglar and that's what made him fall. Or maybe he was pushed."

"Oh, Carole." This was getting outlandish. "Did the police say something was stolen? Is his death being treated as suspicious?"

"No. The policeman I spoke to was rude and dismissive. He said there were no signs of a break-in and that Arthur was old. He implied there was no point wasting their time looking into it and acted like the elderly generation around these parts were always falling over and dying. I'm quite sure they never even opened the case. But something is off and now it's up to us."

I sighed at the thought of being railroaded, which Carole took as acceptance. "Good! Then tomorrow we can go and have a cuppa at Agatha's Teapot Tearooms—Agatha really does know everything and everyone. Then see the solicitor," she said, taking a sip of tea. She plucked a cookie from the tin and pushed it toward me. "Go on, you have one."

I'd no idea how to take Carole's revelation or what she thought I could do about it. Surely it was a job for the police or the Scotland Yard Art and Antiques Unit.

My mind drifted to Arthur's antiques and his shop. Firstly, I had known from working there the shop was a front for Arthur's real passion—hunting down stolen antiques and antiquities. It was a detective agency for the antiques world, one used by police forces, insurance companies, museums and a few private clients around the globe. But I didn't quite understand why he'd told Carole he could help me, when we weren't even on speaking terms. It *was* strange.

I decided that even though I didn't have Carole's "deep-in-my-bones knowing," maybe a little look into things might be a good idea, for her sake.

3

"In my world there's always a favor to repay, Agatha. I told you that."

—Arthur Crockleford

Agatha

Agatha Craven had no idea how to keep her promise to Arthur. The previous Friday he'd handed over a letter and was very insistent that she do exactly as he asked, and it was always hard to say no to Arthur.

Three days later she learned he was dead.

She knew she should've gone to the police. She also knew that if handing the letter over to the police was her intention she would've given the letter to her nephew, who was in the Suffolk Constabulary, when he came around for tea yesterday. But she didn't. When she heard on the grapevine that the police believed Arthur's death to be a tragic accident and he could be buried within the week, Agatha decided there was nothing untoward with the whole situation. It was all a terribly sad coincidence, but she intended on keeping her promise. She waited for Carole and Freya to arrive at the Teapot Tearooms to hand over Arthur's letter.

But Carole and Freya were nowhere to be seen.

It was most inconvenient of them to be late.

The letter had been in Agatha's pocket for the whole weekend. She had considered dropping the letter round to Carole's, but that wasn't what she'd promised. She'd promised Arthur when Carole or Freya came *in* she would hand it over, and Agatha was a woman of her word.

She was setting up for breakfast when she saw Carole's old 1980s Mercedes drive past and park a little farther down the high street. Agatha ran to the kitchen, where her handbag hung on the back of the door, and rummaged around inside until she felt the corner of the letter. The envelope was a little creased, but she blamed Arthur for that—he should've posted it. She stuffed the letter into her apron and opened the front door of the tearoom, the little bell jangling as she did.

Where are they? What if Arthur was wrong and they never entered the Teapot Tearooms ever again?

Agatha breathed deeply, trying to calm her panic, she ran her hands over her head to smooth out her gray bun and headed back to the kitchen. Why did Arthur have to be so mysterious? Not for the first time, she considered steaming the letter open, but she couldn't be sure it would close again and then how would she hand it over?

For now the letter remained a heavy weight in her apron pocket.

4

"We can preserve the past while still striving toward our future."
—Arthur Crockleford

Freya

The Teapot Tearooms was housed in a pocket-sized, pink medieval building in the center of Little Meddington. I'd asked Carole a number of times if she really did want to go there—it was where Arthur used to take her and was one of their favorite places. I was worried it would be too painful for her, but she seemed determined, and I didn't want an argument. I hadn't set foot in the center of the village for a long time. In avoiding Little Meddington I had successfully avoided Arthur, and his shop.

I climbed out of the car and my eyes quickly focused on an elderly man walking toward us. Dread twisted inside me. Was I still trying to hide from Arthur, even though he couldn't possibly have been there?

I made myself take a deep breath of fresh country air and tried to relax. The crisp morning sun lit the village shops on the eastern side of town and I marveled at their old-world beauty. The sight was just as I remembered it—people in these parts didn't like change, preferring the comfort of stagnation.

I'm finally free now that Arthur's gone.

Carole crossed the road and I followed, meeting her as she reached the Teapot door. It was clear she was on autopilot. The bell rang to warn Agatha we were entering.

"Won't be a minute," called Agatha from the kitchen. "Carole, that you?" Agatha's head popped around the side of the kitchen door. Her cheeks were flushed, probably from the heat in the kitchen. "Find a seat, love." On seeing me, she said, "Freya, it's been an age, hasn't it? I'm just *so* glad you're both here." She nodded to herself. "Just as you should be."

I turned to frown at Carole; it seemed like a strange thing for Agatha to say, but Carole was already hovering over a couple of tourists draining the last of their coffee—they were sitting at Carole's table in the bay window. I hung back. In true Carole fashion, she struck up a conversation with the Canadian couple, telling them all about the local attractions and demanding that they see "Constable's church" before leaving the village.

I took a moment to admire the shelves filled with tableware collected from local charity shops. I gravitated toward a delicate 1960s teacup and saucer and ran my finger around the edge of the 1980s Calypso pastel cake plate. It was a nice example and made me think how many pieces ended up at the dump for no reason other than a change in fashion.

The couple hurried off and Carole settled down. We'd spent much of my youth in this café with Bridget, Agatha's mother, the welcoming proprietor. In the winter, Carole would meet me from the school bus and we would huddle next to the log burner in the Teapot drinking hot chocolate and eating toasted teacakes before heading home. It was a sterling plan as Carole was not a talented cook and it wasn't unheard of for her to burn the pesto pasta.

Agatha stood over us with a strange, anxious look on her face.

"Tea and teacake? Or a proper fry-up?" asked Carole.

"Just a coffee would be great." I smiled at Agatha.

"Just like old times, eh, Carole?" Agatha trailed off and frowned.

"Everything okay?" I asked.

Agatha pulled at her apron. "Oh, yes, all fine now." Turning to attend to another customer, who was waving at her for their bill, she said, "I'll bring everything over in just a minute."

In no time, Agatha brought out a coffee for me and a tea and tea cake for Carole. "Sorry it took so long," she said to Carole, although it hadn't been any time at all. She hesitated and we both looked up at her. "I have something for you. . . . A letter."

From her apron pocket, Agatha pulled out a blue envelope that was tattered at the edges, "Carole and Freya" scrawled on the front. She placed the letter against the little vase filled with wildflowers.

We all stared at it as Agatha said, "It's the strangest thing. Arthur came in here last Friday telling me he wanted me to keep this safe and that when you two came in together, I was to give it to you." She nodded to the envelope and Carole snatched it up, giving Agatha a questioning look. "I did ask him, of course. You two haven't been in here together for twenty years. But he was quite adamant you would. Then . . . he . . . well, you know what happened on Sunday night. I've been waiting for you both!" Agatha picked at her nails. "Maybe I should have handed it in or something, but he was *so* insistent."

Carole began to open the letter and smiled at Agatha. "You did exactly what was right. Thank you so much."

Agatha hovered over us, eyeing the letter. Carole stopped unfolding the blue writing paper. "Thank you so much," she said again.

Agatha nodded and reluctantly turned away.

Carole opened the letter on the table so we could both read it. My chest twisted, seeing Arthur's last words on the page.

Dear Carole and Freya,

If you're holding this letter in your hands then it is over for me.

Carole, my dear, dear friend, I shall forever miss your sparkle.

We had some fun. Didn't we? Like that time in Hong Kong for your birthday. It's time to put on those dancing shoes again!

Freya, I know how hard things have been for you. I'm deeply sorry and I have found a way for you to get back to the career that you were made for. But for this to happen you must first finish what I started. It has taken me over twenty years to find an item of immense value. I have been told its location, but it seems I will not be able to retrieve it. Get it back, Freya, and you will have your life and your career back. I'm sorry I cannot be clearer; I have been betrayed and can't risk this letter being discovered. Tell no one. There is no one left to trust. Hunt the clues and you'll find a reservation. I implore you to attend, but be careful. My betrayer will be following your every move.

I always wanted to tell you the truth about Cairo, but I needed you out of the antique hunting game back then, and now it seems fate has decided that I won't get the chance to set it right. You need to see the truth. I hope that in learning what really happened, you'll forgive the choice I had to make.

For your first clue—a bird in the box <u>is</u> more important than two in the hand.

All my love,
Arthur

The room shook ever so slightly, and my hand bumped my cup, making it clatter in its saucer and coffee slosh over the side. Carole reached out, placing a hand on my arm to steady me. It was a lot to take in, Arthur writing a letter to me after all this time, but more than that, it was the end that ripped at me. There wasn't anything Arthur could say to get me to forgive him. My whole world had come crashing down after Cairo—all because of him. I wasn't getting involved in whatever he was up to.

THE ANTIQUE HUNTER'S GUIDE TO MURDER   23

"What is this?" Confusion and annoyance dried my mouth and I lifted my eyes from the letter to my aunt, who was fighting to hold back her own tears. "What has he started that I need to finish? I don't understand. Why now? Why didn't he call me up or . . ." But I knew why he didn't call—it was because I wouldn't have answered.

Carole shook her head and didn't reply.

A lump formed in my throat. I wasn't ever going to be led on one of Arthur's "antiques hunting trips" again.

"And what's that strange line about the bird box? That's not even how the saying goes," I said.

The color had drained from Carole's cheeks. "Something very bad happened in that shop last Sunday night. I'm sure of it," she whispered. "You'll get to the bottom of it, won't you? For me?" Her eyes filled.

I couldn't answer. I would do anything for my aunt. But Arthur calling the shots from beyond the grave?

It was all too much.

5

"To work in this trade, you must have the cunning of a fox and the grace of a bird."

—Arthur Crockleford

I sprinted out of the Teapot Tearooms, my head spinning. I reached the old oak tree next to the library, the one I used to stand beside while waiting for the school bus, and pressed my hands into the trunk, hard, to steady myself; as if the sting of my palms against the jagged bark could push the past away.

Arthur has no right! My heart hammered in my chest. *Not after all this time, not after what he did. He has no right to ask anything of me.* The sentences repeated in my mind over and over. I leaned back against the tree and ran my index finger over the scar on my palm—trying to calm the frightening memories that surfaced of Cairo and of Arthur's betrayal that surfaced. I closed my hand around the scar and resisted the urge to run back to my safe London home. Only, very soon my home would be gone. I wished I'd never agreed to enter the village—even after Arthur's death.

I could've been standing there for minutes or hours, for all I knew, when I heard shouting from behind me. I'd know that deep, husky tone anywhere and turned around to see Carole hurrying toward me—my handbag and hers over her shoulder. The letter was nowhere in sight. She cupped her hands to her mouth, but I couldn't make out what she was saying. Seeing her reminded me why I was there—to help the one person who had never let me down.

I took a few steps toward her, but she violently shook her head and motioned for me to stay put. Carole's shouting was attracting quite a bit of attention and my cheeks warmed.

"Are you hugging the tree, darling? You always loved that tree and it's been a long time since you've seen it."

A couple walked past and began to laugh.

"What?" My cheeks were flaming by then. "I haven't missed the *tree*!"

Carole hurried past me, checking that the people were watching, and headed toward the oak. "Let me show you, and those busybodies, how to *properly* hug a tree."

"What are you doing?" The morning was becoming more and more surreal.

"Come on, we have an audience and I'm still the actor I once was." Carole enveloped the old oak in what could only be described as a bear hug. "You see, darling." She raised her voice so that everyone could hear. "There are wonderful healing properties in tree hugging. I know you were trying, but I didn't think you were giving it your all." She shimmied around the tree in a strange sort of hug-dancing movement.

I cackled, far too loudly. It was a ridiculous sight, but there was nothing I could do to stop my aunt.

When I turned around again our viewing public had lost interest and was gone. Carole winked at me and let go of the tree. I realized she was doing what she'd done when I was a child. Whenever the past had threatened to overwhelm me, Carole had always known how to break me out of it. I now hugged her, instead of the tree.

"Right," she said, straightening her bright blue shirtdress. "Off we go to the solicitor, or we'll be late."

I had totally forgotten about our appointment and I was about to refuse, but I knew that it would be pointless. I'd said I would help, and I wasn't going to let my aunt down.

~

I followed Carole up the steep stairs to the Smith & Sons solicitor's office that resided above the butcher's on the high street. I groaned inwardly as we walked down the corridor; I didn't want to hear anything more about Arthur even if it was to be told that I'd inherited something.

Carole hadn't mentioned the letter again and I was perfectly happy to ignore its existence. The reception was a small room with a large bay window overlooking the high street. There was a metallic whiff of blood from the butcher's shop downstairs mixed with expensive cologne. The spring sun was streaming through the grubby windows, turning the air into a muggy soup. It was an uncommonly hot morning for May, but then, May can be like that, can't it? The month that you rush to unpack all your summer wardrobe only for you to have to push it to the back of the closet again a week later.

Behind the G Plan Fresco mid-century modern desk—which had probably been there since the 1960s—was a woman barely out of school. The teak desk had a floating top and solid legs and made her look like she should've been working at an ad agency in Hackney. I wondered if she knew how expensive that desk was, but she probably just thought it was old and orange. The woman had bright blond hair, deep brown eyes, and pink talons for nails, which tapped as she typed up some handwritten notes. She looked around her computer and smiled warmly at Carole.

She didn't ask my name and clearly knew who Carole was. "He shouldn't be long." She shuffled some papers around. "I'm sorry about Arthur," she said.

"Thank you, Annabelle, that's sweet of you." Carole leaned in. "Do you know why this is all so urgent?"

Annabelle shrugged just as a door opened to our left. A man well over six feet tall and in his late forties stood in the open doorway, his smile white against his slight tan. His shirt, tie, and chinos were expensive and his aftershave engulfed the reception. There was a squeaky polish to him that I didn't warm to but I was sure many of the women in the village were enamored by.

His smile faltered when our eyes met, but he composed himself and held out his hand for a limp handshake that made me shiver. "It's a pleasure to meet you. I'm Franklin Smith, and you are?"

"I'm Carole's niece, Freya Lockwood. Carole told me you asked us both to come to your office as quickly as possible."

Franklin turned to Carole. "Ah yes, I assumed your niece wouldn't be able to make it. If you would come in?" He walked into the office and relaxed into his large, reclining leather chair. "First things first." He intertwined his fingers. "Do you have the keys or alarm code for Crockleford Antiques Shop?"

Carole and I glanced at each other and shook our heads.

"As the executor of Arthur's estate, I need to enter the property, and no one seems to have the keys or code. I'm told the shop door was unlocked when the police arrived. That is most strange, isn't it? Harry, the boy that works there, says the police locked up and he doesn't know the alarm code because Arthur recently changed it. Does that sound right?"

I shrugged and Carole looked confused.

Franklin sighed. "I suppose we'll need to get the locksmith in, and someone to deal with the alarm."

"Is that why we're here?" I asked. "I thought you asked to see us about the will?"

It all seemed very odd.

"Quite right, the will. Arthur came here the day after a friend's death and insisted I draw up a will that very moment."

"Which friend would that be?" asked Carole. "Do you have a name?"

"Lord Metcalf?" Franklin raised an eyebrow enquiringly and we both shook our heads again. "I'm the executor to both estates." He turned to face me. "Arthur informed me that he had written to you about it." His arms were crossed and there was a puzzled expression on his face. "Arthur had been asked to be the verifier for the Metcalf estate. However, he was insistent that you, Ms. Lockwood, should take his place if he wasn't able to. You are mentioned as an alternative verifier for the estate in the Metcalf will, which is most unusual and I can only presume Arthur had suggested this to his late friend. Of course, you absolutely don't need to. I'm more than capable of finding a proper expert to do this."

"I don't know anything about being a verifier for an estate," I replied.

He nodded with satisfaction. "Of course you don't. I have no idea what Arthur was thinking. I will sort it."

I didn't know what to make of Arthur recommending me, so I didn't dwell on it. But I wondered if there was a connection between the two deaths. "If you don't mind me asking, how did this Lord Metcalf die?"

"He was an old man." Franklin checked his watch, and I noticed that it was a cheap reproduction Rolex; the second hand didn't have the sweeping motion. "Long and short of it is, Carole and Freya Lockwood get the building and the business—half each. Though I'm afraid I've spoken to the accountant and the business is going under."

The shop is ours? Why would Arthur do that?

The idea of it made me sick to my stomach. I couldn't even imagine walking through the doors of the building, let alone owning it. Carole and I had no idea how to run the antiques shop, so it was clear we would have to find a buyer at the earliest opportunity.

Franklin pulled open a drawer and retrieved a small wooden box. "And he wanted you to have this." He slid the box across the table to me.

I reached out. "What is it?"

"A plastic brooch," answered Franklin, cocking his head as if he expected an explanation.

"You opened it already?" asked Carole. We all knew he shouldn't have looked inside the box, and I was beginning to wonder if he was entirely legitimate.

Franklin shrugged nonchalantly.

I held the box in my palm, my hand shaking ever so slightly after the news of the inheritance. I creaked open the top and unwrapped a bundle of crisp cream tissue paper that sat inside. A luminous red plastic brooch in the shape of a fox fell into the palm of my hand; the fox's tail curled back under itself, and it had a slender body with feet outstretched like it was running. Without having to look, I knew the name "Lea Stein" was embossed on the silver pin.

"Arthur gave me one like this when I was eighteen." I frowned at Carole.

Why is he giving me another one now? What is he trying to tell me?

My heart contracted as a tender memory came rushing back.

When Arthur had shown me the brooch all those years ago, he'd said, "Tell me everything about this—what it is worth, who made it—and you can keep it." In the days before the Internet, being given a plastic brooch to investigate seemed like an impossible task. But I found I became engrossed in the research, talking to shops in London and reading books on costume jewelry. The more I learned, the more determined I was to uncover the history of not only my brooch but also its designer, Lea Stein. Now Lea Stein was elderly, and her brooches were growing in value.

When I had reported my findings to Arthur, he smiled at me and said the brooch was mine to keep. Soon after, the antique hunting had begun.

"Is there anything else?" Carole asked Franklin.

"Your proof of identification?" Franklin held out his hand to Carole.

She reached into her bag for her driver's license and some utility bills and I did the same, handing them over.

Franklin seemed pleased at last. "It would be best if you understand probate isn't a fast process. I will do my utmost to be swift, but this will take many months—sometimes over a year or more."

We bid him farewell and I left with a sense of unease. There was something strange about him, but I couldn't put my finger on what it was.

I'd taken only a couple of steps out onto the street when I opened my phone and started to search for "Lord Metcalf."

"There is no obituary, nothing about his death. You would think there would be something if a lord died, wouldn't you?"

"I do, darling, I most certainly do."

I considered what we'd learned from Franklin. "It is odd Lord Metcalf, an apparent friend of Arthur's about whom we can't find anything online, dies, and the very next day Arthur hurries to write his will with the same solicitor. *And* Arthur gives Franklin this for me." I held up the box containing the brooch. "If we believe Arthur's death is suspicious, then perhaps the two deaths are related in some way?"

Carole grabbed my arm. "I think it might have been Lord Metcalf that Arthur went to see when he called me. Perhaps after his visit to Lord Metcalf he suspected something or discovered something when he was there? Someone killed them both for what they knew! Arthur was up to something cunning when he left us the letter and that brooch."

Hearing her say the word "cunning" made me remember something. One of Arthur's sayings: *An antique hunter needs to have the cunning of a fox and the grace of a bird.*

I was once a professional antiques hunter with one of the best in the business. Arthur used to say to me before getting on a plane, "Ready for the next fox hunt, then?"

I would smile and reply, "I'm always ready, old man."

The fond memories shocked me, but even more so, I was surprised at how thrilling I found the idea of hunting again. With all the turbulence of James insisting the house was sold, my sadness at Jade moving away, and now Arthur's death, what I really needed was a distraction from it all.

I didn't know where it would lead, or if my skills were still there, but it was an easy decision. I would see what I could uncover.

6

"We begin the hunt at the site of the crime."

—Arthur Crockleford

As soon as we knew there wasn't going to be an official inquest, Carole decided Arthur must be buried immediately. Wednesday and Thursday were spent following my aunt around as she pulled in every favor she could. Arranging the funeral was the most obvious way for her to keep her mind off her loss, and it was a good plan, for both of us. I didn't want to dwell on my past with Arthur or return James's long, demanding voicemail messages. And I was already frustrated by the search for clues. I had read and reread Arthur's letter and gone over everything we'd found out—it was clear Arthur had known he was in danger and his worst fears had come true. But the first clue he had provided was impossible to decipher—the "bird in the box." And without access to his shop, I had no way to start the hunt.

On the day of the funeral I was at the far end of Little Meddington waiting for the arrival of the horse-drawn carriage with Arthur's coffin inside, when Jade called.

"Mom." She'd been away only since last August but sounded more American by the day. "Dad tells me that you're avoiding the real estate agents. Are you all right? I told him he was an idiot—I might have used stronger language than that—for selling my childhood home, but of course he only ever thinks about himself. What the hell did you ever see in him?"

"Jade, he's your father and the house is not your fight. Don't be angry with him on my behalf. I'm fine, honestly. I'm just keeping out of the real estate agents' way." I hesitated but couldn't find the words to tell her about where I was or about Arthur. She'd never heard his name and didn't know about my past as an antiques hunter. "It's not the best time," I said instead. "Can I call you back? But, Jade, I'm so looking forward to you coming back for summer."

"Ah, about that." She took a deep breath. "I haven't been able to sleep worrying how I was going to tell you. I might not. Unless you *really* need me."

I couldn't reply. My heart tightened.

"Mom? Are you still there?"

I tried to sound cheerful. "Yes, love, that's fine."

"It's just I've met someone and she's asked me to . . ." She didn't finish her sentence. "I'm sorry, Mom. I could try. . . ."

"It's absolutely fine, love, I'm fine. You go have the best summer," I said, swallowing down the lump in my throat.

"Great, love you, chat soon." And she hung up the phone.

I hugged my arms around myself. *She doesn't need to spend the summer with boring old me.*

Carole tapped my arm as the horse carriage slowed to allow the mourners to assemble behind. We began our procession down the high street, dodging horse manure as we walked, the pungent smell filling our noses.

"Jade all right?" asked Carole, her voice shaky and her eyes on the coffin. I linked my arm through hers and kept my head down.

"I'm sorry. I shouldn't have answered, but she so rarely calls. . . ." I trailed off, unable to admit just how much I missed Jade. "Jade is fine. I didn't mention I was here."

Carole gave me one of her disapproving looks. "She should know the truth, about Arthur, about who you are."

I don't even know who I am anymore, I wanted to say.

THE ANTIQUE HUNTER'S GUIDE TO MURDER   33

Instead I said, "What good would that do? That's all been over for a very long time."

I saw the post office on my left and knew the antiques shop was now directly to my right. I shouldn't look, but . . . there it was, same as it had always been, and yet faded and smaller than I remembered. I waited for the past anger or the pain to ignite, but all that came to me was the memory of the brooch that was now in my handbag.

What is the "item of immense value" that you want me to hunt down, Arthur? An antique or something similar? And how do I get into your shop to look?

Carole followed my eyes, then squeezed my arm. She must have thought that I was wallowing in the past, but I was quite present.

"In his letter, Arthur says, 'a bird in the box,'" I whispered to her. "What does that mean?"

From under her wide- rimmed black hat she raised one eyebrow at me. "Darling, I'm delighted that you're finally on the scent." She patted my hand. "But I wouldn't know. That is definitely a riddle for you, not me."

The procession arrived at St. Mary's Church. The Reverend Steve Hallberton—a short, round man with a serious frown—ushered the attendants inside. Carole and I rested quietly against the low brick wall that surrounded the ancient graveyard. The morning sun caught the diamond ring on my middle finger and the glint reminded me of the first time I'd seen it.

Around my sixteenth birthday—around thirty years ago—I had started working for Arthur, and when I was eighteen he decided that it was time for me to experience the thrill of bidding at auction.

The South London auction house was a large warehouse by the Thames. It was a cavernous space, cold and musty, but filled with the promise of a bargain. When the auction started, I found it almost impossible to keep up with the lot numbers being called. I was checking the items Arthur had highlighted in the catalogue, but somehow—what with the speed of the auctioneer's gavel hammering down, and my sense of awe at the dealers sitting around me, confidently raising their hands in quick succession—I got lost. I had the numbers muddled and ended up making the winning bid on an extravagant Victorian sapphire-and-diamond engagement ring.

The old ring box was placed in my hand by a smiling lady as I also paid for the items of furniture I'd managed to secure. I opened the old ring box and stared; I was mortified but at the same time I couldn't stop admiring the ring. I'd fretted all the way back to Suffolk, convinced I would lose my job and the trust that Arthur had placed in me. But it didn't turn out the way I feared. Instead, all he'd done was smile and reassure me. "I can see you love it." He said "If you want to keep it, then it will be an early birthday gift from me to you." I'd happily agreed. Arthur was always full of surprises.

That day at the auction house, had given me my first antique and started a yearning for my own collection. I had come to Aunt Carole's as a twelve-year-old girl with nothing but the clothes I wore, after the fire had destroyed everything. If I'm honest, I longed for a keepsake of my parents, but I was afraid of owning something that could ignite my crushing grief with just a glance—I had my scar for that. After the auction house mistake, though, I had my very own piece of history. A *safe* history. It was an engagement ring from the past, but it was someone else's past—I liked to imagine they had a happier ending than my parents. Bit by bit Arthur showed me a world full of history that I felt comfortable immersing myself in. In researching an antique or the theft of one, I'd found a safer world I never wanted to leave.

At least, not until Arthur betrayed me and all I loved.

"We'll be going in soon," said Carole, nodding toward the Reverend Steve, who was giving a drawn-out explanation to the two younger pall-bearers. The youngest was no more than twenty, with fashionable thick-rimmed glasses and an oversized suit.

"That's Harry, Arthur's assistant," whispered Carole. "He looks far too fragile to carry a coffin, doesn't he?"

The funeral directors opened the large, ornate church doors and the pallbearers walked solemnly around to the back of the hearse. Arthur's coffin was pulled out and they heaved it onto their shoulders. My heart tightened and I drew a deep breath. I refused to mourn a man who had taken everything from me.

"Ready?" Carole gulped back her tears.

We followed the coffin down the long, towering aisle. The stained-glass windows lit up the pulpit and the plaques to the wealthy medieval textile merchants whose funds had helped build the church.

"Arthur Crockleford was a well-loved parishioner," Rev. Steve began. "As someone told me yesterday, we've lost not only a dear friend but our very own Indiana Jones—with his antiques and antiquities from all over the world."

As the Reverend Steve continued, I scanned the sea of hats and bowed heads around us. A bearded man standing to my far left, half-hidden by one of the towering pillars, caught my attention. He wore sunglasses, a trilby, and jeans and his hands were plunged into his pockets, not holding a service sheet like the other attendants.

"Please stand for our first hymn," said Rev. Steve.

Carole nudged me and I sprang to my feet, opening the program.

The organ started.

"And did those feet in ancient time
Walk upon England's mountains green?
And was the holy Lamb of God . . ."

Like many in the church that day, I knew the words by heart. I couldn't stop staring at Mr. Sunglasses, and although I couldn't see his face in full because of the beard and sunglasses, it was clear his lips weren't moving. His gaze swept from side to side as if he was scanning the church for someone he knew, and he looked like a man who had lost his dog in the park, not an attendant at a funeral. There was not even a whiff of grief about him.

"What a turnout," whispered Carole, bringing me back to our pew as we sat down again. "Arthur was so loved."

Her comment made me realize that I'd been staring. "I don't recognize many people," I whispered back. "Like him over there. Do you know him?"

I nodded toward the man by the pillar. Carole knew everyone; surely she would know him. She followed my line of sight and bristled, her back straightening. "He's in sunglasses and jeans! I feel that's disrespectful, don't you? I mean, they aren't even black jeans!"

I studied Carole. It wasn't like her to criticize someone's appearance, and her reaction seemed over-the-top. "Do you know him?" I asked again, this time with the feeling that she did. "Arthur told us in the letter that the 'betrayer' would be 'following our every move.'"

"I don't think so." Carole shook her head. "Shush, it's time to pray."

We bowed our heads.

Now wasn't the time to question Carole further, but something was off. She was lying, I was sure of it. I checked on the man again. He was tall and broad, his hat pulled low, but I couldn't see him clearly and I cursed my eyesight—the laser eye surgery of decades ago was failing me now. I must have strained my neck, for Carole nudged me.

"Don't stare. He'll know you're looking."

I readjusted myself, and the hairs on the back of my neck prickled. I felt like Mr. Sunglasses had turned in our direction. I glanced back. He'd leaned forward like he'd discovered the person he was searching for.

Was he looking at me?

An electric shock of horror at being discovered ripped over me and I sank as low in the pew as possible.

Next to me, Carole stood and walked the short distance down the aisle to take the vicar's place for the eulogy.

I looked around to see Mr. Sunglasses was fully focused on Carole at the pulpit. It was obvious he had found his target. It could mean only one thing; Arthur was right. We were being watched. But why?

7

"You're the brightest light I know, Carole. You shine so brightly
that you cast long shadows for the rest of us to hide in."

—Arthur Crockleford

Carole

Carole followed the stream of funeral guests out of the church. She was stopped by villagers and friends, all intent on telling her how very sorry they were. She hurried away—she couldn't let their heartfelt words touch her. She had Arthur's murderer to catch, and until that was done her crushing grief had to be controlled.

Arthur's coffin was lowered into the ground, the magnitude of what she had lost threatened to overwhelm her, but she reminded herself once again. *Not now.*

The dirt was passed around and without thinking Carole scraped her fingers into the cool pile of earth. She hesitated. To throw dirt on darling Arthur didn't feel right. For reassurance she turned to Freya, who placed a hand on her shoulder and squeezed.

By the time everyone had filtered away, Carole was left standing by the graveside, earth still gritty between her fingers, recalling one sentence from the letter.

It's time to put on those dancing shoes again!

Whenever Arthur had used that sentence Carole had experienced the rush of excitement that closely resembled the moment before she walked onstage at the Old Vic. Arthur was telling her that it was time to perform and win the audience over—that it was time for one of their grand adventures. The last one had been in Istanbul a month or so ago, with its wonderful rooftop bars and atmospheric markets. It was clear to Carole there was every possibility she might have just dined with a criminal or two, because Arthur was not in any way fussy about who he dined with. Carole personally never felt one needed to dig into someone's background if it might get in the way of a good time, or some free caviar.

I will dance, darling Arthur. Don't you worry about that. We'll get to the bottom of it all.

It was reassuring to know that Freya was hooked on finding out the truth about Arthur's death. Her niece saw tiny details others didn't, and once on a hunt, she never gave up. Freya might have been born that way, but Carole always thought it had been brought on by her parents' death, though she would never say it to Freya directly. Ever since that tragic fire, Freya had been alert to what was around her, always on the lookout for something that might be wrong, something out of place. Perhaps she thought that if she'd only noticed the faulty electric fire before it was plugged in, then . . .

Carole turned to look for Freya, who was a few steps away. "Are you going to tell me who that strange man was?" asked Freya, leaning close.

"Which one?" asked Carole, although she knew.

"The man with the sunglasses. I'm worried because in the letter Arthur told us he had been betrayed and we should be careful. Then at his funeral a strange man was watching you." Freya anxiously rubbed the palm of her hand.

Carole didn't like to keep things from her niece, but she didn't see the point in bringing up an irrelevant, if somewhat dodgy, acquaintance from Arthur's past. Today was not the day to talk ill of her darling

Arthur. She was quite sure he was just there to pay his respects to Arthur. Best tactic was to change the subject.

"Darling, I've been thinking about the letter too. Arthur told me I need to 'put my dancing shoes on.' That means I'm about to go on a grand adventure." Carole gripped Freya's arm with her other hand. "My Arthur knew we would take this on together and get to the bottom of it."

Carole paused as another realization hit her.

"What is it?" Freya asked.

"In the letter Arthur also mentioned my birthday in Hong Kong. It's the strangest thing because it wasn't my birthday on that trip. Arthur had decided that we would pretend it was to get us some free champagne at a marvelously opulent bar called the Golden Bird. It had wonderful gilded cages and ornate bird boxes hanging from the ceiling. Why on earth would he put that in the letter?"

Freya looked puzzled and Carole congratulated herself on distracting her from thinking about the man in the church. Now all she had to do was get to the bottom of what Arthur's clues meant and uncover his murderer.

8

"The greatest thrill is discovering the provenance of an item, unpicking a mysterious history, piece by piece."

—Arthur Crockleford

Freya

The funeral reception was held at Arthur's favorite pub, the Crown. The building was overflowing with people. It was a rowdier affair than I'd anticipated, but after the quietness of the church it was a welcome relief. The guests were perched on the edges of sofas by the pub bar and others spilled out into the large garden, filled with hundreds of potted plants and flowers. Carole was an expert in events organization, mainly because she loved a good party herself. The mini burgers and hot fries were welcomed by all.

I searched the faces around me, but I didn't see Mr. Sunglasses from the church. Although, if he had removed his glasses and hat, I wasn't sure I would have recognized him.

Carole, already on her second glass of prosecco, was deep in conversation with a young man. They were in the far corner of the restaurant, by the richly colored jungle-themed wallpaper, an unruly palm plant, and a large open window. He was nodding quickly while trying to back away, but Carole placed a firm hand on his arm; she obviously wasn't finished with whatever she was telling him. The only place for the man to go was behind the potted plant—which offered little protection—or out of the window. I decided I'd better go and rescue him before he considered the latter.

Carole beamed as I approached. "Darling, you must meet Harry."

Harry smiled shyly, pushing his glasses up his nose. I recognized him as the tall, pale pallbearer from earlier. "Your aunt tells me I have your old job."

"Which job would that be?" Some of my jobs were more out in the open than others and I wondered if Carole needed reminding to be discreet.

"Assistant at the antiques shop." Harry plunged his hands into his pockets. "I was saving for university."

"I'm so sorry for your loss. It must have been difficult to lose someone when you worked so closely together," I said.

Harry dipped his eyes and scuffed the tip of his shoe on the carpet.

"I worked there saving for university too. Then I came back during the summer breaks," I said, trying to make him feel more comfortable. "Were you there on Monday morning?"

He shifted uncomfortably from one foot to the other. I realized I shouldn't have asked, and I didn't push it any further. When I'd seen my first dead body, the magnitude of it hadn't settled in until I'd returned to our little Cairo apartment. The memory still haunted my nights.

"I'm so sorry." I wondered how I could move the conversation on.

Carole nodded in agreement, sympathy creasing her brow. "We were talking about the antiques in the shop." I could tell that she was coaxing him. "I think things might've been moved the night Arthur died. Some of the vases on the table looked different? If you don't mind, could you tell Freya about it?"

Harry ran his hand through his dark, corkscrew-curly hair. "It hadn't been turned over, not like you see in the movies. I'm not sure anything looked wrong. I don't know anything about vases."

Carole frowned at him.

"The shop was a bit messy, but nothing was missing, I don't think. The police said everything was in order." He paused as she shook her head at him—he wasn't playing along. "Except," he continued, and Carole smiled encouragingly. "I think you *might* be right. Perhaps the silver spoon shelf looked a little . . . emptier?"

"That's not it. I think something bigger was stolen," said Carole.

I opened my mouth to insist we keep our suspicions to ourselves when Harry spoke again. "Perhaps there was a big, ugly bird that went missing? I was working in the shop the Friday before Arthur died and I saw him walking upstairs with one he seemed to think was valuable." Harry waited for Carole's approval, but I responded first.

"What type of bird—like a taxidermy one?" I asked.

"No, I don't know much about antiques." Harry's eyes flitted around the room. "But it was a china thing, like a big sculpture or something. Arthur didn't want it logged on the new computer system so it wouldn't be on there." He stepped backward, obviously keen to leave the conversation.

An image pushed its way into my mind. The only ugly stoneware bird Arthur would care about would be a Martin Brothers one, and there had been a Martin Brothers bird decades ago in Cairo. Was there a connection? I opened my mouth to tell Carole before clamping it shut again. This was between Carole and me and no one else. But I needed to know if I was right. I pulled up some pictures on my phone. "Did it look like any of these?" I asked Harry.

"Um . . ." Harry briefly scanned the images. "Perhaps like this." He pointed at one with a long, blackish beak and an elongated body and its head tipped to one side—it wasn't the same one as in Cairo.

Carole grabbed the phone. "Oh, what a very cute bird—look, that one there is winking."

Not everyone would have responded that way. People often misjudge the value of the Martin Brothers birds, dismissing them as grandma's dark, creepy clay bird pots. I imagined some found their way into charity shops now and then. The images brought back difficult memories for me, but still, I tried to explain to Harry why someone might be carrying one around like the precious item it was.

"They were avant-garde ceramics made in the nineteenth and early twentieth century by four impoverished siblings—the Martin Brothers. The large jars, jugs, and so on were made into animals and, more famously, birds—Wally birds, they're called. But they were no ordinary birds. They have dark feathered bodies, huge smiling beaks, and big clawed talons, some with frowns, some winking at you—like the owl Carole likes. They're truly original, and since the brothers are all long gone, they fetch a good amount."

"Like how much money?" he asked, and I could see why he got on well with Arthur.

"Some around fifty thousand pounds; very fine examples maybe up to a hundred thousand."

Harry had perked up at the mention of money. "Carole says you're going to find out the truth, like you have a nose for finding stuff—that true?" he asked.

I took my phone back, ignoring Harry's question. "If Arthur had found a Martin Brothers bird, he would've been shouting it from the rooftops." It was a lie. I was quite sure he'd have been haunted by that bird as much as I was.

Carole didn't want to change the subject. "She's so like Arthur. Always wanting to know the detailed history of an antique or some such. She'll get to the bottom of what happened in that shop and find what was taken. Leave it to her."

"I'm sure the police checked the security camera and would've kept the case open if they'd seen anything suspicious," I said, unwilling to admit that my mind was already scrolling over everything that had happened over the last couple of days. The letter, the brooch, Mr. Sunglasses in the church, and now the mention of a Martin Brothers bird—I needed to know what was going on.

Carole tutted impatiently; this wasn't the answer she'd been looking for. "The cameras in the shop broke years ago and are just a prop now." She patted Harry's arm. "You've been very helpful."

Harry's shoulders relaxed. "Thank you." He glanced behind him. "There are people I should chat to." He took three fast steps away before pausing and turning back to catch my eye. "If someone was in the shop that evening stealing things, do you think they did it because they wanted that bird thing and Arthur tried to stop them?"

"Maybe that same someone pushed Arthur down the stairs," said Carole.

"Carole!" I scanned the room, checking no one else had heard her.

"What?" Harry went even paler than his normal fair complexion. "We weren't talking about him being pushed. Those steps were wonky and dangerous. You just said you thought it was a burglary gone wrong?"

"Quite right, just a burglary," Carole soothed. "We'll keep all this to ourselves." She waited for him to agree.

Harry straightened, clearly aghast at the mention of foul play.

Carole motioned toward the bar, where everyone always seemed to congregate. "Very good, off you go to your friends."

Harry complied. He had just reached the bar when his phone rang, and at the sight of the number on his screen, his expression fell. He answered and I saw him mouth the word "mom."

I turned to Carole. "Looks like working in Arthur's shop got him out of the house."

"Arthur said Harry's mom was always checking up on him. She really needs to cut the apron strings," said Carole.

But my mind wasn't on Harry. It was swirling with uncomfortable thoughts about the Martin Brothers bird he had seen. It wasn't the same one as we had in Cairo—that would be impossible—but was this the "bird in the box" Arthur mentioned as our first clue in the letter?

"I have a plan," whispered Carole.

"No, you don't. You're not getting involved in this." I wasn't going to encourage her, even if every bone in my body was crying out to know the truth about what had happened in the antiques shop that night. I drained my glass of prosecco and inwardly groaned. Aunt Carole on a mission was a force of nature. "You'll get us into trouble. Like that time you decided to show a prizewinning cow at the Hadleigh country fair— when we didn't even own a cow."

"It's nothing like that. This is a real plan." Carole smoothed her long, deep-green dress and straightened her enormous black hat. "We need to get into that shop."

I shook my head in disbelief, but Carole wasn't wrong. I needed to get into the shop and see if the bird was there. But how?

Arthur had always said, *The greatest thrill is discovering the provenance of an item, unpicking a mysterious history, piece by piece.* What if that didn't apply only to antiques? What if it also applied to what had gone on in the antiques shop that night? If something had happened to Arthur that night, then, even after everything we had been through, I couldn't ignore it. I had to know the truth, and I realized this was always the way hunting started—with a question and a determination to find the answer.

9

"Sooner or later we all leave this earth. What matters is the story
we've left behind."

—Arthur Crockleford

By the time dusk had fallen over Little Meddington, Arthur's
reception had morphed into another rowdy night at the pub. I
couldn't listen to all the anecdotes about Arthur's excellent sense
of humor and his international adventures.

I extracted myself and searched for Carole. I found her holding court
in the back garden, telling stories of Arthur, surrounded by Agatha,
Simon, and Little Meddington's finest. She looked energized for the first
time that day and it didn't seem right to interrupt her.

For over twenty years, Carole and I had agreed to disagree when it
came to Arthur. I had tried to talk to her about the situation but she
wouldn't hear all "the negativity." I was angry and James had insisted that
talking to Carole only made me anxious. He'd suggested we "stop taking
her calls." But then, one Monday morning James was away on business and
four-year-old Jade had broken her arm after climbing a tree. I stood in the
hospital's pale green corridor and called Carole. She had arrived in a whirl
of warm colors and charm, making everyone in the hospital smile, including Jade. It was then that I realized my life had been empty without her—
and that James didn't need to know we were talking again. Carole and I
had come to an unspoken agreement that Arthur was never mentioned.

Now I decided it was time to leave and see Crockleford Antiques Shop for the first time in decades. I pushed my way through the crowds of intoxicated guests spilling onto the pavement and headed down toward the village, stopping at the top of Mill Street. The view from here was splendid and I've always loved the hush of dusk as it settles over the village—its orange glow lighting the medieval wooden shop fronts and Victorian or Edwardian brick houses, interspersed with tea shops and hairdressers.

It was a charming scene and I saw just what Arthur had taken from me for all those years when I couldn't enter for fear of coming face-to-face with him. But on closer inspection, little had changed. In this hidden part of Suffolk, everyone had their favorite hairdresser, café, and pub; you made your choice and you stuck to it. A new shop was seen as a curiosity that needed to be checked out and then discussed in detail; only then could a villager decide if patronage was worth the leap of faith. Little Meddington had the sort of permanence that could be achieved only when people have lived in the same area for generation upon generation, marking their time with subtle changes to architecture and landscape that became a kaleidoscope of social history.

I'd always hoped for a bookshop—one with a coffee shop and a comfy chair to read in; one where I could curl up safely with a coffee and live out an adventurous life full of unsolved murders and espionage, surrounded by other stories just waiting to be chosen. I wasn't the only one who would have liked this, and it was often discussed, but one had never opened. There was a library, and Arthur had a small section of antique books—but a new book was different, wasn't it? The magic of spending hours browsing, running your finger along the shelves, the crisp smell when you flicked through the pages. The satisfaction of discovering a book you didn't know you wanted until you opened the first page of never-before-read paper and dived in. The hunt for a good book was topped only by the hunt for the perfect antique.

The sunset became muted by rain clouds gathering overhead. I hurried across the road and came to a stop outside Crockleford Antiques Shop.

The shop didn't look like the picture I held in my memory. I'd loved the weekends and vacations I'd spent here. I hadn't been a teenager with loads of friends and a constant stream of invitations. When the girls at school talked about their weekend parties and movie nights, I was happy that I had tall tales of haggling with clients at the shop. "Poor, shy Freya," they would say. "She's always working." But from the time I'd arrived in Little Meddington and the kids at school had pointed at my burned hand and whispered behind my back, I preferred the company of adults. I didn't know how to relate to my peers—I had nothing in common with them. I knew if I wasn't at the shop with Arthur, I'd be at home with Aunt Carole's friends or alone while she was out gallivanting. The shop, and the antiques held within its walls, had given me a purpose.

The once gleaming shopwindows and crisp black lettering on the sign above the door were now grubby and the paint peeling. Memories of jiggling the key in the lock and turning over the Closed sign to Open burst to the forefront of my mind.

Is all this really going to be ours?

It didn't seem real, and if it was real—I didn't want it.

Without thinking, I stepped closer, rubbing a clear spot on one of the small panes of glass and cupping my hands to peer through the crack in the curtains. Darkness lay beyond.

"I found you!" My aunt's cry startled me. "And very fortuitous that is too."

I turned to see her waving and charging across the road, holding up her hand to stop the oncoming cars. She was silhouetted against the disappearing dusk and she clung on to her enormous black hat, which was threatening to fly away.

"Sorry, I needed to get some fresh air," I lied as she reached the curb. "What's fortuitous?"

Carole gestured toward the shop. "Fancy having a sneaky peek around?"

I checked Carole's face to see if she was serious. "I intended to keep you out of this." I studied the locked door and wondered what would be the best way in. The skill I'd once held of picking locks was long lost.

Carole lowered her voice into an overly dramatic whisper. "We need to get in there and see if anything was stolen, and if that wonderful bird is still there—take it for safekeeping! Arthur put a bird in the letter after all." She'd had way too much prosecco.

"I think I should take you home." I touched the back of her arm and motioned toward the pub parking lot. I would come back later.

"On we go." She hurried past me. I watched in bemusement as her hat collided with a corner, and then Carole and her hat disappeared from sight. I hurtled after her.

I found Carole in the cobbled alley that ran behind the shops. She had hauled up her dress over her knees and was crouched down next to the back door.

"What are you doing?" I asked.

"It has to be around here somewhere." Carole looked up at me, her eyes crystal clear. Maybe she wasn't as drunk as I thought. "Are you going to help?"

"Help! What are you doing?"

Carole started picking up stones. "I'm sure there's a key hidden here somewhere and that Franklin doesn't know about it." In the darkness I hadn't noticed we were outside the back of Arthur's shop.

"I thought Arthur changed the locks." I gazed up at a navy sky littered with blackened clouds and shivered. The air was heavy with the threat of rain and the earth was ripe with anticipation, and I knew there was no stopping Carole now—not that I wanted to. I scanned our surroundings. The demure funeral dresses and the tottering heels we were both wearing were not meant for such an evening or such an excursion. "Are we really going to break in?"

"It can't possibly be called breaking in if we find a key, and anyway Arthur left all this to us, didn't he?"

She flung a few stones out of her way, and as they tumbled into dark corners farther down the alley, a thought hit me. "Arthur didn't hide the back door key there."

Carole stopped. "Where did he hide it?"

I shook my head, annoyed at myself for not remembering it sooner. "In the bird box! And Arthur wrote, 'For your first clue—a bird in the box *is* more important than two in the hand.' It wasn't the Martin Brothers bird Arthur was referring to—it was where the keys were hidden so that we could get into the shop."

Carole gasped in delight. "We've solved the first riddle! But what bird box?"

I turned away from the shop and hurried toward the ash tree in the corner of the alley. Carole was close behind. In the tree was a small, barely-holding-together bird box. "There." I pointed. I'd misplaced my set of shop keys a number of times when I'd worked there and this was where Arthur had hidden the spare set. Perhaps he stashed the new keys there as well.

"Up you go, darling." Carole nudged my shoulder.

"I'm not a performing monkey," I replied.

"I know that and it's quite disappointing. If you were, we would've already had the keys in our hands."

The bird box had been attached to the trunk so long ago that the tree had taken ownership of it. No one else reading Arthur's letter would've thought to search inside a bird box. *Clever, Arthur*, I thought, and then stopped. It had been a long time since I'd thought a kind word about him.

"Well, don't just stand there." Carole had her hands on her hips. "Or I'll do it myself." She stepped forward and I was pushed into action.

The box was not within arm's reach, but I knew what had to be done to get to it. Arthur used to be abroad a lot and climbing to get the spare set had become an almost weekly jaunt for me. Behind the tree was a Victorian wall with spaces between the bricks that could be used as footholds.

"I just have to put my foot in one of those gaps." I gestured to them.

Carole raised an eyebrow. "Not to be picky or anything, darling, but you're not as sprightly as you once were. I think it's best if I do it."

"Don't be absurd. I'm not letting you climb up there at your age." I sped to the wall behind the tree before Carole could get there and flicked off my heels, placing my toes in the gap where a brick was missing and grabbing the top of the wall. It didn't feel safe, but I couldn't stop now.

"And up we go!" called Carole.

The next thing I knew, she had her shoulder under my bottom and was giving me some sort of lift. It was entirely unwarranted. "What are you doing? Put me down."

"Don't talk, darling, just do!" Her voice was strained and I realized I probably did need her help.

I was teetering between the tree and the wall, with Carole underneath me. This was not what most people do after they leave a funeral. I lifted the once-blue lid of the bird box and ignored the thought of the spider that most certainly lived inside.

"Here!" I called triumphantly as my fingers closed around a key chain. "Arthur *was* telling us where the new keys were. He wanted us to get into the shop."

"Excellent." Carole backed away to see, and my support was gone.

This is going to hurt, I thought, in a moment of pure clarity, as I hurtled toward the ground. With split-second instinct I believed had left me long ago, I managed to land on my feet.

"Off we go." Carole plucked the two keys out of my hand—they shone in the dim evening light—and hurried over to the back door. I followed behind, checking the lane to make sure we weren't seen. Luckily, it was well past five o'clock and the shops had closed. With no sounds from farther down the alley. It was now or never. A rush of adrenaline came over me as Carole placed the key in the lock. I hadn't done anything this reckless since I was in my twenties.

"Hurry, before we are seen."

With a smile, Carole turned the key and the door opened without a sound.

10

"Carole, it's not the darkness that frightens Freya; it's what she imagines exists within it. If she finds her own light, she'll always be able to shine."

—Arthur Crockleford

Carole and I stood just inside the back door of Arthur's shop. Beyond us the corridor was swaddled in darkness. I was pulled forward into the shop, my curiosity taking over.

"It's a bit spooky," whispered Carole.

"It's a bit late to have doubts now. You've already broken in!"

"We, darling, *we* have broken in."

In the corridor, I turned on my phone flashlight. The hall led to the shop entrance on the main high street. I remembered tentatively opening that door in my late teens. I could almost hear the footsteps on the stairs above the shop, Arthur flinging himself around the corner, a large smile on his face. I was surprised, standing in the shop now, how much I longed to be that girl again with all those adventures ahead of her. In allowing that memory in, another blossomed—it was the day he'd told me about the "red sticker" items. If I sold an item with an extra red sticker on it, then it meant "tourist price," or someone that didn't know what they were looking at, and I was to add another five pounds.

Even with the glow from my phone, the shop was dim—the streetlight outside the grubby front windows barely illuminated the place. We weren't going to find anything here without a bit of light, and I reached for the switch to the left of the back door.

"Oh, no!" Carole brushed my hand aside. "We need to do this . . ." She paused, returning to her actor's whisper. "Undercover. Someone could be watching us."

"Like the someone watching you at the funeral?" I waited for her to answer. "Are you still not going to tell me who that was?"

Carole didn't reply and instead walked toward the shop front.

Beep! Beep! Beep!

"The alarm." Panic churned in my stomach. "It's going to go off. Franklin said that no one had the code."

"Franklin didn't get a letter from Arthur." Carole plucked my phone from my hand and hurried toward the alarm. I had no choice but to follow her. The beeping drilled into my ears and I gritted my teeth.

Beep! Beep! Beep!

"Carole." I was about to drag her out of the shop, when she calmly pressed "120908" into the keypad.

The beeping stopped.

"Thank God that racket's over," she said. Then seeing my surprise that she knew the alarm code, she continued, "When you were up the tree getting the keys, I realized the letter held *all* the clues to get us into the shop. There would be no point in Arthur just giving us the keys—so he gave you the clue for the keys and me the code for the alarm."

I nodded, encouraging her on.

"The numbers," Carole explained, "are the date of that wonderful evening we had with friends in Hong Kong at the Golden Bird. Arthur mentioned it in his last phone call to me—'remember when we celebrated in Hong Kong four days before your actual birthday back in 2008?' I am so good at solving all of Arthur's puzzles, aren't I? Now let's look about."

A shiver ran down my spine. I hadn't been in the shop for over twenty years, not since moving to London. My past, the one that I had spent two decades avoiding, seemed to lurk in every dark corner. I walked toward the staircase and stopped at the bottom. I could have been standing at the very point Arthur took his last breath. I noticed a small dark stain on the floor by my feet and a few dark drops on a couple of steps. *Blood?* Goose bumps appeared on my arms and I froze.

I couldn't go any farther.

Carole appeared at my side and rubbed my arms like she used to do after we'd when we had come in from a long, cold winter's walk. "I want to show you what I meant about the vases. Come." She handed back my phone and led me away from the darkness, just as she had always done.

We stopped in the center of the shop, where a round mahogany tilt-top table stood with two cheap reproduction blue-and-white china vases on top. "You don't think these vases weren't here before the night Arthur died?" I asked.

"These vases are the *wrong* vases. These ones we picked up at a rummage sale some years back and Arthur only used for the summer flower displays in the window. They shouldn't be there." Carole turned over the little tag. "Arthur wouldn't be trying to sell them for three thousand pounds each."

I lifted the second vase up and studied it. Carole was right; they were badly done, modern reproductions. "They're newish. Look at the way the figures are painted. Just some brushstrokes thrown around. This is probably based on an Imperial Chinese vase, but the real ones would've taken months to paint and the detail would be exquisite." To prove the last twenty years I'd spent in museums hadn't been a waste, I added, "There are some of the best examples in the London museums where one could see the difference."

"All right, clever clogs. But now you see I'm right."

I nodded. "You think someone entered the shop to steal the vases, or maybe the Martin Brothers Wally Bird Harry was talking about, and Arthur was killed in the process? Perhaps as he tried to stop them or he was startled and fell down the stairs? Then the robber went out of their way to make the place look like nothing was taken and Arthur's death was an accident? But antique burglaries happen all the time and people get away with it. Why go to all the trouble?"

"Indeed. Why would someone break in to steal some vases and then take the time to put other vases in their place?" Carole leaned toward the vases, now in full Inspector Clouseau mode. I was quite sure she would've loved a cape.

I swept my flashlight around the shop, over the furniture, the glass cabinets, and the bookshelves. The layout of the shop was the same as I remembered, but the white woodwork, once painted fresh every other year, was now yellowed, and the carpets were threadbare. "Franklin said the business was going under. This place *does* look run-down," I mused. "Maybe the simplest explanation is the best—Arthur wasn't making the 'fine living' everyone thought he was? Maybe he sold the vases and put these here in their place? And did accidently fall down the stairs." Although as I said it my gut told me that wasn't what happened.

Carole shook her head. "That's not it at all. Arthur had plenty of money. Frankie-boy just doesn't know where it is." Her eyes moved from the vases to the front of the shop. "Perhaps these ones are here to fool anyone looking in the window?"

I had caught the scent of the hunt now. "The lock has been changed and the alarm set, so no one could get up close. The burglar didn't know that you could tell the difference. From the window it might look like everything was fine."

"Exactly."

"What if they weren't stolen? What if someone was here and something broke." I looked under the table and Carole started scouring the surrounding floor.

"Here, under Arthur's desk!" she whispered with excitement. Carole grabbed a pencil and flicked something out from under the heavy mahogany drawers. Straightening, she held up a jagged piece of white porcelain as if she was carrying an Olympic torch.

I shone my light on it. "It looks like blue-and-white Chinese republic-period porcelain. See here?" I showed Carole a scrolling flower. "The detail is clear and well painted."

"What's that?" Carole pointed to the blue painting of an animal.

"It's a Chinese Chi Long dragon—a hornless dragon. They're quite common—to me they almost look like otters." I turned the palm-sized piece over in my hand. "I would say that three thousand pounds is quite cheap if this vase was in perfect condition to begin with and with its pair."

I turned my attention back to the replicas on the table. "Someone broke the original vase—maybe both—cleaned up the mess, and replaced them with reproductions. Hoping no one would notice when they looked through the window." Piece by piece it was becoming clearer.

"Go on, say it," said Carole, almost gleeful.

"You were right," I said. "There is something very wrong here, and we need to get to the bottom of it."

11

"If you keep your eyes sharp at all times, you'll find everything you've ever wanted."

—Arthur Crockleford

A soft patter of rain began outside the shop's large crescent windows. Night had fallen and thunder rumbled in the distance. We needed to be quick.

"Let's hurry," I said. "We should see if we can find the Martin Brothers bird Harry described or the 'item of immense value' Arthur mentioned in the letter."

"Absolutely," replied Carole, buoyed by her recent find. "Maybe they are one and the same?"

I wasn't sure but I began to search. The shop looked like it had been frozen in time, almost as I remembered it, but a lot sparser. I scoured the glass cabinets—dust still waited to be cleaned off the items inside—but there was no Martin Brothers bird or anything of exceptional value. The drawers in Arthur's shop desk were open a crack and his Victorian mahogany bookcase full of guides and auction catalogues looked to be in order, but on closer inspection had been pulled out, just a touch, at odd angles.

Someone was looking for something, just like we are.

I turned to tell Carole and saw that she had heaved a large armchair back to its position next to a table in the small bay window and settled down, her arms wrapped around herself.

"Carole?" I whispered. "Are you all right? Maybe you shouldn't be by the window."

"We used to have our cup of tea or a gin and tonic here," she said, running her hand over the coffee table. "On a winter's afternoon, plotting our next weekend away. Only last month he was talking about an antiques cruise to Jordan."

"I'm so sorry." I went to her and held her hand, which was cold and thin. No wonder she'd wanted to break into the Crockleford Antiques Shop after Arthur's funeral. Today of all days, she was looking for traces of him, but she needed the type of closure that only comes with time.

I waited in silence, until Carole patted my hand.

"Thank you, darling." She rose from the chair, smoothing her dress.

I peered out of the front windows, making sure our presence had gone unobserved. What had started off as a spattering of rain was now a thundering downpour—huge droplets hammered the pavement. Across the road, the post office's hanging baskets began to swing in the oncoming winds. No one was likely to be out for an evening stroll, but in these villages, nothing went unnoticed for long, and I was still worried about Arthur's warning and Mr. Sunglasses.

"If Arthur wanted us, and only us, to find something here, where would he hide it?" I asked.

"We should check upstairs," she replied. "Isn't that where Harry said the bird was?"

I agreed and we headed for the staircase. The long-lost sensation of starting to hunt was taking over and it was thrilling to be pulled along.

The stairs squeaked and groaned as we climbed, but all I could think about was Arthur tumbling down them—I ignored the image and carried on. At the top, there was a long corridor that ran the length of the building with the small bathroom, bedroom, sitting room, and kitchen all opening off it.

We started in the sitting room. The stale air made me want to open the window, but that would be noticed. Instead, I rubbed my nose, trying to free it from the stagnant smell that reminded me of all the abandoned probate houses Arthur and I had ever entered. It was like some houses stopped breathing the moment their owners died. The faded floral William Morris upholstery of Arthur's favorite armchair was now threadbare in places. I ran my hand along the cool fabric and a lump grew in my throat. I snapped my hand away.

In front of the chair was an eighteenth-century pine blanket chest, which was of no real historical importance. Yet I couldn't take my eyes off it, remembering Arthur's training in carpentry and his love of hidden compartments. I opened the chest to see it was filled with blankets, and my fingertips brushed over the boards pitted by woodworm. It was the kind of thing many people used for a coffee table. Years back, it might have resided in a Victorian lady's bedroom, having arrived with her from her childhood home after she was married.

I lifted the tartan blankets and white lace tablecloths out of the chest and carefully laid them on the moth-eaten Persian rug. I shone my phone's flashlight around the inside of the chest. It looked normal, but my instinct told me it wasn't. It was the feeling I always had when something was wrong with an antique. I put one hand on the ground and another in the box—the levels were different.

Excitement pulsed through me. The hope that I was on the brink of a discovery quickened my search.

"Carole, look."

She peered over me. "Darling, I hate to state the obvious, but there's nothing there."

"That's not true." I handed her the phone flashlight. "There should be a small lifting hole or a catch to press if Arthur had modified it."

"Anything?" Carole asked.

"I'm not sure," I said, confused but undeterred. This was the long-forgotten part of the hunt that I loved so much. The single moment of possibility before a find.

Carole shone the light around the very base of the chest as I felt around the bottom. My finger brushed over something metal—a cold, button-like shape. I stopped and caught Carole's eye. We both leaned in. The button was close to the floor and would've been hidden from anyone not looking for it.

"Arthur altered it. In a shop like this I guess the least likely place to search would be the least valuable item." My heart pounded in my ears as I pushed the button inward with my index finger. The mechanism made a *click*, but nothing else seemed to happen. Carole held the light closer. Adrenaline swept through me. The bottom of the chest had popped up at an angle. I placed my fingers under the false bottom and pulled it up, discovering that half of the chest's bottom was on hinges.

Carole clapped and the light of the phone bounced around the room. "Darling, you're a genius!"

Neatly placed along the bottom of the chest were seven leather-bound journals.

I picked one up, the leather soft and cool in my hands, and unwound the strap. Old newspaper clippings fell out and scattered around me. I collected them, knowing that I would study them in detail at home.

"It's just some old journals." Carole's disappointment was evident.

I agreed. "Is this really what Arthur wanted us to find?"

From the street outside, laughter echoed through the rain. I turned off my flashlight and ran to the sitting room window, pulling back the curtain. Below me, a drunken couple was walking away down the high street, huddled under an umbrella.

As my eyes followed them, I saw something else. A movement in the shadows. I strained to see a humanlike shape resting against the post office building. Was it a person? I leaned forward. It was, I was sure of it, and they were watching the shop.

Panic jolted through me. "Someone's out there . . . watching us." Was it Mr. Sunglasses again? I couldn't tell.

A car sped down the high street, splashing the puddles across the pavement. The headlights lit a tall figure in a long coat as they scurried toward the right, down a small alley, deeper into the darkness.

I shivered. "We need to leave."

Carole pointed to the journals. "And take these with us."

"Let's go."

I looked around for a bag to carry the books in, but there wasn't one in sight. I quickly fashioned a cotton tablecloth into a knapsack and was ready to go.

The screech of a cat came from outside, making Carole—who was now standing at the top of the stairs—grab her chest and whisper to me, "Darling, run!"

As we reached the bottom of the stairs and turned down the corridor toward the back door, a shadow crossed the crack in the shopwindow's curtains.

A towering shape was standing at the front door.

It reached for the handle, which rattled.

Then the figure pressed its face to the glass, exactly as I had done earlier, but it was too dark to make out its features.

Knock. Knock.

The sound sent panic shuddering through me and shocked me into action. Had Mr. Sunglasses followed us hoping that Carole had the keys to the shop and would enter at some point? Was he the one Arthur mentioned in his letter? Was he now attempting to get into the shop? If the answer was yes, then we didn't have much time before he came around and tried the back door.

We fumbled our way out of the back, locking the door again, and I stuffed the keys into my handbag. There was no one in the cobbled alley behind the shops.

My phone buzzed in my pocket, startling me. I ignored it and we hurtled toward the Crown and Carole's car, but she stumbled on the uneven, slippery ground.

I gasped and helped her up with trembling hands.

Footsteps were rapidly approaching behind us.

We ran.

I didn't need to turn around to know the man from the shop was closing in on us.

The rain thundered down—rolling off my nose and flooding my eyes as we reached the end of the alley and crossed over the main street and hurried down a small footpath that ran behind some houses, zigzagging our way toward the Crown parking lot. The person was close, but I hoped they didn't know Little Meddington like we did. We picked up speed as the parking lot and Carole's car came into sight. Our funeral clothes were soaked through as we climbed into the car and locked the doors. Carole turned on the engine and we peeled out of the parking space and onto the main road. I watched out of the rear window as we left and saw a shadowy figure, their features still impossible to make out, run into the parking lot.

We were safe, for now.

12

"Always check your exit route."

—Arthur Crockleford

Back in the comfort of the Old Forge I made tea and contemplated how long it would take someone to find out where my aunt lived. But even if they did find us, I was a light sleeper and I practiced the martial art Krav Maga. I'd protected myself back during my antique hunting days, so I hoped I'd be able to now. I should've been fearful, but that's not what was pumping through me. I was excited. In following Arthur's first clue we had managed to get into the shop and find some hidden journals. It was my first hunt in over twenty years, and it had been a success. I was invigorated by it. Now I was quite determined to uncover Arthur's betrayer and what he'd gotten caught up in that could've led to his death.

I placed the bundle of journals on the kitchen table and started opening it.

My phone rang again. *No Caller ID*. I sent it to voicemail and concentrated on the journals.

"Harley, keep watch, would you?" said Carole. Harley opened one eye at the sound of his name but quickly went back to sleep on his bed by the Aga.

Carole pulled the journals toward her. "We have seven journals." She flipped through all of them. "They all contain lists of antiques and the

63

like. Apart from this one. The one labeled 'seven' which is empty. Why do you think that is?"

"Perhaps he didn't get a chance to finish his notes?"

"How strange." Carole showed me the first journal.

Inside the dark-brown leather cover was written, "My Antique Hunter's Guide." Below that, in a different pen, Arthur had written—"Attn; Freya Lockwood."

I couldn't believe what I was seeing. I'd known Arthur had wanted me to get into the shop and find the journals, but I'd never considered that they were directly for me.

I took the journal from Carole's hand and carried it into the sitting room, sinking into the sofa. My finger traced over "Freya" and then up to "Antiques Hunter." Seeing the words together again ignited a small flame of desire in me. I loved the courageous and determined person I'd been back then, before I shrank into James's image of what a wife should be—quiet and unassuming. He had been clear that Jade needed both parents and, "if you leave me," he'd threatened, "your precious daughter will never see her mother again." I didn't doubt him—he had enough money to hire the best solicitors and I had very little. Perhaps I should've been grateful when nine years ago he found someone else who was "more agreeable" and my solicitor could arrange for me to stay in the house until Jade turned eighteen.

Although I regretted almost everything about our marriage, I could never regret it fully—it gave me Jade. But if Arthur hadn't pushed me out of the hunting game, who knew what I might have been? Who might have I become, if I'd spent the past two decades antiques hunting?

I closed my eyes. Arthur had placed a lot of faith in my abilities as a hunter to decipher the clues in his letter. Abilities I hadn't used for a very long time. Perhaps he believed in me more than I believed in myself.

"This first journal has lists of art and antiques," Carole said. "Maybe they're all things Arthur found over the years and he wrote them down for you? Or maybe he wanted you to go and find them?" said Carole.

I took back the journal—or should I call it a "guide" as Arthur had?—and opened the first page.

At the top was written "Copthorn Manor Collection." Then there was a list of furniture, but not just any furniture—truly fine examples of British antique furniture. He'd even pasted in photographs with descriptions. "This entire column is dedicated to Gillows," I said, turning the page to Carole, but she shrugged, oblivious to who Gillows was. "Gillows was a luxury furniture maker in the eighteenth and nineteenth centuries. The Victoria and Albert have some fine pieces. Look at this one." I pointed at a games table with hard stone, fossils, and English marble colorfully placed around the black-and-white-checkered center where one could play chess or checkers. "That would probably be worth over forty thousand pounds."

Next to the image Arthur had written, "Exceptional example attributed to Gillows—a masterpiece."

I ran my finger down the list and over the next few pages, awed by the collection. "This is like a catalogue of some of the greatest furniture makers of the eighteenth and nineteenth centuries. Chippendale, Hepplewhite, et cetera."

There was a blank page, and then another section listing a wide range of smaller items. "It doesn't say if these are part of the Copthorn Collection," I said, showing Carole pictures of a set of snuffboxes, an eighteenth-century barometer, and a seventeenth-century Dutch table clock. "But these are definitely in the six-figure bracket and so, so rare." Next to each photograph was Arthur's handwritten description and a green or red sticker.

"What's the color code for, do you think? Almost all the furniture has red dots next to them," replied Carole.

"In the shop a red sticker means 'tourist price,' but that doesn't make sense here. Why would Arthur go to such lengths to hide these? You would do that only if you thought the information inside was valuable and that others might try to take it. But it just seems to be a list of antiques and there isn't any value in a list, is there?"

I pulled out one of the newspaper cuttings that had been tucked into the back of the journal. It was from the early 2000s and the headline read, "Britain's Biggest Art and Antique Robberies Sweep the Home Counties—Five Police Forces Search for the £80m in Loot."

I remembered the time well. There had been a spate of robberies at stately homes throughout the south of England and millions of pounds' worth of antiques and art were stolen. Only half of the haul was ever recovered. I had followed the case with interest, always longing to be involved. I scanned the rest of the cuttings, then flicked through the pages of the journal. "Many of the items seem to be 'still missing,' but they appear *here* in the middle section of the journal."

"What was Arthur up to?" asked Carole.

"A few of the people arrested didn't even make millions from what they stole," I mused aloud. "They probably didn't know who to sell it on to, so they stashed it in bins in an old container or something. However, the really valuable items were never recovered." It didn't take long for me to come to a conclusion. "Do you think Arthur was hunting these missing antiques? I believe the insurance companies put up a good reward for finding them." I studied the dates of the articles. "I left hunting in April 2002, so most of this was after my time. This one was a year after I'd moved in with James." I showed her another cutting. "I know private detectives were hired. I'd always wondered if Arthur was one of them."

Carole shrugged. "It's possible. Arthur loved the hunt."

I checked the back of the journal and discovered an envelope built into the last page. I looked inside and found a couple of folded, bright white pages.

I unfolded the pages. It was a booking for a two-bedroom vacation cottage on the grounds of a manor, dated for the coming weekend.

It read, "Booking Confirmation for Copthorn Manor—Antiques Enthusiasts Retreat—Freya Lockwood, Verifier."

"Copthorn Manor is where the collection in this journal is." I was excited already. "And we learned from Franklin that Arthur had requested

I value the late Lord Metcalf estate for probate—surely it's not a coincidence. Copthorn Manor must have been owned by the late Lord Metcalf and now Arthur has given us a list of what we are meant to find there. Where did you put the letter? We need to read it again." Carole retrieved it from her handbag.

I pointed. "Here he says 'Hunt the clues and you'll find a reservation. I implore you to attend, but be careful. My betrayer will be following your every move.'"

"Arthur's murderer could be there," Carole said, scanning the confirmation page with a frown. Then she turned to the second page. "Look at this, darling."

❧ PROGRAM ❧

Saturday, May 25

3 P.M.	CHECK IN
6 P.M.	EVENING DRINKS AS THE SUN GOES DOWN
7 P.M.	DINNER WITH EXOTIC MEATS
9 P.M.	ENTERTAINMENT—A BELLY-DANCING EXTRAVAGANZA

Sunday, May 26

5 A.M.	BREAKFAST IN THE MANOR
9 A.M.	ANTIQUES MARKET—LONG MELFORD
12 NOON.	ANTIQUES TALK—VICTORIAN STONEWARE

"Belly dancing," Carole said. "Now, I do really love a good dance."

"Dinner with exotic meats?" The phrase was familiar, but I couldn't place it. "Did Arthur design this program?"

"I don't know," Carole said. "But Arthur's letter helped us to get into the shop. He knew that you'd remember his talent in carpentry and how he loved a hidden compartment. He wanted us to find these journals and this reservation. He was always very fond of an antiques themed retreat and I know that he used to attend some as a verifier so antiques dealers and guests could trade and buy antiques and antiquities. Perhaps this retreat was planned before Lord Metcalf's death and it is now serving as a chance for you to verify the estate? We must trust Arthur and keep going."

But I didn't trust Arthur, did I?

My mobile phone rang. *No Caller ID*. Worried it could be Jade in trouble. I answered.

"Freya?" said James, and my stomach twisted. It couldn't be good news if he was calling.

"Yes?" I tried to sound hard and in control, but somehow James always made me feel small and unimportant.

"We've had an offer," he replied.

"I haven't agreed to that." I reached out for Carole.

"I've been trying to get hold of you, left messages, but you didn't answer or call me back," he barked. "What's wrong with you?"

It was one of his favorite questions.

"Whose phone are you calling on?" I asked, knowing that it was probably a new one.

He ignored me. "The real estate agents say you don't answer them either. I imagine you've run home to your crazy aunt for tea and sympathy. Can't even cope with a few viewings, can you?"

I tried to find a snarky rebuttal, but the words died in my throat.

"Hello?" he huffed when I didn't reply. "Freya, talk to the real estate agents and stop being so pathetic all the time."

He hung up and I chucked my phone onto the coffee table.

Deep down, I worried that he was right. If I couldn't even face real estate agent viewings, why did I think I was strong enough to uncover a murderer?

I woke with the glow of dawn breaking through the living room windows. I must have fallen asleep on the sofa. The first thing I saw was the cricket bat on the floor next to me.

I hadn't been able to sleep last night—James's words had rattled my confidence. I'd distracted myself by emailing friends in London about the antiques in the journals and then, when the house creaked and windows rattled, retrieved the bat from the mudroom. Harley might have slept next to me, but he wasn't the guard dog my aunt considered him to be.

The wood pigeons had started cooing on the oak tree outside. It was the sound of my childhood. I pulled an old quilt around myself and opened the double doors onto the garden. The telephone call with James was still raw, and the sweep of crisp, dew-dampened air soothed me. I slipped on a pair of gardening clogs hanging on the welly boot stand and walked down the path to the fields.

The four apple trees that marked the boundary of Carole's land were covered in white blossoms, and I stopped to admire Suffolk at its best.

I heard Carole's voice and saw her in her long, maroon velvet coat—which should have been worn at a ball—down the garden feeding her fluffy bantams. She was bent over the chicken coop trying to move a hen. "Oh, Marilyn, you broody minx," she was saying as I approached. "Get off the egg."

Carole had always named her chickens after her favorite Hollywood sirens—the white, fluffy one with feathered feet was called Marilyn. Marilyn didn't lay many eggs, but Carole adored her—every few years Marilyn got eaten by a fox or got some illness and was replaced by another Marilyn. And then there were Joan, Bette, Lauren, and Ava.

"Morning," I called.

"Darling, did you sleep on the sofa all night?"

"I'm fine."

She handed me a wicker basket with four small eggs inside and left the coop doors open. "Off you go, then," she said to the chickens. None of them moved. They continued to peck at the ground.

I linked my arm through Carole's, my doubts still lingering. "Are we really going to go to this retreat? It might be dangerous. We've already been followed and Arthur's letter holds a stark warning."

Carole looked me straight in the eye. "Every time you speak to James, I see the spark in your eyes dim. He needed to be in your life when Jade was younger, but Jade's grown now and once that house is gone you never need to talk to him again."

"It's my home," I snapped, but I knew she was right.

Carole seemed to know there was no point in arguing. We walked back to the house in silence.

"Let's have some eggs before packing. I just need to get someone to look after Harley for the night."

"I don't want you in any danger," I said. "Perhaps I should go on my own."

"I am going." Carole broke eggs into a bowl and started to whisk. "His letter was addressed to both of us. It clearly proves he was murdered and points us to this Copthorn Manor, so that's where I'm going."

She was right, and I knew I wouldn't be able to persuade Carole to stay at home. We were both going to Copthorn Manor to catch a killer.

13

"A good estate sale is a dealer's delight."

—Arthur Crockleford

Later that day, Carole and I pulled up to the large black iron gates that guarded an endless drive. "Copthorn Manor" was written on top of the arched gates in gold paint that was flecked with age. I climbed out of Carole's vintage Mercedes, my feet crunching on the deteriorating asphalt, and checked the stonework for a bell or some other way to alert someone that we had arrived.

I turned to Carole, who was readjusting her Jackie O–inspired sunglasses. "Why aren't the gates open? Aren't we expected?"

"The gates don't look locked," said Carole, pointing to the large round handle in the middle. "Just give them a little shove, darling. You know, put your back into it."

I reached out, then hesitated. "Do we have a plan?"

Carole lifted her glasses to check if I was serious. "A plan, darling. What a marvelous idea. I am an absolute genius at making plans. Where shall we start? I've got it." She flicked back her blond hair. "Firstly, I shall be called Marilyn—for obvious reasons."

"Because you look like a fluffy bantam?" I couldn't help myself.

"Oh, a bit of humor from you, how quaint. We shall call you Deirdre—you know, like the one from Corrie." She looked very pleased with her comeback. Then realizing the dig might not land as she

71

intended, she carried on. "Of course, we could've once called you Lara Croft, but you went all *James's wife* on us."

I sighed, not wanting to take this line of conversation any further. "I'll be called Freya and you can pick whatever persona you like. No, I mean a *real* plan. Like finding out what this place really is and why Arthur was so insistent that we attend."

I turned the handle, and sure enough, the gates clicked open a crack.

"I think we need to know a bit of history about everyone here and what they were doing on the night of Sunday, May nineteenth," I continued. "Between . . . what time do we think Arthur died?"

Carole nearly put her hand up. "Oh, I know this one. I'm saying between eleven p.m. and four a.m. Monday morning. Got to be the dead of night or the neighbors would've heard his fall or the vases breaking. And before you ask, when I was at the shop on Monday morning, I overheard the rude Suffolk Constabulary boy asking the neighbors." Carole sounded upbeat but the pain of losing Arthur was etched in her brow. I understood that she was trying too hard to make me believe she was fine. When I didn't react, she said, "What I learned was that the apartments on either side of Arthur's have paper-thin walls. The old man on the right went to sleep at ten p.m. and the couple on the left at eleven p.m. and heard nothing before that time. The old man wasn't a good sleeper and he woke at four a.m., didn't hear a dickey bird after that time. I'm so good at this, aren't I?"

"Oh yes, I don't know why Suffolk even has a police force with you around." I pushed the gate fully open, waited for Carole to drive through, and closed it again. "Right, so that's where we start, finding out who had the opportunity." I got back in the car, my pulse quickening a little. Another hunt was about to begin.

Doubts crept into my mind as I scanned the rewilded fields and overgrown hedges on either side of us, but I wasn't going to let them stop me. At the end of Arthur's letter, he had said, *I always wanted to tell you the truth about Cairo, but I needed you out of the antique hunting game back then, and now it seems fate has decided that I won't get the chance to set it right. You need to see the truth.*

Could my past really be changed by attending an antiques enthusiasts retreat? And what truth could I possibly uncover about myself in a house I had never been to with a dead owner I'd never met?

"Are you sure you want to go ahead with this?" I asked Carole one last time. "That man following us could be here."

Carole patted my knee. "Darling, we're doing this for Arthur. We're going to act like we are having the most fun without a care in the world, get them off guard, and find out all their secrets—you follow my lead." She slammed her foot on the accelerator.

The Mercedes entered a wooded tunnel of trees that lined the drive, just like they did at every National Trust place I'd ever visited. I peered up as the canopy obscured the sky and only streaks of dim daylight flickered through; the touches of sunshine didn't warm the air. The car roof was down even though the clouds threatened rain and I wondered if we were about to be drenched.

We emerged and I blinked in the light. Before us stood a towering manor house, its long shadow swallowing us into darkness once more. Ivy crawled up the brickwork and penetrated through the crumbling windows. A curtain moved on the first floor.

I shivered and reached for my scarf.

A green and motionless lake lay to our left and beyond that overgrown farmland. Across the lake was a figure on a ride-on lawn mower, perhaps a gardener. "This place looks abandoned," I said.

Carole turned the engine off. "I'll go and check. There has to be someone here."

She exited the car, putting on her enormous straw hat and straightening her navy polka-dot swing dress. She looked like a Golden Age Hollywood actress as she sauntered toward the entrance. A paparazzo could have jumped out from behind the line of trees to our left and Carole would've been ready with a huge smile. The manor house's front door was situated between two towering columns, and above, row upon row of windows stretched underneath three gabled rooftops, probably seventeenth century. All the curtains on the second and third floors were tightly drawn. Did one move again?

Carole lifted the large brass knocker and tapped twice. I unclipped my seat belt, ready to rush to her aid if needed.

"Hello?" I heard Carole call through the letterbox.

I was uneasy. Attending the retreat had appeared to be a good idea when weighed against the alternative of going back to London and dealing with the real estate agents. Now, in the presence of an eerie house, I wondered if I was walking my aged—though sprightly—aunt into danger, and all my excitement for the hunt had evaporated.

Carole stepped back from the door and looked up. "Hello? We have a reservation."

As I was debating whether it was best to insist that we leave, the cracked and peeling red front door began to creak open.

I held my breath.

A woman in her forties stood in the doorway; darkness tunneled behind her. Her hair was pulled back in a bun and she wore a white shirt and cropped black trousers with sensible shoes. She didn't look like the lady of the house—based on appearances, that title could plausibly have been given to Carole—but she had the posture of someone who was in charge.

I couldn't hear what was being said and was annoyed at myself for staying in the car. Carole nodded at the woman, then hurried back to me.

"This is it. I've just met the housekeeper, Clare. We're a bit early; most people are arriving this evening for drinks." Carole clicked the seat belt in and started the car. "Lucky I brought you a dress, isn't it, darling?"

"You brought me one of *your* dresses?" I cringed. It would be extravagant and loud and I knew Carole would've loved every second of choosing one for me. "What's it like?"

"Oh, it is *so* you," Carole said as she reversed and steered us down another drive that led around the side of the manor and toward a row of buildings. "Or perhaps the you that you should've been. I am going to let her out into the world. It's a short black number with a plunging neckline, long sleeves, and lots of lovely sequins at the cuffs—it will look amazing. You will be a revelation." Carole beamed at me, then a frown crossed her forehead.

"What is it?" I asked, praying that she had forgotten the dress.

"Clare, who opened the door, said that she knew *you* were arriving as a replacement verifier but didn't expect me. She asked if I knew when Franklin Smith would be here."

"Franklin is also coming?" I hadn't considered he intended to be at the manor this weekend and I wondered who had told the housekeeper I was coming. "I got the impression that Franklin didn't want me to be the estate's verifier and he would have preferred to find someone else. Arthur's letter led us to the shop and to the journals with booking information inside, to make sure we made it here." I looked at the manor behind us. "Are we to believe this house is connected to Arthur's murder?"

Carole shuddered. "I think so, but I do hope we don't meet the same ends."

"I won't let that happen," I said to reassure her, but I didn't have a clue how I could keep us safe. Another thought hit me. "Why did Arthur think I'd be able to be the verifier? I've been out of the game a long time. He was placing a lot of faith in me."

Carole tucked one of my stray curls behind my ear. "You should have faith in *yourself*. It's your passion for all the old stuff and the blind focus you have for it . . . what did Arthur call it? 'The eye.'"

I understood what Carole was saying. Arthur had always said I had an instinct about antiques and antiquities. The way I just knew when something didn't look right. "But I'm not a generalist antiques expert like Arthur was." My stomach twisted. "What if they produce something I don't know? I'll be totally out of my depth."

"You'll be fine as a verifier and it's a good cover," said Carole, parking the car outside the long building with large arched doors. "Looks like this used to be the stable block, and, oh . . . the wonderful climbing roses, Rosa 'Etoile de Hollande,' I think."

I got out of the car and admired the large green front door with red roses arched along the top and stretching toward the first-floor windows. The four cottages were in far better repair than the main house. Recently washed, double-glazed windows were open and a white metal bistro set was placed on the small patio—presumably for a morning coffee.

"Here we are, then," a woman said, appearing from behind them. "I'm Clare, the housekeeper. Let's get you settled in." She motioned to the end cottage.

Inside, I couldn't help but marvel at the tastefully decorated sitting room—modern interiors set against the old stable cobbles. It reminded me quite how untidy and run-down my London house had become. A row of Japanese Ukiyo-e reproduction landscape prints hung along one wall. On my left was a small, contemporary open-plan kitchen and to my right a dining table. Beyond that a huge white sofa in front of a log burner. To be honest, I had always believed a white sofa was the height of luxury. Jade would have loved it and then spilled her coffee down one arm. I regretted not telling her I was away for the weekend. I would've liked to talk it all through with her. I scanned the room again and saw, at the back of the cottage, a staircase presumably leading to the bedrooms.

"This is lovely." Carole gave Clare her most dazzling stage smile. "We shall be *so* comfortable here."

"It's far better than that old, cold place." Clare gestured at the manor. "It needs pulling down." Her soft American accent was evident—it was like she was trying to hide it or she'd been away from home a long time. She held out some keys. "Here you go, then, drinks at seven p.m. in the drawing room and dinner will be at eight p.m." She nodded a goodbye and closed the cottage door behind her.

I watched from the window as she scurried over the cobbled stable yard toward the manor. There was a side door in the back corner of the house that looked so old its hinges were probably rusted shut. Clare jiggled the handle, trying to open it. Her fists clenched in obvious frustration. Rallying herself, she slammed her shoulder into it and it budged just enough for her to squeeze herself through the gap. The hairs on the back of my neck prickled. Something didn't feel right. I looked up. Someone was standing at a first-floor window above the kitchen door—the curtains pulled back—watching us.

14

"Antiques are precious and inspiring, but they cannot set you free. They do not have that sort of power."

—Arthur Crockleford

Giles

Giles was tired. Just the sight of Copthorn Manor did that to him. He hadn't been back in decades and it wasn't a happy reunion. He was just glad there was still a lot of whiskey lying around the place.

What had happened to Arthur had been avoidable. If only he hadn't been so stupid. His death weighed heavily on Giles.

Arthur had sent him a letter telling him where the Martin Brothers bird was hidden. Giles had driven down the long, winding drive, with fields stretching out to the horizon, and admired the barren, unkempt beauty of the place. The manor was so remote it was the perfect place to keep all those treasures.

He'd need to tread carefully and see who turned up this weekend. In his letter, Arthur had been cagey. Giles was now deeply suspicious and had taken greater precautions to hide his identity, even shaving off his beloved beard last week—there were some criminal entities he'd spent a long time keeping away from. His sister, Amy, knew him, of course, but he was making it as hard as possible for anyone to identify him in a lineup if the night went sideways.

He watched from the window as a woman approached the main door while another one remained in the car. The older one, late sixties or perhaps early seventies, looked like she belonged on the French Riviera. The younger one, late forties, was less assuming—dark curly hair, about five foot seven, in jeans and a flowy top.

He knew who they were.

The first time he had seen Carole all those years ago, she'd been sitting with Arthur in a strange bar in Hong Kong drinking champagne for her birthday. He couldn't forget her; she was that sort of woman.

Giles had met her a few times after that; Arthur and Carole traveled together on many occasions. She seemed to be some sort of cover for Arthur, not the type to blend in. She was the type that drew attention toward herself and left others in the shadows. It was perfectly clever of Arthur to think of such a thing. But why was she here, when he was no longer with them? What purpose did it serve? Did she know what Arthur had been up to, and was she now taking his place? *Risky*, was the word that popped into Giles's head. *Risky*.

He watched the car drive toward the cottages, Clare, the new housekeeper, following them. She handed over the cottage keys and quickly retreated. The younger woman lingered at the window. His gaze fixed on her. Did she see him watching her? There was something in her eyes and the slightest frown across her brow that told Giles this woman never missed a beat. He would have to keep an eye on her and find out what she knew. What had Arthur told her? If he'd told her everything . . . well, then, she wouldn't see sunrise.

15

"The start of the hunt is the most exciting and the most dangerous. You always need to get the lay of the land first."
—Arthur Crockleford

Freya

I locked the door behind us and popped the kettle on instead of un-
packing. I'd never seen the point of placing all my clothes in someone else's drawers only to pack them up again—my philosophy was
"hang up the dress and get on with the vacation." Carole, on the other
hand, was upstairs, hanging everything up and using her steamer to make
sure each item was pristine. I sat staring at the unlit log burner in silence,
running through everything in my mind.

When we'd started a hunt for a stolen piece of artwork or antique,
whether it was for an insurance company, a museum, or a private client,
we always approached it the same way. We would sit at Arthur's desk in
the shop reading through the statements and discussing possible places a
criminal could take the item to be sold. Arthur used to ask, *What do we
really know? What are the facts?*

Carole sauntered downstairs.

"Do you have a moment to go through it all—go through what we *really* know?" I asked, reluctantly acknowledging how much I sounded like Arthur.

Before replying, Carole reached for the kettle.

"I've already made a pot of tea." I lifted the pot to entice her over.

"Oh, jolly good, let's get started," she said, relaxing into the squashy armchair next to the window.

I tucked my legs underneath me and allowed my mind to filter through the events of the last week. "A week before Arthur's death he calls you saying he's been to see an old friend who is on death's door, who now we think was Lord Metcalf. I'm guessing that Lord Metcalf told Arthur some secrets on his deathbed. Arthur must have mentioned my name to Metcalf as I am apparently in the will as an alternative verifier and who else would have put me forward. Three days later, on Tuesday, Metcalf dies. The next morning, which is Wednesday, Arthur is in Franklin Smith's office, offering to help with Metcalf's estate and insisting that if he can't do it then I am to be the replacement. He would only do that if he already knew he was 'betrayed' and he might not live to fulfil his role. Arthur also gave instructions for his will to be drawn up there and then. He signs it—with Annabelle, the secretary, as a witness—"

"And he left you the brooch—this is most thrilling," she said. I must have frowned at Carole interrupting my train of thought because she made out like she was zipping her lips shut. "I won't say another word," she mumbled.

"Then on Friday, Arthur gives a letter to Agatha with the clues for finding the shop keys and alarm code. He knew we would start looking around and see something was off. Maybe Arthur broke the vases to give us another clue and then someone tried to cover it up?" Carole nodded enthusiastically. "Where's the letter?"

"I popped it in your handbag," she said. "And you've asked a question. Which means I'm back to speaking." She looked toward the manor. "We must find out what happened here. What happened to my darling . . ." Her voice cracked.

I reached for her hand as her eyes filled up. "No matter what, I will get to the bottom of this, I promise you." I owed my aunt that much.

Carole smiled, but there was still a deep sadness in her expression. "I'm so lucky to have you. We will act like nothing is amiss." She rubbed her eye to hide a tear that lingered there.

I continued, "We believe Arthur died sometime in the middle of Sunday night or before dawn on Monday morning. Whatever Lord Metcalf told him spurred him into action, and he set out leaving us clues that only we could decipher. Arthur told Franklin I should be the verifier here if he couldn't make it. I think this means two things. One, Arthur considered he wouldn't be alive to attend. Two, it implies that Arthur was in some way involved in arranging these retreats."

"So many questions to answer," said Carole.

I checked my email, hoping that one of my suspicions might have been confirmed and was pleased to see I'd had a reply from an auctioneer I'd contacted the previous night.

"Oh, will you look at the smile on your face. Has Jade decided to come back for the summer after all?" asked Carole.

I shook my head. "Not yet." I pushed away the sadness and focused on the hunt. "Last night when I couldn't sleep I emailed a friend at an auction house to check the Art Loss Register for a couple of the items from the second section in the first journal. He's just confirmed they were both stolen back in 2003. I believe this suggests all the antiques in the second section are from the black market."

"Thrilling," said Carole. "And how did you know they might be?"

"The photographs of the antiques in the first journal are not unlike the images of an antique the insurance company or museum would give us when we started a hunt to recover what had been stolen. In the

Copthorn Manor Collection section, the photos look professionally taken but the middle section looks like they could have been taken in secret—some are at a strange angle, others from a distance and the items circled in red. Do we believe all the antiques in the journal are here? That's a lot of antiques. Where would they be?"

We sat in silence, sipping our tea, deep in thought.

I reread Arthur's letter. "Here it says,

"It has taken me over twenty years to find an item of immense value. I have been told its location, but it seems I will not be able to retrieve it. Get it back, Freya, and you will have your life and your career back. I'm sorry I cannot be clearer; I have been betrayed and can't risk this letter being discovered. Tell no one. There is no one left to trust. Hunt the clues and you'll find a reservation. I implore you to attend, but be careful. My betrayer will be following your every move."

Carole's eyes sparkled. "Maybe Lord Metcalf told Arthur the item was here, and you being the retreat's verifier was the cover he gave you so you could find it?"

"I think that's a pretty good bet—and Arthur must've thought if I could retrieve it, then I could use that recognition to get back into the antique hunting world. But we have to be so *very* careful. I'm sure we are being watched and there could be a killer behind any of those manor doors. We will need to ask *subtle* questions at the drinks this evening."

"Darling, I am subtle by nature." Carole rearranged her multitude of jingly bangles.

"You're anything but subtle. You stand out." My aunt lived in a whole other universe sometimes.

"Oh, thank you, darling girl. I stand out *subtly*, don't I? It's my old-world glamour that people just can't help but admire."

"Now that we've come to the agreement that you are not subtle, we need to look around."

Carole downed her tea. "Absolutely. I saw some drainpipes out front that we could climb and search the bedrooms."

I ignored her outlandish suggestion. "I was thinking about a walk around the grounds because I've seen this." I opened the first journal at the beginning of the second section, where Arthur had written:

IMPORTANT—Copthorn Manor Old English Folly—built by the original owner, the Cravens, in 1903. Took quite some time to find, but it's the best place for overseeing events. Would give the Victorian lady something Gothic to see on her daily walk.

Carole reached for her bright red lipstick and reapplied. "A folly, darling, is a tower or grotto or something decorative, and most of them have fallen into disrepair as they didn't have a use other than for being looked at. It's not designed for 'overseeing events.'"

"I totally agree, but I think we should see if one is here. Maybe another clue will be there. And a walk around the grounds won't arouse suspicion, will it?"

"I'll get my coat and some lovely suede knee-high boots to keep the stinging nettles at bay."

I would've protested at the wardrobe change because it was likely to scream "I have arrived" but my mind was too full of unanswered questions. I was beginning to believe that Arthur wrote everything for a reason. "Where would Victorian ladies walk?" I asked.

"Probably around the lake—a folly could've been built there," Carole replied.

Outside, a car door slammed shut and we both jumped. "People." Carole's eyes widened with excitement. "People are always more interesting than a walk."

We hurried toward the kitchen window.

The car was a large silver 4x4 Audi without a speck of dirt on it. Carole and I looked at each other. "From town," she said.

"Colchester or farther?"

"Gut says farther," replied Carole.

We nodded at each other—we were clearly nailing this detective thing.

A middle-aged man wearing ripped jeans ran out of the manor and arrived at the driver's door in time to open it for a young woman, who looked to be in her late twenties. Her dark hair tied in a high ponytail, tight jeans, cream silk shirt, and pointed heels made her look like she had just walked out of a London private members club. The man reached out for the woman's elbow but didn't notice, or didn't care, when she flinched.

I studied him. He looked a bit like someone who'd been slumming it in that very expensive way only the boarding school classes can pull off. He placed a firm hand on the woman's back and pushed her toward the cottage at the other end of the row. It occurred to me that Clare, the housekeeper, wasn't anywhere in sight. I turned to Carole. "I suppose that he has already checked in?"

As they passed our cottage, the woman glanced around, and on seeing the decrepit manor, she shivered and pulled her oversized woolen scarf tightly around her shoulders.

Was either of them Arthur's killer? The question hung in my mind.

"Look like they own the place, don't they?" Carole whispered. "Does he look familiar to you?"

"I'm not sure, but I don't like him. Seems like a bully, doesn't he? And he looks far too old for her."

Carole nodded. "I'm sure we'll meet them at drinks. Now, how about that snoop around?"

"I thought we were calling it a walk?"

"Quite right, just a walk with our eyes peeled." Carole winked at me.

I chuckled and retrieved my coat.

I studied the manor on the other side of the cobbles. There could be a nest of vipers inside. However, it had been an act of desperation on Arthur's part to call on Carole and me to uncover what he could not. I was fixated on the hunt, and I wouldn't stop now.

16

"A highly skilled antiques hunter is like a cat. It stalks its prey
and the victim never knows it's there."

—Arthur Crockleford

I locked the cottage door and looked up at the sky. Dark rain clouds
hung above us. It was one of those May afternoons that threatened to
throw everyone back in time, toward the April showers.

I tied my coat's belt and wrapped my 1960s Hermès scarf around my
neck. Carole, who was never bothered by the weather, hurried ahead of
me with her knee-high suede boots and a bright blue silk kimono with
swirling patterns of the sea.

"What if it rains?" I asked, pointing at her impractical outfit.

"Honestly, where did I raise you! It's Suffolk, one of the driest parts of
the country," she said. "Come on, then." Clapping her hands, she strode
ahead with all the confidence of a meteorologist.

We crossed the drive and headed toward the motionless lake. I
watched in awe as Carole swept over a small wall and landed on the other
side. I did the same, discovering my body remembered past movements
and adventures even if my mind was trained to disregard them. The
glimmer of the memory of who I once was energized me, and the smell
of newly cut grass filled my lungs. The slip of path we walked on hugged
the lake before heading into a thick grove of trees.

The view along the lake was magnificent, with sprawling potato fields, pigsties, and hedgerows. We entered the woods, where soft pine needles blanketed the path underfoot; the scent of the sweet needles and mulch caught my nose. The lake was to our right. I checked behind me to see if we were being followed. Maybe it wasn't wise to go walking about an unknown wood?

Someone could trap us here.

Thunder crackled in the distance.

I searched our surroundings for signs of movement.

"Rain's coming," said Carole, looking totally shocked.

"Let's see how far we can get before having to call it a day?" I said, ignoring the panic brought on by the memory of being chased from the antiques shop the last time it poured with rain.

The deeper we went into the woods, the louder my insides screamed at me to turn around.

A twig snapped.

I froze.

Someone was there.

An old, long-forgotten sensation came back to me—an alertness, a stretching of the senses. I scanned the trees. A blackbird fluttered between the branches. My skin prickled.

"I should take you back," I whispered to Carole, fearful for her safety.

Someone's following us.

Carole paid no attention to my suggestion and walked ahead of me, her nose in the air and her stride determined. "I'm sure the path will lead us on a loop around the lake like the Victorian ladies would have walked. We'll be home in no time. Hopefully passing that folly so we can have a look for more *clues.*"

"Storm's coming," a man's voice called out from the close-knit evergreen trees to our left.

I put my arm out to protect Carole. "If he comes at us, you run."

"Don't be ridiculous. I'm a black belt in tae kwon do and you've become scared of spiders. Stand behind me." Carole stepped beside me, her fists up in the air like a boxer.

I straightened, digging my heels into the soft leaf-covered path. The self-defense instruction of Krav Maga stirred in my muscle memory. *Always try to look strong and in control.* I was out of the classroom and back in the real world. I saw for the first time that I was *me* again—that person hadn't left me; I'd just dived into the safety of my London home and become shrouded within the world of being a wife and mother. But I'd made sure that Jade had started Krav Maga when she was six years old.

Leaves and branches rustled from somewhere between the trees.

I readied myself, adjusting my stance. I was scanning the area for the quickest exit when a tall figure, shadowed by the tree canopy, emerged from the forest.

I tensed.

I'm Freya Lockwood, I recited to myself, *and I've encountered worse than this at the school gate.*

A man stepped onto the path in front of us. I looked him over, trying to assess if he was about to attack. He appeared to be in his early fifties, with strong shoulders. He was wearing old jeans and a ripped padded jacket. His hair was silver and well-kept—he was what some of my divorced friends in London would have referred to as a "silver fox." His ancient wellies were covered in mud. He was probably the same person who had been watching us from the lawn mower when we arrived.

"You shouldn't be here," he said, his eyes boring into us.

"We're just out for a walk," I replied, standing aside, indicating that he should pass us. "We're perfectly fine."

"This is private land. Leave now." He was American, with the deep, soft accent of someone from the South. His manner was harsh and demanding—although nothing like the way James talked to me.

Carole smiled warmly. "We're guests here. Is this off-limits to the guests? Clare didn't say so."

His head tilted with interest. "You're here for the antiques?"

"The antiques weekend, quite right," Carole confirmed, as the first splatter of rain filtered down through the trees. "And you are?"

He relaxed and held out a hand toward Carole. "I'm the estate gardener, Phil." Phil wasn't what I'd expect from an estate gardener. For a start he didn't have a dog, and every gardener I'd ever known had a dog.

The sound of rain hammering down on leaves made us all look up. A few droplets snuck through the canopy. An icy raindrop trickled down my cheek.

"You don't seem like the normal sort." Phil stepped closer to us, but I held my ground.

"I have no idea what the 'normal sort' is," Carole huffed. "Who in their right mind, unless you're a teenager, wants to be normal?"

"I didn't mean to offend you," he said softly.

"A friend of ours booked it for us," I answered, trying to sound chatty and at ease. That was what Arthur would have done, and we were in Arthur's world now.

"And who is this friend?" He crossed his arms.

"A good one, and we're looking forward to meeting everyone later over dinner. I suppose you're used to it all." Carole beamed at him. "I take it you've worked here for years?"

He didn't reply.

I tried a more direct question. "Do you know if there are any notable collections in the manor?"

Phil shrugged, then plunged his hands into his jacket pockets. "As I said, you should leave. *Normally*, people stick close to the house. There's nothing in the woods. You better get back before you're caught in the thick of the storm." And he continued blocking the path.

I didn't move.

Without missing a beat, Carole said, "What a shame. We thought that we could've found a folly around these woods."

"No folly here." Phil bristled.

The rain picked up, and I flipped up the collar of my trench coat, hooking the eyelet in place to shield my neck. Carole didn't seem at all bothered; she merely wiped the rain from the tip of her nose. "Do you live here?" she asked.

Phil frowned. "I do."

"So, you're also here on the weekends?" Carole pressed.

"Yes, but . . . what's this got to do with anything?"

I thought I'd chance a hunch. "Did you see Arthur Crockleford here the other weekend? A man in his eighties, smartly dressed with a brightly colored cravat."

"No. I'm just the gardener." Without saying goodbye, he strode back down the path toward the lake.

We waited a few minutes before continuing around the lake, undeterred by his warning. I let my fingertips brush past some pines—there was an exhilaration in me I hadn't felt since I'd changed the locks, bundled up all of James's clothes, and thrown them out the door—texting him: *your worldly possessions are outside and rain is forecast.*

"He's very handsome, but also very strange," said Carole.

I nodded. "And just because he denies meeting Arthur, doesn't mean that's the truth."

Thunder cracked again overhead and rain broke through the tree canopy. Branches clawed toward us. Birds scattered. Carole turned to me and we both understood that the weather had scuppered our plan. We hurried back the way we'd come until we reached the edge of the woods and had a clear sight of the manor once more.

It was evident that we'd been shielded from the worst of the downpour, and now the force of nature was clear to see. The dark lake danced as sheets of rain fell.

"Better make a run for it," said Carole. "And I'll call Harry when we get back and check on Harley. He might need a hot water bottle if his bed gets cold."

"I don't understand. Who's Harry?"

"Didn't I say? Mary next door was going to dog sit, but then Arthur's shop assistant, Harry, very kindly offered to look after Harley over the weekend. I'm going to call him when we get back and make sure Harley's not too depressed and maybe tell him to skip his Sunday swim."

I studied the downpour, and then Carole and I exchanged a look. We both knew that we were going to have to face the storm head-on if we were going to make it to drinks and dinner in the manor. We had people and antiques to study.

"Ready?" I said, preparing to run.

"As I'll ever be," said Carole.

17

"Sometimes, my dear boy, you just need to look a little closer at an item and you will see what it's truly worth."

—Arthur Crockleford

Harry

Harry was drenched. Rain ran down his face, but he couldn't stop staring at the Crockleford Antiques Shop. About an hour earlier, he'd decided Harley needed a walk. Carole's house was surprisingly claustrophobic—she must have left the heat on.

It was clear by the time they were halfway up the hill that Harley didn't walk much. He was old and slow.

Just like Arthur is. He corrected himself, *like Arthur had been.*

Through the piercing drizzle and whips of wind the shop looked cold. Arthur liked to deter burglars by leaving a light on in the upstairs window when he was away. There was no light on now. Harry would've liked to go inside one last time before he left Little Meddington.

He stepped back as a couple walked around him. The man was wearing big green welly boots, and seeing them reminded him of the argument.

It was rare for Harry to be early for work, but that day he'd really needed to get out of the house. His roommate had his girlfriend over and the kitchen wasn't big enough for all of them.

When he arrived at the shop, he could hear the argument through the front door so he decided to go around the back. He had intended on slipping inside and making a coffee, but on opening the back door his curiosity got the better of him. He had to know what was going on.

Harry stood in the corridor that led to the shop.

"You need to leave. My assistant will be here soon," Arthur was saying.

"Tell me where it is," the man replied.

"This was not part of our agreement." Arthur's voice was low and urgent. "Keep out of it."

Harry crept closer—eager to see who Arthur was talking to.

"Have you found the Martin Brothers bird?" the man asked.

His voice was vaguely familiar and Harry wondered if it was one of Arthur's regular clients.

"No!" There came a thud, as if Arthur had banged his fist into the desk. "I'm demanding that you leave right now."

Arthur wouldn't speak to a client like that.

There was a whisper that Harry couldn't make out, so he tiptoed farther down the corridor.

The bell above the shop door tinkled. Whoever had been arguing with Arthur had left.

Harry was desperate to see who had been in the shop. He stepped toward the end of the corridor. All he could make out was a man walking away with welly boots on. A floorboard squeaked and Arthur, still at his desk in the shop, looked up. He quickly slid a book into a drawer and locked it. "What are you doing here?" he demanded.

Harry stuttered, unable to find the right words. "I-I just . . ."

"I'm sorry, boy, I just wasn't expecting you to be at work so early," said Arthur, calming himself with a deep breath.

Arthur had always been secretive about what he did to make money to keep the shop afloat, but that morning there had been an edge to his voice that Harry couldn't forget. Arthur sounded scared.

Harry shuddered back to the present as Harley pulled harder on the lead. He took one last look at the shop. There was a part of him that missed working there.

He turned in the direction of Carole's house as thunder cracked in the distance.

18

"The winters are long, but spring always finds a way to make everything right."

—Arthur Crockleford

Phil

The path to the gardener's cottage was well hidden from prying eyes. Its location was known only to the late Lord Metcalf and his children. The cottage had low ceilings and small windows, and the plaster had bubbled in places. In Phil's experience, old British houses seemed charming but were not to be lived in if you needed warmth and light to keep you sane. He unlocked the warped door and hurried inside.

He needed to study the photos again to double-check if the women were who he suspected.

Did Arthur tell them about me? The question repeated in his mind as he pulled out the top drawer of his dresser and reached inside the empty cavity. He felt around until his fingers hit on an A4 envelope taped to the back wall.

If Arthur had sent those women here it was exceptionally foolish, but recently, being foolish had been Arthur's main trait.

He tugged the envelope free and shuffled through the papers inside until he found the photos. The first one was of Freya Lockwood. It must have been taken on vacation around twenty years ago—she was on horseback with endless desert behind her. Now Freya was older, but the fiery look she'd given him in the woods was the same.

He turned to the next photo in the envelope, with the words "Carole Lockwood" written on the back. This was a more recent image. Carole was sitting in the window of Crockleford Antiques Shop with Arthur drinking a cup of tea. They were laughing.

He returned the photos to the envelope—they confirmed their identities but that gave him no clue as to the real reason Freya and Carole were there.

Do they have the journals? That was all Phil really wanted to know. He didn't normally attend the drinks party, but he could make an exception just this once, try to befriend them and find out.

And how did they know about the folly? In the end, he had the weather to thank for their retreat, but he was worried all his hard work was about to be undone. He was going to have to watch them.

Six months back, a week after his arrival, Phil had asked Amy if she knew about a folly, and she had replied, "It fell into ruin years ago. I couldn't even tell you where it used to be." At that time, Lord Metcalf was bedridden and there was no one else around who knew the estate, so he was quite sure his hideaway was a secret . . . for now.

The only reason he hadn't had the women removed the moment he saw them was because it was clear Carole didn't recognize him from the couple of times he had been in Arthur's shop. If that situation changed, Phil would have to adapt—he was good at that.

If Freya and Carole had come into Arthur's place, after what had just happened to him, they were either incredibly brave or incredibly stupid. Either way, he was going to have to be alert.

Phil pulled off his boots and sodden jacket. It was a couple of hours until the meeting drinks, enough time for a warm shower and a quick iron of his shirt. He wanted to go back to the folly and make a quick phone call, tell them that Arthur's old colleague had turned up, the one he used to repatriate antiquities with in the Middle East. But there wasn't time for that; the weather wouldn't allow a quick trip—nor would the last of the daylight.

The small sitting room smelled of stale wood smoke. An old armchair sat beside the unlit log burner. Phil sighed deeply; his job wasn't easy. The chair was simple to flip onto its back—he was well practiced in the motion. The fabric covering the underbelly of the armchair pulled away easily thanks to the Velcro he'd added. He reached inside and lifted out a bag.

The pair of black leather gloves came out first and then the gun. The gun needed to be clean and ready to go.

There's a strong possibility those women won't get out of this alive.

19

"The other way to hunt is to circle your prey like a shark. Explore all sides of a job before you jump to a conclusion."

—Arthur Crockleford

Freya

We were late for evening drinks at the manor. Carole's "quick soak in the tub to warm up" had taken hours, and to pass the time I'd lit the log burner and inadvertently dozed off. I woke with a start, disorientated—thinking at first that I was on my sofa in London and looked around for Jade. Until the heartbreaking truth hit me—Jade was grown and far away and my London house would probably belong to someone else by summer. I pushed aside my despair and focused on the faint buzz of a hair dryer drifting down the pine staircase. My shoulders relaxed and I was standing up to go and join Carole, when something near the door caught my eye. It was a small envelope.

I opened it and retrieved a slip of paper that said, "LEAVE NOW."

A desperate impulse to know who'd sent it made me hurtle toward the curtain covering the door. I peered out. There was no one in sight.

One of Arthur's sayings came back to me. *Fight or flight? The decision can be life-or-death.*

"Carole," I called. "You need to see this."

She hurried downstairs and I showed her the note. "We're onto something, then," she said.

I traced the scar on my palm. "I don't want you in any danger."

Carole touched my shoulder. "If we play dumb, we won't seem a threat. And anyway, at my age, death could be around any corner. I won't let that stop me."

I didn't answer. I hated to think about my aunt's age or anything happening to her, natural or not.

"If we get the slightest whiff of danger, promise me you'll leave?" I said. *Flight was the safest answer.*

Carole frowned. "We always knew this would be a risky mission. Arthur warned us."

I agreed and picked up the first journal, scanning the pictures again, wanting to make sure I had the items memorized so I could identify them quickly. I ran my index finger over the finest examples of Gillows and Chippendale furniture. The Copthorn Manor Collection finished on an ornate silver tea-and-coffee set with repoussé decoration (hammered into relief from the reverse side) of herons, dragonflies, and fish. It was an exceptional piece of silverware. As was the pair of Meissen parrots sitting on white tree stumps—with their bright green and red plumage and their beaks slightly open as if they were talking to each other. The items in the journal were of the highest quality, and they were inside the manor over the road from me. It was like a private museum. I had to see them in real life, even if someone was telling us very clearly to leave.

"Shall we go?" I asked, hiding the journal as best I could behind the wood pile next to the log burner.

"Absolutely. We're off to uncover the monstrous person that killed my darling Arthur," Carole replied. "I'm going to draw from all my acting experience and give the performance of a lifetime!" But the worry line on her face gave her away.

However much I wanted to see the collection inside the manor, I was scared of what I might find beyond the front door. Holding the note of warning in my hand, I realized we weren't safe in the cottage either. Danger lurked in every dark corner. I took a deep breath and buried my fears as best I could.

~

With evening setting in, Carole and I ventured toward the manor. The rain had stopped and large puddles filled the potholes on the drive, and the air was thick with the threat of another downpour. I was looking over at the luminous lake when Carole tapped my arm.

"I've been thinking about the handsome gardener," said Carole.

"I'm not going on a date with him, if that's what you're going to say."

"Darling, I would never suggest such a thing." But she winked at me. "I was actually going to say that he seemed familiar, maybe I saw him around the area?" She frowned like she was running Phil's face through an internal Rolodex. "Or he just has one of those faces?"

"Perhaps." I wasn't sure. I considered that it was quite likely Phil could have lied to us about not knowing Arthur. "Considering Arthur had a connection with Copthorn Manor and Lord Metcalf it would stand to reason he could've come into contact with the head gardener here. Tomorrow morning, we should get out early and search for the folly again."

Carole's eyes blazed with excitement. "And there is something else that came to me in the bath—as all the best ideas do, of course."

"Of course, and?"

"That young woman we saw arriving in the Audi; I think I've met her somewhere before as well—maybe it was on vacation with Arthur. I can't place her. It's like she's had a haircut or something."

"Then she'll be the first one we talk to. Find out who she is and what she was doing the weekend Arthur died." The adrenaline for the hunt overtook any hesitation and I quickened my pace before I changed my mind.

When we reached the door, I raised a tentative hand to knock before realizing it was ajar. "Hello?" My voice echoed throughout the space beyond.

I paused, not wanting to enter without being invited, but Carole had no such reservations. She pushed the door open and swept past me, glid-ing down the cavernous hallway, her red heels tapping on the flagstone floor. I hung back and searched for any exits should we need them. A huge stone fireplace filled the wall to our left, a fire blazing inside, and farther down was a large mahogany door, half-open. A warm glow of light and a murmur of voices came from the other side.

"On we go," Carole whispered with a wink, and I knew she was get-ting ready to charm whoever was inside. She strode toward the light like a soprano about to sing her first aria and disappeared through the door into the room full of strangers.

I didn't feel as confident. I readjusted the dress Carole had lent me—I was uncomfortable with the tightness of the fit and the black plastic beads at the cuffs. For decades I had made my life a quiet one. After Cairo—my career ended and James proposed—I threw myself into the opportunity of a new life being a "good wife and mother." I never considered what would be on the other side of it. Hearing the laughter ripple out from the room be-fore me, I understood how small my life had become. If I had continued to build my career as a hunter of stolen antiques, if I'd found a way to continue my career without Arthur's mentorship and ignored James's objections, I believed I would have walked into that room with my head held high. Had I really missed so much by hiding myself safely away?

I took a step toward the door, my curiosity giving me all the courage I needed; just like it had all those years ago. I decided it was time to awaken the rest of the skills I'd developed in my twenties. I needed to find out whether all the aspects of my antique hunting ability were still there inside me—it was the only way to discover the truth.

Carole's forced laughter filled the corridor. I could hear her introduc-ing herself and her husky voice repeating the names as she was told them. I breathed deeply.

It's time.

I walked inside, the words "LEAVE NOW" echoing in my head.

20

"First we trust our instinct and then we trust our knowledge."
—Arthur Crockleford

The drawing room had high ceilings and ran the length, front to back, of the manor. Maroon silk curtains cascaded down each of the three sets of French doors. The enormous room had been zoned into separate seating areas; a pair of Victorian armchairs and a chaise longue circled the nearest French doors. It made me imagine long summer nights with the doors wide open to allow in the sweet, flowery breeze from the rose garden. In the center was a round table, perfect for afternoon tea or canapés in the evening. On the table was an ornate nineteenth-century silver ice bucket and an open bottle of bubbly with 1950s-looking champagne goblets next to it. One had a small chip on the edge, which was a shame as the whole set would be devalued.

I decided not to go over to Carole and the rest of the guests by the drinks table. I needed to study these people before I interacted with them. What small tells or ticks of character could I see when they weren't aware they were being watched? It was what I would have done all those years ago.

I moved quietly to the bookcase that was partly hidden by the open drawing-room door—it was the best vantage point I could find in such a large, open room. Carole was standing by the circular drinks table in the middle of the room. Phil was to her right, and another glamorous woman to her left. Opposite her, with his back to me, was the man I'd seen earlier heading toward the vacation cottages. He was tall and well-built with salt-and-pepper hair, clad in a polo shirt and jeans. He stood next to the younger woman, who I assumed was his girlfriend. I didn't like the way he kept his arm firmly around her waist.

I pretended to study the leather-bound books, glass, and porcelain on display. I was undetected thanks to Carole being the star of the show, keeping the guests enraptured in one of her stories.

I scanned the room for the Copthorn Manor furniture collection that was mentioned in the journal. To my left, underneath a window overlooking the lake, was a side table that could be attributed to Gillows. I was eager to see it—for surely this was part of the collection Arthur had talked to Franklin about? It looked wrong. I ran my finger over the top and it *felt* wrong. On closer inspection, there was nothing masterful in its craftsmanship—it was a cheap reproduction. I was snapped out of my confusion by hearing a familiar voice behind me.

"Giles, it's been a long time," said Franklin, entering the room.

I sped back down the wall to my somewhat hidden position by the drawing room door, hoping Franklin didn't notice me. He beelined for the tall, well-built man named Giles, who stepped away from the group and shook Franklin's hand.

I slipped farther back and picked out a book from the bookshelf, listening intently.

Has he seen Carole?

The book was covered in a thick layer of dust, which told me Clare wasn't a great housekeeper.

"I was sorry to phone you about your father and then Arthur's demise," Franklin was saying. "Arthur mentioned to me that you two were acquaintances."

Is Giles Lord Metcalf's son? If so, it makes sense that he would be here, but why is he staying in the cottage? Surely he's lord of the manor now?

Out of the corner of my eye I saw Giles's large biceps clench. He took a sharp breath and twiddled his signet ring on his little finger. The crest etched into the ring must be a family one, but I was too far away to make it out clearly.

"I only knew Arthur in passing, but he was a wonderful man by all accounts." Giles tried to smile but it didn't reach his eyes.

"I'm so glad that Arthur pointed you out to me in the Crown last Sunday or I wouldn't have recognized you this evening," Franklin said. "Your father had given me the impression that you and your sister didn't get along, so I was a little surprised to see you both having dinner together." He was trying to sound casual, but there was an edge of intensity to the words.

"I'll just get another drink," said Giles between his teeth. "If you'll excuse me."

He headed for the drinks table and filled his glass to the brim with red wine.

Carole headed toward me carrying two glasses of champagne. Franklin saw her. His shoulders tightened and eyes narrowed but he made no movement to greet my aunt. Instead he turned his back on her and followed Giles to the drinks table.

"Well, this is quite a gathering," she said, handing me some champagne. "I see Franklin is here. Isn't he rude for not saying hello?"

"I just overheard that Franklin saw Giles and his sister in the Crown in Little Meddington on Sunday—and we know that Arthur probably died in the very early hours of Monday morning. One of them at that dinner could have stayed in the village and gone to the shop. But who's his sister?"

Carole gripped my arm. "Darling, you are fabulous. But do you see, that means Franklin was also there."

We both took a sharp breath.

"I heard my name. Good evening, ladies," said Franklin, joining us. "I noticed you're here. I thought we'd agreed you wouldn't be attending?" He took a long gulp of wine.

"We never said so," I replied. "I said I hadn't valued anything in a long time. But I've decided that since Arthur asked you to offer me the job, then I should accept. Out of respect for our departed friend."

That should do it.

"You're actually going to value these antiques?" He threw his hand around the room.

I glanced at the reproduction Gillows table again, realizing Franklin did not know antiques. "That's right."

"You said you *weren't* coming," Franklin insisted, his right fist clenching ever so slightly.

"We changed our minds at the last minute." The atmosphere was becoming icy. I pulled another beautifully bound leather book from the shelf and said, "Lovely chatting. I'll just be evaluating the books, if you please."

Franklin shook his head and stormed off. I flicked through the pages—the book looked Victorian or Edwardian and was in German. I pulled out a third volume, then a fourth, a fifth. They were all in German and the last one looked like a Victorian manual for housekeeping, if the drawings were anything to go by.

I lowered my voice so only Carole could hear. "I've been in a room like this before when some banker had bought an old country house and needed it to look authentic—it didn't matter what was *in* the books, only what they *looked* like on the outside." I ran my finger along the spines. "If Lord Metcalf wasn't German then this seems to be staged to look like a nineteenth-century library, but why?"

Carole frowned. "The journal details a huge collection. I thought this was it." It was clear that to a layperson the room probably did look like it was full of expensive antique furniture.

Arthur knew nothing in the room was original, and he wanted me to see.

"My gut says this is all wrong," I whispered. "Where are all the real antiques?"

Before she could give an opinion, the glamorous woman I'd noticed earlier hurried over. She was in her late fifties and, I noticed, dripping in Joseff of Hollywood costume jewelry.

"I'm Amy Metcalf." She held out her hand to Carole, then to me. *This is the sister*. She was tall and slim, and wearing a black silk blouse and black chinos with red high heels. I envied her style and confidence. "Welcome to my humble home. I'm told by my housekeeper, Clare, you're here in Arthur's place. How fascinating . . ." She paused and her deep brown eyes looked me over, stopping at the black plastic beads and sequins surrounding my wrists. I smiled in reply, and she continued, "I know my father liked Arthur's eccentric flare of calling these weekend meetings a 'retreat,' but I'm hoping that we can do without that now and get down to the valuation tomorrow morning. Unfortunately, we need to start closing the old family home," she said.

"Are you selling?" I asked.

"Selling? Lord, no, we are . . . you know, putting sheets over everything." She flung her arm around the room. "Until we come back."

"Where are you going?" I asked.

A momentary frown crossed over Amy's forehead, but she made herself smile. "I love to travel and now that my father is gone there is no reason to stay."

"Of course. I'm sorry for your loss," I said quickly.

"If you will excuse me, I shall check on dinner." Amy floated out of the room.

Carole nodded toward the drinks table as the young woman who had been driving the Audi approached it to refill her glass, and I remembered our plan to talk to her. I threw my head toward her and Carole got the hint. Within seconds she'd brought her over to me.

"Bella, darling, you must meet my *wonderful* niece. I've been telling Bella what a star you are, jumping in to cover for Arthur at the last minute."

I didn't know what to say.

"She's very modest." Carole pointed to my black dress with sequins at the cuffs. "It's one of mine."

"Oh," replied Bella, not making eye contact. Her shoulders were hunched and her hair was falling over her face.

I smiled and extended my hand. "I'm Freya."

She kept her head down.

Giles joined us, and in a swift motion, he fixed his arm around her waist. His fingers seemed to dig into her side, as if claiming her back from my aunt.

I fidgeted with the clutter of black plastic around my wrists. Uncomfortable with what I was witnessing, I ran through the options of how to help Bella.

A swift chop to the neck to wind him might do it. The thought shocked me. Not because I didn't know how to do it, but because I instantly remembered what action I would take.

"We need to talk to my sister," said Giles. "Good evening." He pulled at Bella's arm.

But Carole, it seemed, was having none of it. "Very good, off you go." She grabbed Bella with one hand and with the other dismissed Giles.

I had a feeling that Carole was quite ready for a tug-of-war.

Giles eyed my aunt and then me—he could easily win any war and we all knew it. Instead of causing a scene, he let go. "Keep an eye on her," he said, then strode away.

There was a collective sigh. Bella straightened a little and her large brown eyes met mine. She was as tall as a model and looked like she was from the Mediterranean somewhere with her tanned skin and dark hair.

"I'm Freya," I said again.

"I'm Bella. . . ." She paused. "I'm so sorry, he can be a little grumpy when he's around family."

I held out my hand and she shook it warmly. It was a simple interaction, but it made all the difference to me, and I realized that meeting new people wasn't as hard as I feared.

"Do I detect a London accent?" I asked.

Bella nodded. "I grew up on Green Lanes in Tottenham, in the Turkish community there—my mom was Turkish. Now that I'm with Giles I move around a lot." She looked over at Giles, who was deep in conversation with Amy in the doorway.

Even with the few words that Giles had spoken, it was quite clear his accent was definitely not inner-city London; it was more . . . home counties private school. I watched him as he whispered something to Amy. Their family resemblance wasn't obvious.

"Amy and Giles are siblings, do I have that right?" I asked Bella.

She nodded. "And Lord Metcalf, the owner of this house, was their father. It probably wasn't wise to leave the place to both of them when they hate each other and both hate this house."

"They seem to be getting on fine now," I replied, considering what I'd just heard Franklin say about the siblings having dinner together. I said as much to Bella now.

She smiled at me and took a sip of her champagne. "I don't know about any dinner. This autumn we're getting away from here and going to see that place in the Indiana Jones movie—do you know the one I mean? Arthur said it was breathtaking."

I straightened at the mention of Arthur, but I tried remaining casual. "Do you mean Petra? I've always longed to go," I lied. I found it was always best to ignore the three years I'd hunted antiques around the world, including in Jordan, in my twenties. It stopped the unwanted questions that always came. "And you knew Arthur?"

"Petra, yes," said Bella, clapping her hands. "Arthur told me all about it last winter and said I had to go with Giles if I could. But Giles is always so busy. Normally I'm a lone woman at these things." She tipped her head toward Carole. "Though of course, sometimes you came too."

Carole beamed. "That's it, darling, I just knew we had met before. It was at that Scottish castle, wasn't it? We danced at a ceilidh—flung ourselves around the room." Carole twirled, her bangles jangling.

"I'll confess to being a little tipsy." Bella laughed, until she saw Giles shaking his head at her, and she coughed down the chuckle.

"And we will dance again tonight, won't we? It says there is belly dancing after dinner." Carole grabbed Bella's hands. "Get him drunk and away we go."

"If only it was that easy," she replied. "Anyway, that stuff about a 'program' was just a joke that Arthur used to find funny. No one ever expected any of it to actually happen."

I was right. Arthur did write the program.

Carole's face fell. "No belly dancing?"

Bella looked like she was about to laugh again, but she caught herself. "No, there won't be," she muttered. There was something strange in the way she controlled herself so easily that felt wrong. Perhaps she was used to hiding her emotions around Giles?

Laughter erupted from over by the drinks table and I spun around. Phil the gardener, Giles, and Franklin were enjoying each other's company. Phil's shirt was tight enough to see the strength in his arms. I realized that if I found him attractive there was definitely something wrong with him—after my mistake in marrying James I was quite sure I couldn't trust my taste in men. Was he Arthur's murderer? Carole smiled at me, then headed over to join in the merriment—leaving me with Bella.

"She's great, isn't she?" Bella nodded toward Carole. "And seems to be handling Arthur's death so well."

"She's stoic," I replied.

Bella took another sip of champagne. "Franklin tells us that Arthur left the shop to Carole and you. And that you'll be the valuer for the estate tomorrow morning?" She checked the room, then whispered, "Normally there are quite a few people at these weekends, way more than now. You know, chatting over drinks, doing deals over dinner, and then the next morning trading items that Arthur had authenticated and valued." She lifted her goblet to the room. "But that's not what's happening, is it?" She smiled innocently, but I understood what she was saying.

That this weekend was different from others that had gone before, and that Arthur was up to his neck in it. But was it illegal or merely secretive? I was desperate to know the answer.

My mind whirled with questions. Where was the furniture from the journal? Was Arthur's murderer really here? Who wrote the "LEAVE NOW" note?

"Here comes my boyfriend." Bella tried to smile.

Someone brushed past me, and I jumped. Giles was standing to my right. "What were you both discussing?"

I met his intense stare with a smile. "We're both Londoners, and it's always nice to reminisce, isn't it?"

"Sometimes." He took a large swig of wine and looked me up and down, his gaze stopping at the dazzling cuffs of my dress. I tugged the right sleeve down over my hand and the scar on my palm. I didn't like Giles. For all his chiseled chin and expensive country clothing, there was nothing appealing about him at all. And if there was something bad going on at the manor, I would bet money on the white male privilege standing before me swimming in it.

I'd excused myself to rejoin Carole when my eyes caught a bad reproduction of a Chippendale chair in the far corner of the room. It was the third item that didn't look right. The world seemed to slow. I took in as much of the room as possible with one sweep. To my right, on the bookshelf, a mantel clock ticked. My eyes jumped from one guest to the next. Franklin. Giles. Bella. Amy. Phil. And somewhere in the kitchen was Clare. There was something about each of them that wasn't quite right—just like the chair. Arthur had been correct to tell us to be careful. Nothing at Copthorn Manor was what it seemed, and any of the people inside could be his murderer.

21

"Amy, you must cherish the items of the past, for sometimes they are all we have left of those we love."

—Arthur Crockleford

Amy

Amy stood in the large kitchen of Copthorn Manor. Clare was proving to be a terrible cook, and Amy wondered why Franklin had recommended that she cook for this weekend. The pan of watercress soup bubbled like the witch's cauldron in *Macbeth*. It crossed Amy's mind that perhaps Clare was here to poison her and steal her jewelry, which Amy loved more than almost anything.

The pop of a champagne cork echoed down the corridor. Amy wanted to get back to playing hostess—it was one of her favorite roles.

"It's all edible this time, isn't it?" she asked Clare, opening the oven and checking the lasagna wasn't burned.

Clare ignored the insult and started serving the soup.

"No!" shrieked Amy. "The guests need to be seated first or it'll get cold. Honestly, don't you know anything?"

"Sorry," mumbled Clare. "It's ready, so . . ."

"Yes, yes. I'll get them to the table."

Amy left the kitchen and marched down the corridor to the drawing room.

Why did Franklin put Clare here? What's his game?

As she pushed open the door, she saw Carole laughing in a way that reminded her of Arthur. He had no right to offer Freya's antique valuing services to Franklin. Franklin was an idiot to allow her to be here.

Amy stood in the doorway watching Freya fiddling with the sleeves of her ghastly dress. She seemed quite . . . bland, but there was something in the way she paused to look at each item in the room that made Amy nervous.

She sees things others don't.

Amy cursed Franklin again. She had enough on her plate without having to watch everyone, but she also prided herself on being equal to any situation.

"Dinner's ready, if you would be so kind as to follow me," she called to the room.

Carole hurried toward her, and her perfume brought back an unwelcome memory. A week ago, Amy had driven to Little Meddington to find Arthur. She'd sat in the car just outside the post office, across the road from his shop, and waited until the shop was empty. It had taken two hours and twenty-five minutes for Arthur and Carole, who were sitting in the two armchairs near the window, to drink their tea and for Carole to leave.

When Amy had entered the shop, the Chanel N°5 was still lingering around the doorway. She had to admire Carole's grace and confidence. It was almost as well rehearsed as her own.

She'd found Arthur sitting behind his desk.

"Arthur, darling," she'd said, closing the shop door behind her. "How are you?"

He sprang up from his chair the moment he'd realized who she was. "Amy, how nice of you to drop by," he said.

"You went to see my father." Amy smiled sweetly at him.

Arthur tried to smile back. "It was just a chat between old men. He was quite circumspect."

"He's dying, Arthur, and I will inherit everything he has." She knew he would understand what that meant. "I'm taking over now. My father insisted that you work for him; now I'm insisting you work for me." She ran her hand along the desk and picked up a small vase with a barnacle attached.

"A piece of shipwreck ceramics?"

Arthur stiffened. "I'm retiring. Please don't touch those."

"You love your work far too much to retire. I can make it worth your while. Pay you a lot more than my father did."

She knew that would do it and was pleased when his eyes lit up. Amy believed that most people could be bought—it was only ever a matter of how much for.

Amy stepped around the desk and pressed herself up against the old man. There was a whiff of mint tea on his breath. "Arthur, darling, everyone knows you're the best in the business and I only work with the best. You will consider my offer, won't you?" She gave him her very best smile and pecked him on the cheek.

"Of course," Arthur said, his smile faltering.

Now, in the drawing room doorway, Amy watched Freya walking toward her.

Is she really a valuer? If she is, then perhaps she can be useful. . . .

22

"There's always a clue to follow even if it's not the one you're looking for."

—Arthur Crockleford

Freya

Carole and I followed Amy out of the drawing room and across the back of the entrance hall. Dim light filtered through the large hallway windows and lit the stone floor in the entrance hall. I guessed we were heading parallel to the front of the building and toward the side that faced the vacation cottages.

I nudged Carole and said, "We know most of the guests here were around Suffolk the night Arthur died. But we haven't asked Phil yet. Let's now focus on who had an issue with Arthur?"

Carole rubbed her hands together. "Leave it to me. Before the entertainment arrives—which I am *so* excited about, aren't you?—I'll get everyone's dirty little secrets. Every last juicy bit."

"Oh dear," I mumbled to myself. The last thing we needed was Carole's version of the Spanish Inquisition.

"I heard that. You know, there is still a huge ton of glittery showbiz in these bones." Carole stuck her chin out. "Arthur knew I would be here, so it was time to up the game and provide some dancing. Like in Scotland."

"I meant the questioning of people," I replied. There was no point in telling Carole again that there wouldn't be any entertainment. She only ever heard what she wanted to.

"Watch and learn, darling." Carole caught up with Amy farther down the corridor and, looping her arm through Amy's, she whispered in her ear.

I heard footsteps close behind me.

"You shouldn't be here," whispered Franklin.

I strove for calm. "I changed my mind. I will verify whatever you need me to. Will I be paid for this job?"

Franklin glared at me.

I peered over his shoulder. Behind us, I noticed Phil and Giles were leaving the drawing room. I couldn't see Bella; she was probably behind Giles somewhere.

Giles's head moved from left to right, checking the hallway, and I froze. There was something in the way he was standing. His face was in the shadows, but I knew him—he was Mr. Sunglasses from the funeral. He might not have had the beard he did last week, but it was definitely the same man. I wiped my clammy hands on my dress. Why had he been at Arthur's funeral searching for Carole? I wondered if he was the man who tried to get into the shop and then chased us. I shuddered—this was a deeply worrying discovery.

"Are you listening to me?" demanded Franklin, gripping my arm. He glanced at Phil and Giles, then spoke quickly. "This is a mistake. There's no need for you to be here. I have it all under control. Just as I told Arthur."

The warning note that had been pushed under the cottage door screamed at me. Had Franklin spotted us earlier in the day and written the note, and was he feigning surprise now seeing us here at the drinks gathering?

"And what was Arthur's reply?" I asked, knowing Arthur had never taken kindly to being told what to do.

Franklin's eyes narrowed. "He shouldn't have—"

"I imagine he insisted," I interrupted. "And when he thought you might not inform me, he found a way to get me the information himself."

Franklin sighed. "There's nothing for you to do here. Tomorrow I have instructions to retrieve some items and send them on to some individuals. These individuals insisted the items be verified by Arthur Crockleford or no one at all. You must leave."

"You didn't perhaps slip a note under my door to that effect?"

"What note?" asked Franklin, his brow furrowed. "I have better things to be doing."

His reaction seemed genuine; I was inclined to believe he hadn't written the note. But that didn't mean he wasn't a murderer.

~

The dining room had a long table stretching down its center. At one end of the room was a roaring fire, flanked by fitted bookcases with drawers underneath. Each shelf was empty and the starkness made me shiver. This room had probably once been the library but had been converted into a dining room, for it was easier to heat on a damp and chilly spring evening. The curtains were still pulled back and the hazy glow of the moon stretched down the table. Small flames flickered on a couple of the candlesticks and the large candelabra—with their wax pooling on the tablecloth. The only other light in the room came from a large, modern lamp on a side table. It was either romantic or spooky, I couldn't decide. Phil entered the room and our eyes met. Embarrassed by the awkward moment, I walked over to the window to draw the curtains. It was an old habit; James always demanded the curtains were closed at dusk. From where I stood, I could make out the lights in our cottage over the drive.

At my feet, the navy carpet had been devoured by moths. I scratched my foot along it as a thought niggled at me. So much of the Manor didn't make any sense. Before we arrived, I had googled it and found that the house had been purchased thirty-five years ago for a fortune. People with that sort of money surely had the funds to do it up, but the house didn't look like a home. And yet a family had lived here for decades. Unhappily, it would seem.

I overheard Amy making a dig at Giles: "Why don't you take the head of the table this once, Shanks?"

Giles gritted his teeth and Amy didn't wait for an answer before leaving the room, looking pleased with herself.

"Shanks" wasn't a great nickname, was it? Wasn't a shank the part of the human leg between the knee and ankle? Why call someone that? Unless... Long ago, when we tracked the most notorious art-and-antique thieves across the continents, they all seemed to have nicknames or aliases. A shiver prickled down my back. Maybe someone got the nickname of "Shanks" because they liked to break that part of the body? Or ...

A prison knife is called a shank.

How dangerous was Giles? What did his sister know?

Before Giles could take his seat, Franklin positioned himself at the head of the table, looking right at home, and I wondered why he'd taken such a liberty. Giles glared at Franklin as he put his paper napkin on his lap.

Carole must have registered the palpable tension in the air because she directed him to a seat next to her and opposite me. "Do you know when the entertainment is arriving?" she asked.

Giles shook his head and his jawline softened. "It's just an old joke of Arthur's."

"Oh, Arthur did have a grand sense of humor." She patted his arm, and as he pulled away, I saw a scar along his right palm. It wasn't like my own. My scar was a burn; his looked as if it had been made by something sharp and jagged.

I coughed to get Carole's attention.

To my right, Bella sat down. "Are you okay?"

"I'm fine, thank you," I said. "Just need a bit of water."

Across from me, Carole was focused on Giles. "Hurt yourself?" she asked.

"An accident long ago." My hand closed around my own scar, and I momentarily sympathized with Giles—scars are hard to hide from.

Amy and Clare returned with the soup course, but Giles pushed his away, turning to Franklin. "Why don't you tell the table why we are not all walking around the vaults at this very moment," he said. "I could make you open them."

Silence.

Everyone looked at Franklin, who shifted in his seat.

"As I've already said, you will enter the vaults tomorrow morning when the van arrives. Your father gave me very clear instructions." Franklin picked up his spoon. "I've placed the keys somewhere safe, and if something happens to me then you won't get them."

"There are many ways to get information out of a man," said Giles. "Do you like your fingernails?"

My eyes widened at Carole. In sitting next to this man it was very clear she might be in danger.

"Enough," snapped Amy. "Why do you always have to be so crude? We'll deal with the vaults tomorrow and that's final."

Were they talking about bank vaults? Copthorn Manor did not look like a bank. I wondered if all the items from the journal were in these vaults—*they would have to be very large to fit in all that furniture.*

"Vaults! That is most exciting. Is that where my darling niece will be needed as valuer? In a vault. This is most thrilling. Isn't it, darling?" Carole winked at me for the whole table to see. "Of course, after we've had some of the 'exotic meats' mentioned in the program!"

Vaults? Exotic meats?

A memory shot to the forefront of my mind—the Picasso case! I knew that part of the program Arthur had given us along with the reservation had sounded familiar. It was another clue.

6 P.M.   EVENING DRINKS AS THE SUN GOES DOWN

7 P.M.   DINNER WITH EXOTIC MEATS

The Picasso case was one of my favorite assignments that Arthur and I had worked on together. It was the moment, two years into hunting for stolen antiques, when my training and experience collided. We had arrived at la Coucher de Soleil, a villa in the region of western France called Charente—the villa's name translated to "sunset." On breaking in we were confronted by an elderly housekeeper who threatened us with a broomstick, shouting, "Out, roast beef, out!" Arthur was offended at the remark and had replied, "My dear lady, if I were to be compared to an animal, I would be something fabulous, perhaps a flamingo or a lion." Arthur had charmed his way in and to a cup of coffee. We had joked about him as an exotic meat ever since. But why would he lead me to that case?

I explored the memory again. The Picasso case was one in which an original sketch had been stolen from a Greek museum and then was hidden *behind* a modern-day Picasso print of the same sketch. I had found it in a box in the cellar along with some other priceless art. A piece finally slotted into place—the vaults must be in the cellar, and perhaps the real antiques were also there.

Clever, Arthur.

Franklin cleared his throat, breaking through my thoughts. He smiled at Phil sitting down opposite him, at the other end of the table. "You work here—do you know the lands well?"

Phil winced. "I haven't been here long. Still getting my head around the job." He turned to focus on Carole. "I'm glad you both got home safely this afternoon."

"We did, darling, yes. Thank you for your concern. You're quite a charmer, aren't you?"

Phil nodded politely. "Where I'm from we make sure a lady gets home. It's difficult when they're as headstrong as you and your niece."

"She is marvelous and *single*." Carole raised her eyebrows at me, and I shrank down in my seat. She was probably setting me up with a murderer for all she knew.

"Do you understand what's going on here yet?" Bella whispered. I looked at her in confusion. Was she trying to tell me something? She swept her eyes around the room and they rested on the empty shelves.

"I thought there would be lots of lovely silver photo frames with family pictures inside," she said to the table. I noticed her motion toward the last drawers underneath the bookcase by the window.

"Shut up," snapped Giles, and Bella dropped her gaze to the soup.

My mind was spinning. Bella was right; I hadn't seen one personal item in the house. It reminded me of the old country houses that had fallen on hard times and the owners had started selling everything off and replacing it with cheap reproductions—just like the Gillows-looking furniture in the drawing room. It struck me again that it was like we were all walking through a film set, but on close inspection almost everything in the manor could have been bought cheaply at auction and put up in days. It was like the Picasso case. I just needed to find the genuine item behind the copy.

"What were you going to say?" I asked Bella. "Something about the family pictures?"

"Don't listen to me. I just go where Giles tells me to and lap up all the free wine." She gulped down half her glass of white wine. Giles's eyes were shooting daggers at me. "I am excited to go to Petra, though. Have you been to the Middle East? I don't think you said."

Giles muttered something to Franklin, who went ghost white. His spoon clattered in his bowl.

"Is everyone finished?" interjected Amy.

"I am," Carole said.

"Be good to go on a vacation," Bella was saying. "Giles is always very busy on these things and I get time to explore."

I nodded. I saw Giles lean in toward Franklin again. I heard him say, "Perhaps we need a new solicitor?"

I couldn't hear the next comment as Bella was rattling on. Then Franklin pushed his seat back abruptly and hurried from the room.

"I've always wanted to see the pyramids," Bella continued, oblivious to Franklin's hasty departure. "That's where I really wanted to go, on one of those boats down the Nile."

I realized she was waiting for my response. I replied without thinking, "Well then, first you would need to fly into Cairo and see the pyramids. Then you could fly to Luxor and jump on a boat up the Nile. There are lots of tourists if you don't go in the shoulder seasons, but it's magical nonetheless." As I spoke, the memories of those adventures filled my mind—it was a time when I had felt truly alive, courageous, free the way one could feel only when young and childless.

Maybe that was why Bella was putting up with Giles; perhaps he was a means of escape from something even worse than she had left behind. It reminded me of my daughter, Jade, and her new and exciting life at university. The emptiness since Jade left threatened to open up inside me.

"So you've been to Egypt?" Bella said, eyes wide. "Can you tell me everything you remember about your time there? Who did you go with?"

I took a long drink of wine and tried to concentrate on the bad reproduction candlesticks in front of me. "It was a very long time ago. My memories are so distant. . . ." I couldn't think of Cairo. I had lost Asim in Cairo. My throat was thick with emotion. Asim. The one person in the world who had chosen me. He had understood me. The first day we'd met we had sat in the café and talked and talked and yet he never once asked about my scar. . . . Now I ran my index finger over my scarred palm just like he used to. He wanted to know about me, which antiques I loved and why. . . . I couldn't let those memories out of the cage I had locked them in, and I cursed Bella for prying.

"Freya, are you all right?" She touched my arm, but I shrugged her off. "I'm fine."

I looked around the dinner guests again, and Arthur's warning came back to me.

It has taken me over twenty years to find an item of immense value. I have been told its location, but it seems I will not be able to retrieve it. Get it back, Freya, and you will have your life and your career back.

How could I ever get my old life back, when I could never get Asim back? I had never been able to forgive Arthur for putting him in such danger. If only Arthur were here, I would've made him tell me everything instead of following all these strange clues.

Which one of you here was Arthur talking about? I thought, scanning each face. *Which one of you betrayed him? Who killed Arthur so that I couldn't get the answers I need?*

23

"My dear girl, you have such talent and such a future ahead of you. Don't waste it."

—Arthur Crockleford

Bella

Bella watched Giles, who was deep in conversation with Carole across the table. Perhaps Carole didn't recognize him? He did look different without his beard. Bella had been with Giles only a few weeks when he'd taken her to a grand Scottish castle outside Edinburgh last spring. Arthur had made a beeline for them and introduced himself. Later that night, while Giles was talking business, Arthur had counseled Bella to leave him—that "for all the money in the world, it isn't worth putting up with a man like that."

Of course, Arthur had forgotten what it was like to be all alone. He had Carole and his shop and all his village friends. Bella didn't have those luxuries.

Carole was now telling Giles some story about a famous musician and he was smiling. A wave of hatred swept through Bella, but she pushed it away. If he saw anger in her eyes the retaliation would be swift.

Just after Bella arrived at the manor, she'd overheard Amy and Giles discussing Arthur's journals. If Arthur had written everything down it would be valuable information. Giles's plan was to retrieve some precious antique, and that was it, but he could be unpredictable. Carole needed to be careful.

Bella studied Freya again. Did she know where the journals were? Another question rolled around in her mind—was Arthur's insistence that he hadn't spoken to Freya for over twenty years a lie?

Bella had tried to throw Freya a bone by mentioning the family photographs. She'd even gestured in the direction of the drawer she had opened earlier, but Freya didn't seem to get what she was trying to say. Bella had also tried to get some answers by asking Freya about the Middle East, in particular Cairo and Jordan; Freya had bristled at the mention of Egypt, but hadn't dropped her guard.

Arthur had told Bella quite a bit about what had happened that weekend in Cairo twenty years ago. People thought that she never listened, but she did.

Freya was not as Arthur had described her and so she wasn't what Bella had expected. She'd envisioned someone in combats and a tight white T-shirt, with her head held high and a fierce glare—the look of someone ready for any eventuality. Instead, sitting next to her now was a middle-aged woman in a dated black velvet dress with over-the-top sequins and beads at the wrists who was staring blankly at the candlesticks. If Freya *was* meant to be taking Arthur's place as a verifier, Bella found it odd that she hadn't asked where the Copthorn Manor Collection was.

Nothing about this trip to Copthorn Manor felt right, and perhaps she shouldn't have agreed to go. But saying no to Giles wasn't an option. He was what Bella's mother would've called a "meal ticket," and she wasn't about to let go of him until she had what she wanted.

She turned to Freya. "These old manor places always make me shiver. All this really old stuff on the walls." She nodded at the candelabras. "All the fancy candlesticks and furniture."

"They look like reproductions," said Freya, the corners of her mouth turning into a slight smile. "Strange for an antiques retreat, don't you think?" She met Bella's eye.

Bella shrugged and the lie came easily. "I wouldn't know what was real or not."

Freya is clever, she thought. *Just like Arthur. Perhaps she'll work it all out soon enough.*

She glanced at Giles again, then checked her watch. The game was about to begin.

24

"Freya, you need to look beyond the obvious to see what's hidden."

—Arthur Crockleford

Freya

Clare started to pile empty soup bowls on top of each other. The ceramic clattered together as they wobbled in her hands.

"Where's Amy?" asked Giles.

Clare glared at Giles. "In the kitchen micromanaging me."

She turned to leave and met Franklin in the doorway. There was an awkward dance, and I presumed Franklin would come back to the table—he didn't. They stood whispering together. Then Franklin followed Clare back into the corridor.

Carole and I exchanged glances—something about their interaction had been strange. Did Clare find Franklin attractive?

Amy strolled in and gripped the back of her dining chair. "I'm just going to be direct. Everyone here knows Arthur. Therefore, do you know where Arthur kept his logbook? He told my father about them, and my father asked for the books to be returned as they logged the antiques here. Arthur didn't keep his word and return them."

Carole's eyebrows were nearly in her hairline. She couldn't have looked more suspicious if she had tried. Amy searched Bella's face and then my own, working her way around the table.

Silence.

I shook my head, not knowing what to say. Everyone seemed surprised, but from their expressions it seemed as if they all knew what Amy was talking about. If that was true, the first journal hidden in the cottage was not safe. How far would any of these strangers go to get them from us? Giles had already threatened Franklin for some keys . . .

Had Arthur been killed for his journals? And now that Carole and I had them, would we be next? I rubbed the sweat from my palms, fighting the urge to grab my aunt and leave.

"No? All right, then, I'll get Clare to hurry the main course along." Amy walked away.

A gust of rain swept past the windows and ivy pelted the glass. I jumped. Too jittery to stay seated and worried someone would ask again about the journals, I rose from the table and went to the window, pretending to readjust the curtains. I noticed that a drawer under the bookcase—near where Bella had motioned to—was open slightly, and there were photos inside. Had it been like that when I'd closed the curtains earlier? I didn't think so.

Bella's comments about there not being a family photo in the house pushed me on.

What was she really getting at?

I checked that no one was watching, then pulled the drawer open a little more. Inside were a few unframed family photos—a baby photo, an old wedding photo. I withdrew a photo. It had been taken in the room where I was now standing.

I know who that is. I held my breath. *I knew him long ago.*

I peered closer, not caring now who saw me. The photo had probably been taken around twenty years earlier, judging by the clothes. There was a man, in his fifties, sitting at a desk. I flipped the photograph over and in the right-hand corner "Lord Mark Metcalf" was scrawled in a black pen. I was looking at Lord Metcalf, Amy's father. A wave of understanding turned my stomach. Twenty years ago, I knew him as Mark Maben.

The hairs on my neck prickled and I turned around as Amy arrived and stood at the head of the table with a large tray of lasagna in her hands. Clare had also returned and was standing next to her with the plates. The warm smell of baked cheese and ground beef filled the room.

Amy's eyes bored into me holding the photo. "Clare, start serving," she said, her casual charm from earlier cracking. Her eyes flickered to a spot behind me—as if there was something there. I looked, but all I could see were curtains. "You've forgotten the salt and pepper. I'll go get them," she said, leaving the room in a hurry.

I focused on the photo again.

Decades ago, "Mark" had hired Arthur and me to retrieve his stolen Martin Brothers bird, which he believed was being taken to Cairo by his son to have a copy made. He'd never explained why he knew that, but he threw a lot of money at us to get it back. Arthur was desperately broke and needed to keep the shop afloat. We rarely took jobs from private clients—preferring museums, galleries, or insurance companies—and I wasn't happy about working for someone we knew nothing about. I was sure this was the same man who had come into the shop looking for Arthur.

It has to be connected, doesn't it? What happened in Cairo and what happened to Arthur last week. Why else would he have sent me here? I remembered Arthur's "a bird in the box" clue; it had pointed us toward the shop keys but what if it was also directing me toward a Martin Brothers bird? The real question was, which bird—the one Harry had seen at the shop or the one from Cairo?

What had Arthur been playing at by getting Carole and me to come here? I studied Giles. He was the son Mark had mentioned; he had stolen from his father. My body tensed and my hands clenched—he was the monster who started it all.

I made myself look back at the photo for fear I would say something that would endanger us further. On the shelf behind Lord Metcalf's large Victorian partners desk was a dark statue, tall and thin, and I could just make out a few talons. *The Martin Brothers bird.*

A memory of Asim began to surface along with a lump in my throat. The Egyptian Museum in Cairo was cool and quiet. I'd arched my neck to take in the high ceilings. Asim had taken my damaged hand and pulled me farther into the galleries. "I want to show you something. You're the only woman I know who'd love it too," he whispered. I'd looked into his deep brown eyes and . . .

I dug my nail into my palm and made the fond memory retreat.

"Freya?" my aunt called, but I was lost in swirling emotions of anger and pain. "Freya?"

I shook away the images and looked up to see the table of guests staring at me.

"As the entertainment is not on the way, I suggest we get the party started ourselves. . . . Perhaps we could play Who Am I?—you know when we all stick paper to our forehead and everyone has to guess? I'll be Marilyn Monroe." She clapped her hands together in an overexaggerated motion—she was acting, trying to draw the attention away from me.

Crash!

I jumped and the photo flew out of my hands.

Clare had let a couple of plates collide as she served them out.

I looked around the dining room. *Where is Franklin?*

"Right, dinner is here," Clare said. She pointed to my seat, insistent. "Before it gets cold."

I scanned the floor. Where had the photograph gone? I decided not to draw attention to it while Clare was watching me—*I'll pretend to drop something in a bit and go on a hunt.* I took out my earring as I headed back to my chair, ready to say I'd lost it.

The wind rattled the windows and the ivy scratched across the glass again.

"Storm's coming," muttered Bella as I took my seat.

"Shouldn't we wait for Franklin?" I asked Clare. "And where's Amy?"

"They'll be here in a minute," said Clare, leaving the room. Now there were only five of us around the table: Giles, Phil, Bella, Carole, and me.

"I do love a good storm, don't you?" said Carole, turning to Giles.

Giles looked like his mind was elsewhere. "Problem with these places is the lanes and dirt roads get flooded and trees come down."

"I think you're being a little dramatic. We have big old storms from time to time and it's really just an excuse to light a fire and a scented candle. Isn't it, Freya?" Carole was still trying to lighten the mood.

I smiled at my aunt. "Of course."

A thundery gust whipped down the chimney behind Carole. Bella shuddered. The air gave the fire a new life and it popped and fizzled. "Best we put some more logs on," said Carole, stretching her arm out toward Bella to reassure her the countryside wasn't as fearful as she might believe.

"I'll go and get some more from the hall." Giles sprang up and left the dining room.

The lamp light flickered, and thunder rumbled. Phil poured Bella, Carole, and me some more wine.

Bella leaned in toward me. "You shouldn't be here," she whispered.

Carole threw the last log on the fire, sending shards of embers into the room, and her face glowed.

"This place gives me the heebie-jeebies," said Bella. "I think I'll go and get my coat." She shivered again and left the room.

A few moments later the lights went out.

A candle on the table flickered and my eyes met Phil's. I realized that Carole and I were alone in the room with him.

Where had everyone gone?

A door was opened somewhere and a squall of damp wind swept into the room.

The candles went out.

Darkness ebbed around the edges of the room. The dwindling fire was our only light, and it was of no comfort.

Silence.

"Carole?" I whispered.

Out of the inky blackness, there was a shout.

And then a scream rang out.

25

"Keeping yourself calm in a heightened situation is the greatest talent."

—Arthur Crockleford

I sprang to my feet, my chair clattering to the floor.

"Who screamed?" Carole asked Phil. "It sounded like a woman's scream."

Phil wiped the sides of his mouth and placed his napkin by his plate—judging by his actions, it was as if the evening were a perfectly normal one. It was almost like he had experience of such situations. "I shall have a look." He rose and strode toward the door. "I can't see anything."

Franklin and Clare barged into the room past him. "Which one of you is frightened of the dark, then?" asked Clare, looking between Carole and me.

"It wasn't us, darling. It came from out there. Was it you?"

Clare shook her head.

Giles came in carrying a large bundle of logs and threw them onto the hearth. The clattering of wood made us all jump. As if nothing had happened, he sat down and started to eat his lasagna.

A match fizzed and Phil's face was illuminated by the orange glow. He calmly reached over to the center of the table to relight the candles.

No one spoke.

Bella slipped into the room and righted my fallen chair, taking a seat next to me. "Are you all right?" I asked, thinking it must have been Bella who'd screamed, considering she was the nerviest of the group.

"I'm fine, why?" There was a bead of sweat by her ear like she'd been running.

The only person not in the dining room was Amy. "If it wasn't any of us that screamed it had to be Amy," I said. "Do you think she's hurt?"

Carole grabbed her table knife, holding it out. "Right. Off we go. Best we see what's happened." She tutted at Giles, who hadn't moved. "Are you a man or a boy? Freya thinks it was your sister that screamed."

Giles took a long drink of his wine. "You've no idea who I am." He wiped his lips.

"I'll go and see," I said to Carole, before she could give Giles a lecture on being a gentleman.

I grasped one of the single candlesticks. The thought of what could be beyond the dining room made my heart pound in my ears. If Arthur's murderer was now at Copthorn Manor, perhaps they'd struck again.

On seeing Carole and me spring into action, Phil picked up the reproduction candelabra from the center of the table. "I'll see what's going on."

"Excellent, we'll all go," Carole said, but I shook my head. I did an overexaggerated look around the table and she got that I was trying to say—*watch them*. She nodded and moved to sit in my seat between Bella and Franklin.

I took a breath for courage and stepped into the corridor, glancing back at Carole. By the way she flicked her hair I knew she was telling one of her stories—my aunt really was marvelous in any situation. I wished I'd retained my hunter's confidence like she had retained her stage presence.

Phil had gone ahead and I hurried to catch up. The metal in my palm was cold, and the hot flame before my eyes made it hard to see any distance. Shielding the flame, I made out the fading glow of Phil's candles down the hall. He'd stopped in front of the last door in the corridor. The fluttering light of the large candelabra caused his shadow to dance on the floor behind him.

"The kitchen," said Phil, pushing the white fire door open. I noticed it was on large hinges that allowed it to swing each way. Phil snapped around. "You should go back. I can handle this. She's probably just dropped something."

Darkness crept around my shoulders and my hands shook as the memory of a different kitchen haunted me. Could I keep it together if I discovered another body, in another kitchen, twenty years on? I doubted it. I had tried to forget, but ever since Arthur's death the painful details of what had happened in Cairo had been seeping into my consciousness. The photo of Lord Mark Metcalf was still clear in my mind. What was the connection between Cairo and Metcalf's death and Arthur's death?

I needed to uncover what was going on.

"Are you sure you don't want to stay with your aunt?" Phil asked. Concern crossed his brow and made me uncomfortable.

"I want to check Amy's okay." I forced myself forward. I tried to remember who I once was and what that woman would have done.

Once inside, I held my breath, readying myself for the horror that might be there. It was hard to see the huge kitchen clearly. There was a small light coming from a fire alarm on the ceiling and our candles. I hardened my grip on the candlestick. This time I wasn't listening to anything but my own instincts. This time I was going to make a different choice. This time perhaps the outcome would be different.

Flashes of the past came rushing back: Asim lying lifeless on the restaurant's kitchen floor. The muggy Egyptian heat making the air hard to breathe. Pieces of stoneware dispersed among the pool of blood.

It's not that kitchen, I told myself. *It can't be the same.*

A gust of damp air crept around my neck. Was a window open? Our candles flickered violently.

"Hello?" I called.

I strained my eyes, searching the tiled floor for signs of a body.

Nothing.

I relaxed.

"There's no one here," said Phil, waving his light around.

The back door—the one Clare had struggled to open when we had arrived—was now ajar, the gap wide enough for someone to fit through.

"Do you think Amy's all right?" I asked.

"She's probably gone to check the fuse board or something," Phil replied, placing the candelabra on the stainless-steel island. It created a dim glow.

Of course she would have. Maybe the scream had been one of frustration at the power going out.

"Best to look for flashlights—there must be some here," said Phil.

I walked around the kitchen, searching for signs that someone might have accidentally hurt themselves—anything to explain why Amy would have screamed like that.

I noticed the mess of pots and pans, the soup bowls piled high by the side of the sink, the dirty knives on the chopping board. Clare was the messiest housekeeper I had ever met. *Is she even a housekeeper?*

Another draught sped through the open back door. I walked over and spotted a puddle of water on the tiles. I peered outside. There was a flash of lightning and a crack of thunder. In the brief light something glittered on the ground.

"Got some," said Phil, holding out a couple of flashlights. He managed to get them working and gave one to me. "Best you and your aunt get back to your cottage. It's not safe here in this weather."

I set my candle down on the nearest countertop and shone the flashlight toward the back door, when a clatter came from behind me. I jumped. Clare had slipped back into the kitchen carrying dirty plates and some had fallen into the sink.

"Let's go," said Phil to me, picking up the large candelabra. He handed his flashlight to Clare. "Will you be all right in here?"

"Of course, but I'll have to leave all this"—she flung her arm at the mess—"until morning."

"I'll just close this door," I said.

Behind me, I could make out Clare and Phil muttering something to each other. What was Clare up to? I looked back and they stopped. Clare left Phil by the kitchen door and began loading the dishwasher.

So much for leaving it until tomorrow.

Turning to the back door, I tried to pull it shut, but the door was warped and its hinges were almost stuck in place. Wind whipped strands of hair across my face and the rain pushed me inside.

"Did you open this door?" I asked Clare.

"Not me. I made the mistake of opening it earlier and it was a nightmare to get closed again," she said.

So it must have been Amy, I thought. But I didn't understand why she would have opened it.

My shoe kicked something. I directed the beam of the flashlight down and it caught the glass of a cell phone; it was damp with rain. The corner was cracked. I pressed the button to turn it on.

The beginning of a text flashed.

We've run out of time. DO IT NOW. Time to se . . . I couldn't read the rest of the sentence without unlocking the phone. The phone number didn't have a name allocated to it.

"Amy!" I called, but there was no reply; just the howling wind and a dog barking in the distance.

It was then, in that darkness, that the memory I'd kept shut away for so very long came crashing back.

26

"We are the best in the business—we can track down anything—
and now we are going to get the recognition we deserve."
                                        —Arthur Crockleford

I first met Asim when I was twenty-two, a year into my antique hunting career. I was late for a British Museum lecture on how objects of
Middle Eastern heritage can be used as a starting point for historical
debate and inquiry. The Lecture Theatre was full, the speaker was checking her microphone, the men and women around me had hushed their
voices. I had nowhere to sit. I saw an empty chair but I couldn't get to it
without disturbing the whole row. I scanned the room for another space.
My palms were sweating. I caught the eyes of a young man at the end of
the row and my cheeks reddened as my heart warmed.

"My friend is here; would you be so kind?" he said to the row, and
motioned for them to move along.

"Good afternoon, ladies and gentlemen." The speaker stood at the
lectern and the room quieted.

I had my seat.

"Thank you," I whispered.

"It's no problem," he said. "I'm Asim."

"Freya."

"I'm sure this is going to be one of her best lectures," Asim whispered,
nodding toward the lecturer.

Afterward, we talked for hours. He was utterly charming. His depth of knowledge on antiquities greatly outweighed my own, yet he never made me feel ignorant. The way his eyes locked on mine made me feel like I too was a rare find—much like the items he loved. I had never experienced anything like it before. Asim was studying in Cairo and he told me he was in the UK to further his learning: attend lectures and visit museums. He taught me about the ancient world as I showed him the wonders of London's museums, galleries, and theaters. I admired his knowledge as much as I admired Arthur's. I found it intoxicating.

It took a lot for him to tell me how he paid for his university tuition. It was our secret and it bound us together before it broke us apart.

We had spent the night at his small B and B in Paddington. The next morning, we were entwined under the duvet.

"I'll tell you the truth and then we are real to each other, but it is the point in our relationship we differ the most," he said, pulling the duvet farther over our heads.

"You can tell me anything." I had no idea what this admission would lead to, but it wouldn't matter. To me it wouldn't change a thing.

"Very well. I take a real antiquity and I make an exact copy, then the real thing stays in its rightful place and the copy gets sold."

I was shocked. "You're a forger?" Asim was the type of person we hunted, a person that was on the wrong side of the law. Yet he was the person I loved.

"In your eyes, my love, not in mine," he murmured.

I was disappointed. Angry. But he spent that evening pleading his case—explaining his reasons. He believed that in making illegal forgeries in his family's workshop, he was giving the West what it so desired and keeping for the Middle East what should be kept. Asim's passion ignited my own belief in the necessity for items of cultural value to reside within that same culture. He passionately believed that people should have easy access to their own cultural history. That the worth of an item is not just what someone was willing to pay for it; it also holds a priceless cultural value.

Asim made me promise not to tell anyone about his illegal trade and I agreed. I was deeply worried what Arthur would do if he found out.

We spent as much time as we could together—mainly in the UK; a couple of times in Cairo. When we were apart my longing grew. I hadn't seen Asim for two months when Arthur was offered the job to retrieve the stolen Martin Brothers bird from Cairo for Mark.

I didn't trust Mark Maben and had asked around. A week after he had hired Arthur, I arrived at the shop to confront Arthur on his choice of client. "There're rumors he's probably a money launderer or some such, and some of his antique collection is from the black market."

"I don't think you're in a place to be judgmental," said Arthur.

"What are you implying?" Panic rushed through me. Was he talking about Asim? I turned away, heading toward the shop's kitchen to put the kettle on.

"I know what your boyfriend does. You're not the only one who can investigate things," Arthur called after me. "If you didn't want me to know, you shouldn't have told me the name of his family business and where it was located!"

Cold dread swept over me. I'd told him the name of Asim's family's business—A. A. M. Egypt—*before* I knew what the company actually did.

"You'd be able to see him if you came with me. Mark said the job would be all-expenses-paid. I would like to be introduced," said Arthur.

If only I'd kept my mouth shut Arthur wouldn't have joined the dots and discovered A. A. M. Egypt was the big forgeries workshop everyone was looking for.

My back was rigid and my nails dug into the scar on my palm. "I have no intention of introducing you. What would you do? Shop him to the police or make him your informant? For me, please, keep Asim out of what we do."

But saying no to Arthur was never an option—he had a way of persuading me his plans were always the best ones—and after a meeting with Mark, he was convinced the thief of the Martin Brothers bird would seek to have the bird copied. He "just wanted to ask Asim a few questions," so I agreed to let them "meet" over the phone. That was another mistake.

I had insisted on being present for the telephone call, which started innocently enough with Arthur explaining what the Martin Brothers bird looked like. But then Asim told Arthur his workshop had been given one only days before. Arthur instantly took the phone off speaker and had excitedly started making plans. Plans I was not part of. It wasn't until much later that I'd understood I had also been left out of many other discussions surrounding the Cairo trip.

Over the course of the next week I had asked Asim what Arthur really wanted him to arrange for us in Cairo. His vague answers filled me with dread. He told me not to worry, that Arthur had made the very best deal for them. I pestered Arthur over and over about what this deal was, but I was always brushed off with the same "you will get to see your lover" and "won't it be nice to be in Egypt again," and "getting the bird back will be such a coup."

The only way I thought I'd find out what was really going on and the only way I could protect Asim was to go on the trip.

A week later, I was on a red-eye flight to Cairo in a seat next to Arthur.

~

Before dawn, Arthur and I had left our downtown Cairo serviced-apartment block and hurried through dusty street after dusty street, heading to meet Asim in a café near Talaat Harb Square. The cool morning air was a welcome relief, and the roads were empty except for an occasional stray cat. I hadn't seen Asim in eight weeks and I'd missed him with a longing I couldn't admit to.

Arthur was gleeful that morning. "My dear, with your boyfriend's help we could bring down a prominent British forgery ring. He says he will get us the Martin Brothers bird *and* it has given him a clue as to who the international-forgery big boss is."

With every step my dread grew. "Is that what you've arranged with him behind my back?" My pulse picked up. "When I asked you to keep him out of it!" I stopped and Arthur tapped my shoulder to get me to keep moving. "I knew you were both keeping your plans from me but this . . . this puts Asim in danger!" I grabbed his arm. "Listen to me. I called Asim before we flew out and he sounded strange. He thought he was being followed."

"This was all Asim's idea, my dear. The workshop never had direct contact with the big forgery boss they manufacture for. It was only when someone turned up at Asim's father's house asking about a bird, that the clever boy took a photograph of the man and ran back to the workshop to take the Martin Brothers bird for us."

"Why didn't he tell me?" My heart twisted. "Why didn't *you* tell me?"

Arthur was too excited to listen to me. He was always like that on the hunt. "He'll give us the Martin Brothers bird and show us who the head of the forgery gang is, and I will get him the money he needs for a new life." He laughed. "Who would be crazy enough to think of copying one of those birds?"

The coffeehouse was on the corner of a small alley. The owner was an old school friend of Asim's and had opened early for us. We pushed the mahogany door open, the little brass bell tinkling about our heads.

"Are you sure?" I whispered to Arthur. "I don't like this."

"It'll be a win-win, my dear, just you see. I'll make sure the FBI Art Crime Team pays Asim well for the information he gives us, and he can do his archaeology degree at University College London like he longs to."

I knew that Asim would be thrilled with that deal. I was not—it didn't feel right to me.

"And Mark will get his beloved Martin Brothers bird back." Arthur looked around the small coffee shop. The chairs were still on the tables. There was no smell of fresh coffee, and the lights above the bar were turned off.

I was alarmed at the stillness inside the café. By the expression on Arthur's face, I knew he could sense it too.

Arthur put a finger to his lips and motioned that he was going to check in the kitchen, and I should stay put. "If you hear me shout, you run. You know the drill."

The stifling heat made me undo my scarf, and I pulled the hair off my neck.

Arthur disappeared into the kitchen, and I checked out the front window for signs of movement. The odd person wandered by, but no one seemed to notice we were inside. I checked my watch—6 a.m. We were on time. I gripped the café curtains.

Where's Asim?

Minutes passed. After fifteen, Arthur still hadn't come back. "Arthur?" I whispered.

Nothing.

I crept toward the kitchen and placed my ear to the door. There was no sound. I pushed it open. The kitchen had been turned upside down, pots and pans on the floor, broken eggs on the stainless-steel work surface. "Arthur?" I called again, a little louder.

Just then Arthur reappeared, walking through the rear door of the kitchen, which exited onto a back street. "Go now. Get on the next plane out of here." His voice was strained.

I went to him.

"No!" he cried, but it was too late.

On the other side of the stainless-steel kitchen island, Asim was lying on his back.

His eyes were open, locked on the ceiling.

Dead.

My stomach churned. I couldn't believe what I was seeing. I clamped my mouth closed as bile rose in my throat. I reached out to him, lightly touching his arm. It was cool. He didn't move.

There was a pool of crimson blood covering his neck.

I staggered backward and into the kitchen island. I bit my lip and the metallic taste of blood filled my mouth.

"What happened?" I whispered.

I looked around for Arthur. But I was all alone. I ran toward the back door, where Arthur had been standing. I opened it. The grimy alley behind the building was empty.

My legs were weak with grief.

Who would've done this?

Where did Arthur go?

I checked the whole café and no one else was there.

However much I desperately wanted to help Asim, I knew there was nothing I could do for him, and no good would come from being found by the Egyptian police. I was meant to be in Cairo as a tourist visiting the pyramids and I knew the well-rehearsed escape plan—I'd used it before in Jordan.

I ran back to the apartment as fast as I could, my hood pulled up tight and head down. When I arrived, I waved at the porter and headed for the elevator. I needed to find Arthur.

The two-bedroom apartment was exactly as we'd left it, but nothing was the same.

The image of Asim wouldn't leave me and the adrenaline that had gotten me home, pumping through my veins and moving my legs, had turned into a shaking grief.

There was a knock at the door. I ran into Arthur's bedroom and searched for the gun he told me he'd hidden under the mattress. It wasn't there. Did Arthur take the gun with him this morning? I didn't hear a shot in the café and I wouldn't believe Arthur capable of such a thing.

"Miss Freya, is everything all right?" It was the porter's voice from the other side of the door. "Mr. Arthur called and told me to check if you were okay. I have a taxi outside to take you to the airport like he asked."

I slipped the flimsy chain across the door and opened it slowly. The porter said again, "Everything all right, miss?"

"Yes, I'm fine, thank you." But I wasn't.

Who killed Asim?

I was convinced Arthur didn't kill Asim, but he *was* responsible for his death. He had gone behind my back and now Asim was lost to me. Arthur's greed had taken Asim from me. "Please tell the taxi to wait a few minutes while I pack."

Asim . . . Kind, funny, quick-witted Asim, who spoke three languages and loved his family, spoke of his sisters with such warmth and affection. He had wanted to save so many antiques for Egypt, had wanted to see so much more of the world. We were supposed to see the world together. And he had been ripped from me, from his family, far too soon, and so brutally.

The only way I had managed to cope with losing Asim was to scrub the memory of Cairo from my mind, but Arthur's clues and their connection to the past were making that day crash into me over and over again.

27

"If something looks wrong, run."

—Arthur Crockleford

Sheets of rain battered the drive outside the door, pulling me back to the present. I touched my cheek and found damp tears—I'd been soundlessly sobbing. Then I looked down at the phone in my other hand. Reality set in. If I had dropped my phone, I think I'd realize pretty quickly and go look for it. Was this Amy's phone?

Phil opened the kitchen door. "Are you coming? I think we should get back to the others."

"Yes," I replied, slipping the phone into my pocket without thinking. "I was wondering if Amy went out this way." There was something wrong—I didn't want to go back to the others; I wanted to look around the manor to see if I could find her.

On seeing me hesitate, Phil said, "No one uses that door. I tried it when I first arrived and it almost fell off its hinges."

"I made the same mistake earlier," Clare said, rattling cutlery.

"Why would Amy open it?" I asked.

"Perhaps she was trying a shortcut. Maybe she couldn't get it closed again?"

"Maybe." I wasn't convinced. It seemed to me that something had frightened Amy and she'd left the kitchen in a hurry.

146

With my flashlight in one hand and the candlestick in the other I followed Phil out of the kitchen and back to the dining room.

As I entered, Carole came toward me, trying to hide the worry in her eyes with a smile. "I'm so glad you're back. I was just saying that at my age I get awfully tired." She glanced at Giles.

It wasn't like my aunt to go to bed early if there was company, but I didn't think much about it; I was still worrying about Amy. I turned to face the other guests. "Do you think that we should arrange some sort of search party for Amy?"

"Nothing to worry about. My sister's always fine," said Giles.

"But where did she go?" I asked again.

No one answered me.

Bella shivered and concern etched her brow. She glared at me in a way that made me realize what Carole was suggesting was a really good idea. It made my mind up. I would take Carole back to the cottage, get her settled, and then return to the manor to look for Amy.

"Our coats are still in the drawing room. Shall I go and get them?" I said to Carole, then I remembered the photo of Lord Metcalf and his family—I needed to retrieve it. I tugged at my earlobe. "I think I've lost an earring—give me one minute."

I looked under the table, around the curtain, in the drawer. The photo was gone.

Carole looped her arm through mine. "Let's go now," she said.

I didn't argue. "We're going to head back to our cottage and light the log burner, get some warmth into the place," I said to the table.

Bella rose. "Good night, then." She gave me a hug and whispered, "Lock the door."

I addressed the room: "Good night." Carole and I stepped into the corridor.

"Let's get our coats and get out of here." I hesitated, remembering something. "A gust of wind blew out the candles, didn't it? That could have happened only if the kitchen door was held open long enough for the outside air to make it from the back door all the way into the manor. I think someone hooked it open. But why?"

"When we heard the scream there was only you, me, and Phil in the dining room—any of them could have hurt Amy. Also . . ." Carole's eyes fell. "When we get to the cottage I have a confession." She didn't wait for me to question her further and hurried toward the drawing room.

"Tell me." I hustled after her. This wasn't going to be good; Carole was one of the most upfront people I know. It meant that she was fearful.

The drawing room was lit by only a few scented candles on the table. The curtains were all open, stirring in the air coming in through the drafty French doors.

Carole was pulling on her coat. "I know Giles. I've met him a few times with Arthur, on a cruise ship and in that bar in Hong Kong. I'm not sure what he does; he was always very vague. But Arthur and Giles had a strained relationship—they were never easy in each other's company."

"You're implying Giles is dodgy in some way. Like, involved in the black market for antiques?"

Someone coughed farther down the corridor.

"*Hush.*" Carole grabbed my arm. "Let's get back to the cottage and talk about it there—not here. I know what you're going to say. You think Arthur was into that black market stuff as well. But it was just that one Cairo job. You of all people know how desperate someone can become when they're about to lose everything. What would you do to save your house? Did you decide to go and see Franklin Smith with the thought that you might inherit a business from a man that you supposedly hated? Would you do that to save your home?" She raised an eyebrow and I turned away, pretending to hunt for my coat to mask my shame.

It was then I glimpsed taillights in the distance through the French doors.

"There's a car driving away," I said, scurrying over to the doors for a better look. I guessed that the car must be nearing the tunnel of trees before the front gates.

Carole rushed over. "Do you think it's Amy leaving?"

"It can only be Amy. Everyone else is here, aren't they?"

The red lights flickered through the trees as the car entered the tunnel.

"Guess she's gone." Carole shook her head, moving away. "Very strange that she didn't tell us!"

Then the car lights stopped.

"Carole." I beckoned her back. "Look. Have they stopped to open the gates?"

"Weren't the gates left open?" Carole squinted. "I can't see. It's dark and so far."

I heard footsteps behind us. "Everything all right?" said Phil, entering the room. He grabbed his Barbour jacket from where it had been flung over an armchair in the corner.

"Absolutely," said Carole.

I pulled on my trench coat and tugged up the collar to give me some protection against the weather outside. "Have you got everything?" I asked Carole.

"I suppose you'll be going to the Antiques Fair tomorrow morning?" asked Phil.

I had totally forgotten there was a program of events. What did it say? I pulled out my phone and looked at the picture I had taken of the itinerary.

5 A.M.	BREAKFAST IN THE MANOR
9 A.M.	ANTIQUES MARKET — LONG MELFORD
12 NOON.	ANTIQUES TALK — VICTORIAN STONEWARE

The time of the breakfast seemed far too early. What was Arthur playing at? The "Victorian Stoneware" was probably a talk about Martin Brothers birds—perhaps because Lord Metcalf loved his one so much.

And what could Arthur have meant by putting an antiques market in there?

"Maybe Arthur chose this weekend specifically to coincide with the fair? It's the first time a fair has been on the program," said Phil.

"You said that you didn't know Arthur." I waited for an answer.

"Did I?" Phil shifted from one foot to the other.

Liar.

"When did you and he first meet? My aunt and I love a story about Arthur. It keeps his memory alive." I tried to smile at him.

Phil sighed. "I met him only once. A couple of Saturdays ago, I think. I saw him knock on the manor door but no one answered, so I went over to see if I could help."

Now I knew he was lying because Franklin had told us Arthur did see Lord Metcalf that day. And Carole believed Arthur had called her when he arrived at Copthorn Manor to see Metcalf.

"You were watching him?" I asked.

"Not at all." Phil checked his watch. "It's late, and I know you're tired. Good night." He left quickly.

"What should we make of that?" Carole asked.

"He's lying. But I think we should check out this antiques fair. Arthur put it in the schedule for a reason. Perhaps it's another clue."

"Perhaps the murderer will be there?"

"If there is anything there, we have to find it," I said. "Tomorrow is the last day of the retreat and we have to speed up our search. Time is running out to catch Arthur's killer."

28

"Sooner or later someone always slips up. Secrets are hard to keep and people are nosy."

—Arthur Crockleford

By the time Carole and I left the manor it seemed everyone else had decided to retreat to their rooms. I had made one last check of the kitchen and dining room, but everyone had probably arrived at the same conclusion we had. It was time for bed.

The wind and rain howled around us as we rushed across the drive to the cottage. Tree branches crashed together, leaves rustling, and a bolt of lightning cracked in the distance.

The hairs on my neck prickled. Were we being watched again? I scanned every empty black space for signs of movement but couldn't distinguish anything.

I wiped the sodden curls that clung to my face as I unlocked the door to our cottage. The first thing I saw was the upturned armchair by the fireplace. The "LEAVE NOW" note had been taken from its envelope and left open on the coffee table.

The cottage has been searched and we are being warned.

My eyes met Carole's—did they find the journal?

I hurried over to the woodpile. What if it had been taken? That journal could be the only record of the real Copthorn Manor Collection—

the only images of stolen antiques after the time they were taken. What if I had ruined everything by not keeping it safe?

Another of Arthur's sayings came back to me: *When in doubt, always hide the items of true value. Those are the ones people want to take.*

"Is it still there?" Carole whispered.

With shaking hands, I pulled the logs away and lifted the old newspaper beneath them. My eyes locked on the journal and relief washed over me. "Yes!"

We both searched the rest of the cottage but nothing seemed to have been taken. I collapsed back on the sofa and Carole lit the fire. I was shivering, but the pop and crackle of the newly lit logs held no comfort. I couldn't decide if it was adrenaline or fear that had shaken me up so much. Darkness shrouded Copthorn Manor and all the guests inside it.

"They did a thorough job searching the place," said Carole, returning to the sofa with a pot of tea and two teacups. "Thank all the heavens they didn't pull out the logs." She pointed to the journal in my lap. "We need to be more careful."

"I agree. Shall we recap?" I asked, wanting to focus my spinning thoughts. "And after that, you will need to tell me all you know about Giles. No more secrets."

Carole gave a solemn nod.

"I found a photo of a man in the dining room this evening," I began. "I recognized him as Mark, the man who employed Arthur and me to recover his stolen Martin Brothers bird about twenty years ago. Now I know he was Lord Metcalf, the father of Giles and Amy."

"And Harry saw Arthur with a Martin Brothers bird in his shop the day before his death," Carole said. "It is all connected."

"Yes, it has to be," I replied. "But I don't think it's the exact same bird—there are many Martin Brothers Wally Birds in the world. A dealer once told me that the brother who ran the shop used to hide his favorite birds out of sight so that only the collectors he liked or the ones who paid the most money would have them. Those birds seem to inspire something in collectors . . . Lord Metcalf was almost hysterical when he came to Arthur begging him to help get his back. He said it had been stolen by his estranged son."

"Giles."

"Giles stole the bird from his father and sent it, or took it, I don't know, to Egypt for it to be copied by one of the best forgery workshops in the business."

"And your old boyfriend worked there?" asked Carole.

"Yes, Asim, who stole the bird from the workshop to hand it over to us. He was killed the next morning . . . I never found out who killed him." I focused on the dancing light of the fire. I didn't want to see the sympathy in my aunt's eyes. "When Arthur and I didn't come back with the bird, Mark was livid. I'm surprised Arthur remained friendly with him after that."

"I knew the job had gone wrong in Cairo and that your boyfriend was killed." Carole looked out the window toward the manor. "So, this is where it all started."

"And will it all end here?" I sighed. "Arthur knew how this puzzle joined together, but we don't have all the pieces yet."

"You will." Carole tapped my knee and smiled with the utter confidence that only a mother figure can hold. "Who do you think was driving that car earlier? It wasn't the belly dancers, that's for sure." She winked at me as she poured more tea into our cups.

"First, let's ask why everyone is here. It feels very much like Arthur orchestrated it this way. We know from Franklin that in Metcalf's vaults there are items being stored for certain individuals. Which is strange in itself. Franklin was given the keys to the vaults by Metcalf on his death . . . but how did he get them?"

"I don't follow," said Carole.

"I think Metcalf gave the vault keys to Arthur when he came to see him a week ago. Perhaps he didn't want his family getting in the vaults, and we should then assume there is only one set. I believe Arthur handed the keys over to Franklin at their meeting. And what's inside the vaults that Giles wants so badly? I suppose they're all waiting to get in there tomorrow? Except for Bella; she seems to be here just because Giles is. And Amy's a strange one. She knows about the journals—she asked the whole room about them and now she's disappeared." I paused.

Carole smiled. "I knew you'd get back into the swing of things."

"It seems clear the only thing we've learned is that Arthur was right: no one here is to be trusted. The program says breakfast will be at five a.m. That's very early for breakfast. I think something is happening at five a.m. and Arthur wanted us to know about it."

I returned my thoughts to Arthur's final night. I knew from my hunting days that when an antique was ordered to be stolen, then it was planned weeks in advance—this type of robbery was recognizable, because only a few valuable items were missing. The "enter and grab what you can" type of incident, where every last silver-looking piece of cutlery was taken, looked chaotic in nature. The scene at Arthur's shop hadn't been chaotic; it was staged, just like the manor. For the first type of crime, antique hunters looked at who was around the property weeks before. For the second type, it was days before. I realized that this theory could also be applied to Arthur's death, couldn't it?

"Before Arthur died, he was pottering along, writing all those stolen items down in his journal, booking vacations," I said. "And then he spoke to Metcalf and everything changed. Amy asked about the journals; what if the information inside the journals could damage the Metcalf family or uncover someone's wrongdoing? That would make someone very intent on finding them. Franklin? Giles and Bella? Amy, or Clare?"

"And the handsome gardener, Phil. Just because he's a looker doesn't mean he's not a killer." Carole beamed at me and I chose to ignore her.

"We've assumed that Amy, Clare, and Phil were here the day Arthur came, but Franklin could have also been here." Questions were spinning in my mind. I needed facts. I opened the calendar app on my phone.

"Arthur died sometime on the night of Sunday, May nineteenth. Let's work backward. Almost two weeks before, on Saturday, May fourth, Arthur goes to see Metcalf, and they talk. Then Metcalf dies. On Wednesday, May fifteenth, Arthur goes to Franklin to draw up his will and signs it. He tells Franklin he knows about Metcalf's instructions to open the vaults after his death and he gives Franklin the keys then. I think we can assume that Metcalf had also told Arthur what was in his will. Arthur helps Franklin book the transport for this weekend, and everyone is informed. Arthur doesn't trust that Franklin will tell us about the retreat, so on Friday, the seventeenth, he writes a letter. By this point Arthur is worried he's being watched so he gives the letter to Agatha on the sly. But I'm not clear why he didn't post it?"

Carole breathed deeply. "The letter was an insurance policy *if* something happened to him. I think he wanted to find whatever was hidden here at the manor, but he knew he was in danger. If he was all right in the end, then he would have gone and retrieved the letter from Agatha. He couldn't do that if he had posted it to us."

"Clever."

"Oh, he was just the best, darling." Carole sighed.

"We still don't know what happened on the night Arthur died," I said. "Amy and Giles were at the Crown. Franklin was there too. . . ."

Carole pointed her finger in the air and exclaimed, "They were all in on it! Amy, Giles, Franklin, Phil, and Bella—they all killed my poor darling Arthur, and now we will take our revenge!"

"Really?" She was getting ahead of herself. "Arthur was at the Crown too. We don't know where Phil was. And Bella said she was in London but she might not have been. They probably all had the opportunity."

"We are exceptionally brilliant at this, darling. Don't you think?" said my aunt. She was always very modest.

I crossed my arms. "Now, let's hear about Giles."

"I met him years ago." Carole settled back on the sofa. "I used to join Arthur on his exotic business trips and, on occasion, Giles was there. He seemed to be invited like Arthur had been. It took me a while to recognize him tonight, darling, as he used to be a lot more suave, with a lovely big, trendy beard—shiny shoes and the like. Maybe he's fallen on hard times."

"Did you recognize him at the funeral?" I demanded.

"Well, I wasn't *sure* it was him. And I thought it best not to bring up Arthur's business . . . contacts." She took a sip of her tea, avoiding eye contact. "You're quite touchy about all that and it was a lifetime ago."

"What did Arthur say about him?" I demanded.

"Arthur called him a 'dealer friend,' but he once told me Giles's father was an antiques collector—'dripping in dodgy money'—and that Giles was the one who acquired things for him. Made me think he was a 'take a painting from a museum' type of thief and not a 'bid at an auction' dealer. Giles was quite happy to sell Arthur information on other sketchy goings-on if it meant he could wipe out some competition."

It made sense. "Arthur always had informers—it helped him massively when he was on the hunt for a stolen item. But why would Arthur have anything to do with a man who stole a Martin Brothers bird from his own father?" I asked. "Especially as that deal ended . . . badly?" I wondered.

"I think it was sometime after Cairo, when Arthur was hunting down some stately home burglaries in 2003, and he came across Giles again," replied Carole.

"The ones mentioned in those clippings we found in the journals. I remembered those burglaries, of course, but they happened after I'd left hunting. Perhaps Giles was one of the thieves?" I asked.

"I don't know about that, exactly. Recession had hit hard; the shop was on the verge of being repossessed. Giles came to him trying to sell an item that had been stolen, and Arthur noticed what it was, bought it, and claimed the insurance reward. Giles came back again with another item and cut a deal with Arthur, that's what I think. Arthur told me that 'Giles saw a gap in the market' that would make them both some money. Arthur was just trying to save the shop."

I sighed, understanding what had probably happened. "Back then it wasn't the insurance companies' job to catch criminals; they cared about getting the items back so they didn't have to pay out on the policy. What Arthur and Giles were up to was a scam."

Carole hung her head. "It was a different type of hunting," she mumbled.

My fist clenched around my scar. "If Arthur was in on it, and if this was going on after Egypt, then he didn't stop when he promised you he did. Did he?" Anger quickened my pulse and I breathed deeply trying to stay calm. "Arthur crossed over into the black market of the antiques world—he worked for criminals and traded in stolen antiques." I stood up. "You didn't tell me." I knew why. We'd had an unspoken agreement never to talk about Arthur, and Carole had always longed for Arthur and me to reconcile. "In that world people don't value human life. People get killed. . . ." I grabbed my cup and took it into the kitchen. I needed space from my aunt and her defense of Arthur. Memories of Asim threatened to resurface and I closed my eyes.

"But people did get back their stolen items and he did do legitimate hunting after you left. . . ."

I whipped around, fury bubbling inside me, intent on telling her how very wrong Arthur had been in Cairo and ever since, when a howling wind shook the front door.

Rain beat against the windows. Concerned for our safety, I hurried over to check that the cottage door was locked.

Carole followed me and looked out the window. "Oh gosh, darling, what's that?" she asked, pointing to something outside.

Was she trying to change the subject? I took a few deep breaths and tamped down my anger at our argument. I couldn't ignore the thought she had seen something, and I cupped my hands to the glass.

There was the beam of a flashlight inside the manor.

"Someone's there," whispered Carole.

My hunter's instinct ignited and our argument paused for now. "Perhaps it's Amy." I stepped back, not wanting to be seen at the window even though the manor was quite some distance away.

I caught my reflection in the glass, eyes wide and bright, mouth determined, hair pulled back in a bun, all businesslike. *Alive.* That was the word that sprang to mind; for the first time in a very long time, I looked alive. I straightened and breathed deeply. *I've missed you.*

There was another flash of light in one of the windows of the manor. "That's in the kitchen."

The phone. Perhaps Amy had come back and is looking for her phone?

Light flitted out through the crack in the back door of the kitchen.

"Arthur told us he was looking for something here that he desperately wanted to find and when he thought he might not be able to, he left as many clues as possible for us." I watched the light grow dimmer. "I should find out what's going on."

"It's not a good idea now, darling. The storm is picking up again," Carole said, returning to the log burner and placing another log on the fire.

I was about to join her—if Amy was back and looking for her phone then I could give it to her in the morning—when I saw a tall, slim woman dash across the drive toward the manor.

"Where's Bella going?" I said, almost to myself.

Without waiting to hear Carole's objections, I slipped on my coat, Amy's phone in my pocket, pulled on my sneakers, and unlocked the cottage door.

"Where are you going?" called Carole.

"I'm going back." I silenced her with a look. "I've done this before." I reached into my handbag, retrieved a couple of bobby pins, and put them into my coat pocket, hoping I would remember how to pick a lock if necessary.

I quietly closed the cottage door behind me, checking that no one was around. It took only a couple of puddles soaking through my socks to realize that this might not have been the best idea. But I was *alive* now, wasn't I? I would just pop over and see if Amy was around and return her phone to her and maybe double-check what Bella was up to. I took in a lungful of air and ran toward the manor.

29

"Our time has come, dear boy, to right the wrongs of the past."
—Arthur Crockleford

Giles

Giles was the last one in the manor. It was the way he'd planned it—telling Bella to go to bed. He'd even made sure that nosy gardener, Phil, had left through the French doors in the drawing room and watched those other women scurry back to their cottage.

On arrival at the manor, Giles had thought he recognized Phil, but that couldn't be right, could it? Giles hadn't been back to Copthorn for a long time. But it did make him wary of Phil. Something wasn't right about him.

It had, however, been a pleasure to reacquaint himself with Carole. Arthur had introduced them somewhere in Asia a couple of decades ago and they had met at different venues all over the world since then. She was always charming company, unlike her niece, who . . . wasn't. Freya Lockwood was going to have to be dealt with—it was clear she knew too much.

Reassuring himself he was unseen, Giles returned to the dining room and retrieved an old family photograph. He slid it out from its hiding place under the tablecloth and stuffed it into his shirt pocket. Freya had seemed fixated by what she saw in the photo, and that worried Giles. It was why he'd thought it best to collect it from where it fell.

He hoped she hadn't identified everyone and *everything* in it. He didn't know where the photo had come from; he had thrown away any images of his father's old Martin Brothers bird. That bird was cursed.

Next he hurried upstairs to find Amy. She was going to tell him where the new entrance to the vaults was. There used to be stairs leading down from the kitchen, but those had been blocked up. The old man would've told his favorite child where everything was kept, and Giles was going to get it out of her.

In his message, Arthur was very clear—*It's in the vault and it will be open on Sunday, May twenty-sixth at 10 a.m. when the van arrives.*

The Martin Brothers bird had been haunting Giles for most of his adult life, and it would haunt him still until it was destroyed. Arthur understood how important finding it was. That Martin Brothers bird might once have been worth up to sixty thousand or higher, a drop in the ocean to Giles, but its sentimental value was priceless. He'd been looking for the bloody thing ever since Cairo.

Arthur was the only one who'd really cared about the antiques. Everyone else here just cared about the price of them, and Arthur was the verifier—the one who could say if something was genuine or a fake. Giles had always considered that it would've been hard for a man as honorable as Arthur to verify stolen antiques for the criminal underworld, but Arthur needed the money. And he didn't have a choice.

Giles walked through the ink-black corridors of Copthorn Manor and hoped Amy had her own set of keys to the vaults. If she did, he didn't have long to get them from her.

He reached the kitchen door and propped it open with his foot, the large hinges wanting to swing the heavy door back into position. He swept his flashlight around the room. There was a draft from the back door, which was still open a crack.

"Hello?" he called into the room. "Amy? I'm just checking you're all right."

There was a squeak of floorboards from the floor above him.

"I always hated this house," Giles muttered. "You had to make me come back, didn't you."

His left hand clenched and his thumb found the back of the signet ring on his little finger. For the hundredth time he wished his mother hadn't given it to him, for then he could have thrown it away.

If Amy's still in the manor, then she would've retreated to her bedroom.

Giles passed the hall fireplace and picked up one of the pokers, the roaring fire flushing his cheeks for a moment. He turned the cool metal around in his hand. It would do.

The two large double doors leading to the main grand staircase were wide open. Giles grabbed the banister, which he used to slide down as a child while his mother waited to catch him at the bottom, then turned off his flashlight and crept up the stairs. He stopped on the balcony, his heart pounding and lungs gasping. He wasn't as light on his feet as he'd once been.

He listened.

Waited.

Silence.

The only light came from under Amy's bedroom door.

She's in there.

Earlier, Amy had been on the phone when he'd gone to get some oat milk for Bella. She was screaming at the person on the other end. Telling them to hurry up and get to the manor. That there was no way she could do this on her own. He'd assumed she had meant hosting the retreat, but now . . .

Giles approached her bedroom door and reached for the round brass handle. It was ice-cold. He turned it as slowly as possible, trying not to make a sound. He wanted the element of surprise.

Click.

Annoyed at himself, he shoved the door open. It crashed against the wall.

The room was lit by candlelight and a few camping lamps. Amy was rifling through a chest of drawers. She spun around. "What do you want?" she said, straightening her shoulders, her eyes boring into him.

Giles mirrored her and planted his feet on the old navy carpet. "The guests were wondering if you were all right. You seemed to disappear. I thought I'd come and check." He tried to sound concerned.

"You thought you'd go sneaking about in the dark. Didn't you?" Her tone was emotionless. "What are you looking for, Shanks? The vaults? He moved the entrance so you would never find it. Imagine going to all that trouble so your own son would be kept in the dark."

"Don't call me that." His grip tightened on the poker. "I own half this place now." He noticed a bandage on her arm.

Amy followed his eyes and shrugged. "Just a small cut." She pulled her sweater down over the bandage. "Have you seen a phone? I can't find mine."

"No." Giles looked around the room, which was almost empty apart from storage boxes. Clothing was strewn over the floor, and what looked like the contents of a handbag were scattered on the bed.

Amy walked toward him. "Well, as you can see, I'm perfectly fine." She motioned to the door. "I'm going to get some sleep. I'm sure you can remember your way out, and where your old bedroom is over the hall."

Giles shivered at the mention of his old room. He wanted to get out of there, but not without the bird. "Do you have the vault keys? I want what is mine. My debt is paid!"

Amy smiled warmly, like one would to a toddler. "I've no idea what you're talking about. As I said, I'm off to bed." She eyed the poker in Giles's hand but didn't flinch. "Tomorrow we are closing up the house and all this will be over."

Giles knew she was no match for him. He was taller and broader than her, and with a flick of his arm he would be past her and into the room. But he hesitated and contemplated retreating. There was no point in playing his hand too soon. Once he had the bird then everything would

30

"Always be ready for the tide to turn."

—Arthur Crockleford

Freya

I slipped into the manor. The hallway was lit by the soft glow of fire-light, but the open doorways before me were gaping black holes. I shone my flashlight into the darkness—as far as the light would stretch—looking for Amy or Bella.

Danger, my senses screamed at me. *Careful.*

There was a murmur of voices above me, and I hastened toward them, coming to a stop at the bottom of a grand staircase. There was no light up there. I waited, listening.

Was it in my imagination?

Floorboards creaked.

Turn around. My fear pulsed through me. *Go back.*

But I didn't go back. Instead, I reminded myself of all the houses I'd slipped into unseen during my hunting days with Arthur. I'd never turned back then. With each step I took up the staircase in Copthorn Manor I was discovering my courage again. I thought bravery had deserted me, but it hadn't. It had been swallowed by grief, and now I was slowly emerging from that pool.

164

THE ANTIQUE HUNTER'S GUIDE TO MURDER   163

change. There was a niggling question—why did Arthur think the bird would be here? Surely his father would've hidden it on foreign soil far, far away?

He got the sense someone was listening, and scanned the corridor before wedging his foot against the door so that Amy couldn't close it on him. He needed answers and time was running out.

I knew what Arthur had been implying when he sent me the fox brooch. It wasn't just "go and hunt again." It was "go and find that girl inside you who loved the hunt," the eighteen-year-old who had ended up in Paris at the fox brooches' designer Lea Stein's door, wanting to know everything there was to know about jewelry making. A young woman hungry for answers, with a life full of adventure ahead. I didn't know how the fire that killed my parents had started, but there were other questions that *could* be answered. And now Arthur had left enough clues, hoping I wouldn't be able to resist the urge to find out the truth. I should have been livid at the manipulation, but I wasn't, for it was only now that Arthur was gone that the drip, drip of fond memories of the person I once was had started to come back to me. Arthur had played a part in making that person who she was, and I couldn't hate him for that, could I? I had loved the old me.

I stepped slowly and quietly like I used to. I'd be in and out before anyone knew. A wave of adrenaline tingled over me as I placed my foot on the next step and then the next. At the top, there was a flare of a flashlight down the corridor. Perhaps Bella was also looking for Amy.

If it was Amy, I'd ask if the power outage had been reported and give her back her phone. If it was Bella . . . I'd tell her I was looking for Amy. My plan was watertight.

I reached the top of the stairs. The voices were clearer now. It was a man and a woman—that didn't make sense. I placed my sleeve over the flashlight, dimming the light, and stayed close to the barren walls. The hallway was bare, no occasional tables with photo frames or objets d'art, no paintings or pictures on the walls. I passed a window and realized I was at the back of the house and there were no curtains.

This confirmed my instincts had been right. The house below me was staged; downstairs rooms that entertained guests were furnished and made to look "old," but the rest of the house was seemingly empty.

There was a warm glow of candlelight stretching out from an open door. I switched off my flashlight and crept closer, feeling my way along the wall. My wet sneakers squelched, and I prayed no one else heard.

There was a tall figure of a man standing in the doorway.

"The bird belongs to me." It was Giles. "I stole it for Mom in the first place."

I held my breath. Was Giles looking for the Martin Brothers bird Harry had seen Arthur with?

I pressed my index finger into my scar and closed my eyes to push away the memory of Asim's death. It would not help me find Arthur's killer, would it?

I turned my focus to who was talking. It was Amy. "Arthur came here asking to look in one of the vaults that he wasn't privileged to enter. Now you? What's so special about Vault Four?"

The question echoed through the darkness, as did the name—Vault 4.

Giles didn't answer.

"I never understood why you cared so much about that thing; it's ugly as all hell. Why send it to the best workshop? Stupid move: you must've known Arthur could track it there."

"Shut your mouth, you old hag." I could see his back tighten and his biceps twitch. He had a poker in his hand.

"These things of Dad's are just wood stuck together or dirt made into a jar. I'll never understand why people are stupid enough to pay good money for them."

"It's not about the money." Giles stepped forward.

"Oh, I know, I know," Amy's voice whined. "It's because Mommy loved it and Mommy was the only one who loved poor little Shanks. It's lucky she didn't see what you became, isn't it?"

"At least someone loved *me*. Now, where is the entrance to the vaults?" Giles raised the poker.

"Arthur should've kept his mouth shut." Amy slammed the door into Giles's foot.

He didn't flinch. But he raised the poker in the air like he was about to bring it crashing down on Amy's head.

Amy stepped backward.

I readied myself to pounce on Giles from behind, but then he twiddled the poker in his hand and lowered it to his side.

He's showing her who's really in control. I relaxed and retreated into the darkness.

"I'll be seeing you tomorrow morning. I believe Arthur said the van was arriving at ten. Then these games will all be over," said Giles.

He stepped into the hallway. I panicked and stumbled backward toward the nearest room and hid inside. I swung the door silently shut behind me, relieved I'd escaped. In the cold darkness I could barely see the room, empty except for a dusty toy train on the windowsill.

Giles's footsteps passed by in the corridor. I considered going to ask Amy if she was all right, but then I heard the scraping of something heavy being moved. Amy seemed to be barricading herself in her bedroom— *she's right to be afraid of Giles.*

I needed to get back to Carole and tell her what I'd heard. I peeked out of the room, checking that there was no one was about, then started back down the hallway.

Outside, a car door slammed shut and tires splashed through a puddle.

Was it the same car from earlier or had someone else arrived? Or was someone else leaving?

I hurried down the stairs, my pulse racing, searching every corner with my light. At the bottom a wooden floorboard creaked behind me.

Danger.

I started to run, but a hand grabbed me, and I was thrown sideways, my flashlight crashing to the floor. The air burst from my lungs as I slammed into a cold and musty wall. My arm blazed in red-hot pain.

"Get off me," I tried to yell, but only an airless whisper escaped.

The person pressed their body into mine. "Be quiet," a man's voice said in my ear, stale coffee breath hitting my face. I couldn't see who it was, but the voice told me it was Giles. "We need to talk."

"Get your bloody hands off me before I scream."

"Don't make a sound and do as you're told. Deal?" He released his grip a fraction.

I nodded in agreement—anything to get out of there.

He let me go and picked up my fallen flashlight, spinning it in his hand. The poker was nowhere to be seen.

"What are you doing?" I asked, straightening my back. I couldn't let him see my fear. I'd been in worse situations than this, I tried to remind myself.

"Me? What about you? This is no place to go sneaking about. Didn't Arthur tell you what to expect?" Giles seemed shocked to find me standing before him and I wondered who he'd expected.

"I don't . . ." I didn't go on; I didn't trust him. "You were at Arthur's funeral."

"I was paying my respects; Arthur was an old friend." He glanced up the stairs.

That wasn't the impression I'd gotten when I saw him at Arthur's funeral, but I kept this observation to myself. I rubbed my throbbing arm. "Why are you grabbing women and throwing them against walls like that?"

"You're sneaking about. You could've been anyone." He looked around again. "We should talk."

"Not here." I wanted out of the manor, and I needed to get back to the safety of Carole. "I'm going back to my cottage. Unless you're going to stop me?" I stepped toward him, trying to look unafraid.

Giles put his hands up like I was holding a gun to his head. "Of course not. I'll walk you there." It sounded like a demand, not an offer.

I didn't argue. He gestured for me to go ahead, then closed the manor door behind us. Outside the storm had passed and I looked around for a newly arrived car but there wasn't one in the driveway. Perhaps I had imagined it. And where was Bella? I had seen her running toward the manor but I had never seen her leave—was she still inside? And was Franklin in his cottage? I realized someone else was unaccounted for . . . Clare. She'd been in the kitchen when I found the phone, but I hadn't seen her again.

31

"There is no greater thrill than finding what has been lost, either a ten-pound note or a hidden Ming vase."

—Arthur Crockleford

I entered the cottage to see that the electricity on the estate grounds was still out, and Carole was curled up on the sofa with a novel in one hand and a flashlight in the other. The log burner had made the room furnace-hot, but she was still covered in a blanket. She sprang to her feet, her hand gripping her chest. "Thank God you're home, darling. I thought I was going to have to call the . . ." She stopped when she saw Giles behind me.

Giles slipped off his coat, beaming at Carole. "I'm so glad we can talk away from everyone else."

Carole nodded in agreement, but there was no welcoming smile.

"Do you mind if we sit for a moment?" asked Giles, making himself comfortable on the sofa.

I closed the door but didn't lock it.

"This will probably require some tea." Carole swept into the kitchen, filling a pot with water and lighting the gas with the fizz of a match—even with the kettle out of action due to the power outage, Carole still found a way to make tea.

I hadn't moved from my position by the front door. Giles looked like someone who spent a lot of time in the gym, and his obvious strength made my stomach tighten. It would take a lot of skill to take him on. I moved to sit opposite him, my back rigid. I couldn't relax with a man who had just thrown me up against a wall in such a swift, well-practiced action. A clattering of spoons came from the kitchen.

"Are you all right?" I called to Carole.

"Yes, darling, if you wouldn't mind coming to help me carry the pot."

I hurried over and picked up the steaming teapot. Carole pulled open a drawer and slipped a carving knife under a tea towel and placed it on the edge of the workspace nearest to the sofa.

She nodded to me in a way that said *if there's a problem, run for the knife.*

Once we were all seated again, I said, "Giles pounced on me as I was coming down the stairs, and now he's insisted on speaking to both of us." I waited for him to elaborate.

"I didn't know your niece was following me around. I thought it was . . ." He caught himself.

"I wasn't following you. I saw a flashlight in the manor and thought that Amy might've been there. I was going to check if she was all right." I was about to add that I had intended to give Amy her phone back when I decided Giles didn't need to know more than was absolutely necessary. I was still wearing my damp coat and I reached into the pocket to check that the phone was still there.

Carole poured the tea and looked Giles up and down. "I think it's time you told us what is so important that you needed to barge into our cottage."

"You're messing around in things you don't understand—you must leave. I'm warning you as a favor to Arthur. But it's the only warning I'll give."

He sat very still, and I worried for my aunt.

"Arthur was my closest friend, darling," Carole said, smiling at Giles. "I traveled with him everywhere, as you know." She paused for one of her "dramatic effect" moments. "Arthur told me *everything.*"

Giles cocked his head and studied her. It was clear he was trying to decide if she was telling the truth. I frowned at her, but she remained stone-faced. I didn't know if she was acting or not.

"Why are you here?" asked Giles.

"Arthur sent us here to verify the estate's antiques for probate," said Carole.

He frowned. "I don't believe that."

"Of course, we didn't realize the antiques would be in vaults, did we, Freya?"

I took my cue and tested Giles. "I believe it's number four we need to verify?"

"That's the family vault," Giles said. "You don't need to go anywhere near there. My father was stupid enough to give Amy the keys to the vaults on occasion, but he'd obviously come to his senses if he changed the locks and left the only set of keys with Arthur before he died."

I nodded. He had just confirmed that the Copthorn Manor Collection of furniture must have been replaced with the reproductions in the manor and stored in the vaults. I remembered something else I had overheard and made a guess. "Arthur told us there was quite a collection inside Vault Four."

"He didn't tell you that." Giles's shoulder tightened.

I've pushed too far.

"He told us everything, darling," Carole lied. "We are quite trustworthy."

There were times when my aunt could be as nutty as a fruitcake, but this was not one of those times. She was really quite marvelous when she wanted to be.

"Well . . ." Giles relaxed back into the sofa cushions. "I suppose if Arthur told you everything, then you know who I am?"

It's a test, I thought. *What on earth is Carole going to say?*

"Of course. You're the clever one of the family; they just don't know it yet," Carole said.

Of course! With a nickname like Shanks, he probably *wasn't* the brightest one—Carole was stroking his ego.

"You're bloody right. My sister doesn't know what I've had to do to keep the business going. While she swanned around getting her degree, I was keeping the business alive as my father's health got worse. Then she comes back a year or so ago to save the day."

We were getting off topic. "What's in the vaults that's so important to you?" I asked.

"What's in the vaults that's so important to *you*?" he parroted.

He was playing games.

When I didn't answer, Giles shrugged. "It was something of my father's, and as he's no longer with us, now it's mine. Arthur said it was here—and I want to get it before anyone else." He clenched his fists. "Do you know where the entrance to the vaults is? It appears it has been moved!"

"Oh, we don't, darling. Arthur didn't tell us *that* much," soothed Carole. "We thought that you'd know where it was?"

"Then you're no good to me." He glared at us but said nothing more. The silence hung in the air.

I picked up my cup and pretended to take it to the kitchen so I would be near the knife.

Giles rose slowly. He cracked his knuckles. "You need to go. Now!"

He turned on his heels and left.

Carole locked the door behind him and we both let out a long shudder of air. "Thank the heavens he's gone. I think we can safely assume he sent the note?"

"I don't think note writing is his thing," I said. "He seems to be someone who prefers physical action over the written word." I collapsed back on the sofa. "Before he spotted me, I overheard Giles and Amy talking. I believe he's looking for the Martin Brothers bird from Cairo and there must have been a reason for Lord Metcalf locking it away.... We need to get into Vault Four before anyone else. Giles told Amy that the moving van was arriving at ten a.m., so we can assume that's when Franklin will be opening the vaults. But in the program, Arthur wrote that breakfast would be at five a.m. I'm going to set my alarm for four forty-five a.m. and be on the lookout for anything suspicious."

Carole patted my arm. "We're finally going to get to the bottom of all this."

≈

Before bed, I stood in the bathroom doorway, because there was "no room for both of us, darling," watching Carole's evening beauty routine.

"Do you really think that Giles killed Arthur?" said Carole, retrieving a pot of moisturizer. "You should invest in some of this. I think it's laced with gold or something." She rubbed it in and picked up a jade roller. "And this would stop you looking all puffy." The roller made little squeaks as it went up and down her neck and cheeks. "It must have been Arthur that told Giles the vaults' entrance had been relocated so he probably trusted him."

"Giles seems very focused on getting the keys and discovering how to enter, and if we think that Lord Metcalf gave them to Arthur first . . . perhaps Giles tried to get them off Arthur in the shop on Sunday night." It was a grim thought, and it made me grateful Giles was no longer in our cottage.

"He is definitely very dodgy and has a horrendous nickname—we can only speculate where he got that from." Carole took out her toothbrush.

"Can we talk honestly about Arthur for once?" I snapped. "Arthur was *dodgy*. For all we know, the stolen antiques in the journal are items *he* was selling on the black market. Anything can happen when you're dealing with criminals. We know that Giles was a thief and maybe Arthur was too."

Carole glared at me, and I knew I'd gone too far. I had broken the unspoken rule—we didn't talk about Arthur like that.

She swiped a hand towel across her mouth and flung it down. "I won't hear of it. Just because he knew Giles doesn't mean he was *like* Giles. This is why I didn't tell you it might have been Giles at the funeral." She threw her toothbrush into the nearest glass and barged past me, grabbing my flashlight. She hated hearing a bad word said about Arthur, but this time I couldn't let it go, and I followed her into her bedroom as she pumped lavender sleep spray onto her pillows. "You need this to relax." She squirted the spray in my direction.

I choked as the lavender hit the back of my throat. Carole looked pleased with herself.

"I'm fine, by the way," I coughed.

"Excellent. It's bedtime, darling."

"Listen to me. One of the explanations for the list of stolen antiques in the journal is that it is a sales log, and the antiques shop would be a good cover for that, wouldn't it? When I overheard Giles and Amy talking, he said he had stolen the Martin Brothers bird for his mother. The Martin Brothers bird Arthur and I hunted down in Cairo was never legally Lord Metcalf's." I filled Carole in on everything I had heard Giles say and his actions toward Amy. As I was talking it through, another thought came to me. "Wait. There is a question that we're not asking. It's a question I didn't ask back in Cairo as I was in such a mess."

Carole put the top back on her sleep spray and waited.

"How did Giles know to send the bird to Asim? How did Giles know Asim and his family's workshop was one of the best in the business when that information was a closely guarded secret?" My mind began to go over everything from the day Asim died.

Carole looked confused. "Go on."

"Arthur said if we retrieved the bird and talked to Asim we would bring down a big forgery ring, and it would give us a reputation as some of the best hunters in the business. But the only way a Martin Brothers bird could bring down a forgery ring is if it's proof a forgery ring exists. If Lord Metcalf ran the forgery ring . . ."

"Giles was told about the forgery workshop in Cairo by his father," replied Carole, her eyes wide with excitement. "And then Giles took the bird there without Lord Metcalf knowing."

But I shook my head. This didn't solve anything. "How does this connect to Arthur's death, and why did he send us here?"

"My darling Arthur was so clever; he must've had a very good reason." Carole pointed her flashlight at me. "And so we're clear, darling, Arthur did that job for Lord Metcalf just once to save his shop from being repossessed, but when that poor young man—"

"Asim was the love of my life!" My anger surged.

"You know I'm so dreadfully sorry that you lost him. But after your poor boyfriend died, Arthur *never* went down that road again." She nodded like that was the end of it.

It had been a long, long time since we'd talked about what happened to Asim in Cairo, but the sickness swirling in my stomach was back. An all-consuming grief as if it had happened yesterday.

For the first time I didn't hold back with my aunt. "That's not true. Arthur should've gone to the forgeries workshop *himself* to get the Martin Brothers bird back. He shouldn't have told Asim to take it from his family's very illegal forgeries workshop and bring it to us. We found him dead in that restaurant's kitchen probably because someone found out he was going to report them and then they killed him because of it!" I was trying to keep my voice calm, but my fists clenched.

"We can't discuss this if you're going to get angry." Carole flung the flashlight in my direction and I instinctively reached out to catch it. I pointed the light at her and she turned away. "Good night, darling. Shut the door, would you."

I knew the conversation was over, but I wasn't finished. Now that Arthur was dead, I wanted it all out in the open. I wanted my aunt to take my side just this once.

I scrubbed away an angry tear.

Arthur was dead.

Asim was dead.

Lord Metcalf was dead.

It was all connected, but I didn't see how.

I closed Carole's bedroom door and went back downstairs. The tension in my muscles made me grip the banister harder than was necessary.

The fire had burned down to embers. I didn't see the point of putting another log on, so I pulled the blanket over me and reached for the journal that I'd hidden under the sofa cushions. Arthur's letter fell out and I read it again.

I always wanted to tell you the truth about Cairo, but I needed you out of the antique hunting game back then, and now it seems fate has decided that I won't get the chance to set it right. You need to see the truth. I hope that in learning what really happened, you'll forgive the choice I had to make.

For your first clue—a bird in the box is more important than two in the hand.

I had thought that I knew the truth of what happened in Cairo. But if Arthur's letter was to be believed, there must've been a lot he didn't tell me. We had exchanged harsh words on the phone just after I arrived home. "It's all your fault," I had screamed as soon as I'd answered his call.

"You dated a criminal," Arthur said. "No matter how lovely he was. He understood the risk. I didn't mean . . ."

"For him to die. It's on you!"

"I didn't do it! How could you think that? It was Asim's idea, his plan . . . his way to get to you. If you weren't dating him, he wouldn't have been there. You compromised yourself and your career. If you can't see that then you shouldn't be hunting. You should never work again!"

I'd hung up. I'd taken every ounce of Arthur's criticisms, and we never spoke again.

Did he say that just to get me to quit? A lump built in my throat at the memory.

I read the letter again. I'd been so angry and hurt back then I had never looked any deeper into what had happened. Without my hunting job with Arthur and not being able to run to Little Meddington and Carole, survival was my only priority. Lying in bed crying stopped being an option when the gas was cut off. I found a job in a small café at the end of my road. Making coffee and sandwiches and never leaving the area became my new normal. The customers became my new friends. James turned from customer to lover to boyfriend to husband without much thought. I'd lost the love of my life—no one could compete with that—so I settled on someone who was there.

In trying to hide my past, I willingly played the part of being the incompetent and needy wife. But slowly, as my true self began to creep to the surface—telling Jade to climb the highest tree or stand up to the bully—our marriage began to crumble.

If only I'd focused on trying to find out who had killed Asim instead of running away from it all. If I'd had answers back then, perhaps I would have made different choices. However, the past week had taught me that not everything was lost. It had just been buried. I might not have been hunting for over twenty years, but that didn't mean I hadn't been studying. It didn't mean I couldn't remember.

I looked at the journal in my lap.

What have you really been up to, Arthur?

I scanned the pages, desperately wanting to know where all these priceless items were. My eyes locked onto the manor. Was Arthur looking for some sort of redemption in handing this over to me and possibly the location of all those antiques and antiquities?

My phone rang in my handbag. "Hello?"

"Mom, I've been trying to call you," said Jade.

Her voice took me into mother mode. "Jade, how are you, my darling? How's LA?"

"I'm bloody pissed off at Dad. He says he's about to take an offer on our house! You're going to stop him again, aren't you? Mom, that's my childhood home."

I was about to say the things I always said: "over my dead body," "he's taken so much," "he's not having the house." But I realized I hadn't cared much about James or my home for days. "I'm sure it's going to be all right."

"Are you *kidding*? Are you all right? What's going on? You're making me panic and you know that's not good for me."

"I'm absolutely fine. Perhaps the house isn't everything."

"OMG, you're *not* okay. I'm going to call Aunt Carole and have her come to London to visit you." She hesitated and I remembered I hadn't told her where I was. "I mean, I would come, but Izzie—my new girl-friend; you're going to love her—and I are going to Lollapalooza in July. We have tickets and everything—it'll be our first trip away together."

"Jade, it's only May."

"Oh, well, at least you know what month it is. That means you might not be too bad." Jade breathed out.

"Darling, it's very late and I'm on the hunt for a murderer." I chuckled to myself. I couldn't help winding her up a little.

"What! Mom. Mom. Has Dad finally pushed you over the edge?"

"I'm fine. I'll call you tomorrow afternoon. And Jade, don't worry about the house or me. It's going to be fine." For the first time in years, those words didn't sound like a lie.

I heard chattering voices in the background at the other end of the line. "Okay, good. You really shouldn't worry me like that. I'll call soon. Love you."

The phone went dead, but I couldn't put it down. Jade's absence had created a gaping hole in my life. It was like my purpose had flown away with her. But I understood I'd been missing her for years before she actu-ally left. James traveled a lot and so she was my partner in everything. She was the little hand I held to cross the road, the hug at the school gate, the sharing of an ice cream when the sun came out. She was the teenager I went to the cinema with on a Monday night when she didn't have plans. I'd been determined to bring her up independent and strong because I was adamant she would take on the world and never hide from it. I was proud of being her mother, but I'd never stopped to wonder who I'd be when she ventured out into the world on her own.

I pulled a blanket over me and opened the first page of the first jour-nal. It was time to prepare for what would be in the vault tomorrow—I began to memorize every item inside the journal.

32

"I think the saying goes, keep your friends close and your enemies closer, and Giles, you have more enemies than friends."

—Arthur Crockleford

Giles

The moment Giles opened the bedroom door in the cottage, he
knew an argument was brewing. Bella was different this weekend, less attentive, and he didn't know why. He only knew that
he wasn't going to stand for it.

Talking to Amy and then those women had made his blood boil. He
was proud of himself for keeping his cool with them all, but the bubbling
anger wouldn't stay down for long—"the venom," he called it. Being at
Copthorn Manor again was bringing it all back to him.

"You're a damn sneak," he spat at Bella. "What were you doing going
over there in the dead of night? If she finds out you know anything, you
know what will happen."

Bella cowered. "I wasn't doing anything, just looking for some food."

"After dinner?" Giles frowned. "I saw you talking to those women.
Did you find out about the journals or the vault?"

"I didn't. They seem clueless." Bella bowed her head.

"You talked a lot tonight and you couldn't even get that out of them." Giles stepped toward her.

"You asked me to chat with them and see what they knew. That was all I was doing. I promise." She was using that calming voice, the one she used when things were about to turn nasty.

"Did you get *any* useful information?" he demanded.

Bella didn't reply.

"No, you didn't. I had to go and confront them myself. Idiotic women for coming here. Idiotic Arthur for giving Franklin the keys to the vault...." All Giles needed was to keep his cool until he had the Martin Brothers bird and received his inheritance. After that, Franklin would get what's coming to him, and Giles would really start making a name for himself.

"I was wondering how long we might be staying here?" asked Bella.

"We go when I say so." Giles slumped onto the bed.

"Did Amy or the women tell you anything useful?"

"Those women don't know anything about the vault, but I'm quite sure they know about those journals. I need to go back to Arthur's shop, break in, and have a look around."

"Freya didn't say anything about a journal," Bella said. "Why would she agree to take Arthur's place? Did Franklin tell Freya your father had put her as an alternative verifier in the will?"

"Perhaps Franklin wants something to happen to them so he can profit from Arthur's shop in some way. He's a slippery one." Giles caught Bella's eye and it obviously unnerved her. She rose quietly and hurried toward the stairs.

"Do you want your whiskey?"

Giles nodded and relaxed a little. "Freya Lockwood being here is a liability," he said.

"You're going to hurt them?" she asked.

The question echoed in the space between them; it wouldn't be the first woman he'd hurt.

Bella filled the silence the way she always did. Nervy, that's what Amy called her. "Freya doesn't know anything. She's totally out of her depth and they don't belong here."

"Doesn't matter. She needs to disappear." He closed his eyes; the conversation was becoming boring. "Go and get my nightcap."

"Do you think there'll be some sort of scrum to get into the vaults tomorrow morning?" said Bella. "It might be quite a fight. You will be careful, won't you?"

She was asking too many questions. He sat up and glared at her. "Just go and get my drink."

Finally she left the room. Giles was glad his laptop still had charge and he could get back to work.

"You better be ready to leave when I say," he called down to her, wondering if he needed her anymore; perhaps it was time to move on with one of his other women.

"Of course, love," Bella called back.

33

"A wolf in sheep's clothing is still a wolf."

—Arthur Crockleford

Franklin

The dawn chorus called through the branches as Franklin woke and quickly dressed. His weekend bag was packed and waiting by the door. The job was nearly over, and then he'd be free. It was time for a new life in a new place. He was bone-tired of it all. Some cold canned coffee that could be gulped down quickly would help him with this morning's job, but he had forgotten to bring any with him. The electricity seemed to be back on, but there was no time to make some real coffee either. He looked out the kitchen window toward the manor and checked his watch; it was 5 a.m.

He pulled on his raincoat and wrapped a silk scarf around his neck. If Lord Metcalf hadn't insisted Franklin oversee the opening of the vaults, he could have just handed over the keys to Giles, but there was a possibility that Arthur had sent those women to check up on him. When dealing with black market clients, you could never tell who knew who. Why did those women turn up?

Franklin hadn't told Freya and Carole Lockwood that Lord Metcalf had also appointed Arthur as executor of his will. Nor had he told them

183

Arthur had been given direct instructions by Lord Metcalf, because by the time it might have mattered, Arthur was dead. Franklin had wanted to keep Lord Metcalf's estate at arm's length—he knew it wasn't exactly aboveboard, but it wasn't safe to ask questions. Arthur and Franklin had argued about this in his office on the day Arthur asked him to draft his will. It should've been Arthur's job to sort out the vaults, but Arthur was as stubborn as they came and demanded that Franklin keep to the letter of the Metcalf will and oversee the emptying of the vaults. He had begrudgingly agreed.

In a matter of days, he would see the back of Suffolk and its inhabitants for good. He wasn't one for country life, which had become clear about a week after moving there—too much greenness and idle gossip with the odd backstab for good measure. He preferred the city—the constant movement and alertness. The medieval villages of Dedham Vale and out toward Long Melford and Lavenham were picturesque, but the sleepiness was wearing. John Constable might have loved the area, but Franklin Smith liked neither Constable's paintings nor the places he had once frequented. Franklin was going to make a tidy sum from the estate and then he could set up somewhere else and start again, perhaps somewhere warmer.

It had been prudent of Arthur to arrange for the van to arrive early, while everyone was sleeping. Franklin knew only too well what a pain the probate process could be, especially with a criminal element involved. He didn't like to be involved in any shootings or murders, not if he could help it.

There was a screech of brakes and Franklin knew they were here. He picked up his bag and strode out the door, locking it behind him and placing the key back through the letterbox. He paused to check the other cottages for signs of movement.

All clear.

The morning air was dew damp and the first rays of sunlight reflected on the lake. Franklin could have done without the sun. Last night he had found a nice bottle of whiskey in the kitchen before heading back to the cottage and had indulged a little too much. His hangover was turning in his stomach and pounding behind his eyes.

A large moving van had stopped outside the manor. Franklin approached the driver as the cab doors opened and two large men jumped down. The older one was called Jim, but he didn't know the other one.

"We moving the lot, then, like Arthur said?" said Jim, nodding toward the house.

"Everything in Vaults One and Two." Franklin took a few steps to show them the way, and then remembered. "Do you both have flashlights? There was a power outage last night and it is back on in the cottages but I'm not sure about the manor."

"Sure, we got some head ones in the front. Give me a sec and I'll go grab one," said Jim, turning back.

The other man was shorter than Jim, and wider. "That's odd. You've thought everywhere would've been out."

"What do you mean?" Franklin looked him dead in the eye.

"We stayed at the pub in the village last night and they had electricity. Did you have trees down?"

"It's possible," said Franklin, making light of it.

He walked faster than he normally would, eager to check that everything was still in order, leading the men through the front door of the manor and down the corridor toward the drawing room. Lord Metcalf had taken pains to show Arthur where the new entrance was and how to get inside—and then Franklin had made Arthur tell him. Amy knew where it was, but not how to open it, because Metcalf had had some of the locks changed like Arthur suggested. Arthur, it seemed, liked to change the locks on everything. Franklin had the keys in his pocket. He reached the drawing room and made sure all the curtains were closed. He retrieved his flashlight from his coat pocket and clicked it on.

A section of wooden paneling came away from the wall with ease, and the white keypad lit up. He tapped in the code. The secret door opened—a door no one would ever suspect was there. It was three inches thick and reinforced with steel. There was a landing beyond the door and then an open elevator—it looked like one someone would use for a wheelchair.

"That's no good, then, with no electricity, is it?" said Jim. He spoke to his colleague. "This is going to be one of those trouble jobs, Ben. You mark me."

Ben grunted and Franklin's shoulders tightened. He just needed to be sent professionals that didn't moan and groan like a plumber looking at a kitchen sink that someone else had installed. Out of annoyance, he pressed the red button on the side to turn the elevator on, not expecting it to work.

The elevator shuddered awake. "Guess there's power back on, then?" Ben opened the gate and stepped onto the platform.

Jim, with his headlamp blazing from his forehead, looked left and right until he found a light switch. "Let's get some light in here."

The space around Franklin lit up. He closed the steel door behind them.

"We don't have all day if you're to catch the ferry," said Franklin. "And will you please keep your voices down."

The elevator descended and clanked to a stop. There was a gate on the opposite side and Franklin opened it. "Right. The ones for moving have been wrapped and packed in Vaults One and Two." There was a long-arched corridor with four metal doors along it, two doors on each side, all with a number above them.

Franklin hurried to reach the first door on his right with the number two above it. He put his brass key in the lock. The door clicked open. He smiled; this was all going very nicely. It would take an hour or so to load the crates and then he could be on his way. Job done. "Be as quiet as possible. Best we get as much of this done as we can before the family comes snooping around."

The three men stepped into the vault.

"Looks like these crates have been opened," called Jim from the far end of the room. "You need to come and see this. I'm not getting into any trouble if they think I was messing with the crates." Jim leaned forward.

Franklin's stomach turned again and this time it had nothing to do with the whiskey. Someone had been down here, and they had been rummaging through the boxes.

Heads will roll, he thought. *And I'd better make sure mine isn't one of them.*

34

"Fear is a choice. Choose courage."

—Arthur Crockleford

Freya

I awoke to the sound of my alarm. I was dressed and waiting by the downstairs window when a large moving van arrived without any headlights on. Franklin approached the van and spoke to the men who climbed out of the cab. They all went into the manor.

Is this what you wanted me to see, Arthur?

I checked my watch. It read 5:05 a.m.

Didn't everyone say that the van was arriving at 10 a.m.? I was right. Arthur hadn't gotten the times wrong on the program. He was telling me that a van was arriving at 5 a.m.

I had to find out what was going on, and if Franklin was about to open the vaults, I needed to get inside.

I ran into Carole's room expecting her to be up and dressed but she was sound asleep with a leopard-print silk eye mask covering most of her face.

"Carole, did you set your alarm? Are you awake?"

"No, darling, I decided last night that nothing could possibly happen at such an inhuman hour."

"But something *is* happening. Arthur was giving us another clue. A moving van has just turned up a lot earlier than planned. Franklin Smith met them like he knew they were coming. I think they're opening the vaults." Excitement swept through me.

Carole peeled one side of her eye mask up. "Are you sure? I don't like to be up before nine a.m., as you know. If I get woken up before then I'll look shoddy, and no one wants to be a shoddy version of themselves. Do they?"

"I know." I raised my hand to stop her giving me a talk on always looking your best. "It takes time to look fabulous. But sometimes, if we don't have time to look fabulous . . . we just need to *act* fabulous." It was something I'd said to Jade many times throughout her teenage years when she was late for school. Carole flung back the covers and pulled off her eye mask. "Well, if you're sure?"

"You watch. Here." She rummaged in her handbag and pulled out her bird-watching binoculars. "Keep an eye on them from the safety of the window and I'll have a shower. Shout if anything interesting happens." She grabbed her towel and headed for the bathroom.

I was impatiently scanning the area with the binoculars when I saw movement inside the manor. As someone passed a window, I focused in—they were dressed all in black with a hood pulled up and gloves on. I couldn't see their face. I had no intention of being left behind because my aunt needed to finish her beauty routine. And there was a small part of me that was still annoyed at Carole for taking Arthur's side again last night.

I didn't have time to wait.

"Carole, I'm going," I said through the bathroom door.

I pulled on my sneakers and coat and ran toward the manor. The kitchen back door was still wedged open.

Inside, the kitchen smelled of cold grease, and the breaking dawn stretched in through the dirty bay window. Muffled voices came from the corridor.

Even though they were quiet, the new arrivals wouldn't evade detection for long.

Adrenaline pumping, I inched open the kitchen door to the corridor. Two men were carrying a large crate out of the drawing room.

What's in those boxes?

When they exited through the main door, I ran toward the drawing room.

It was deserted.

Perhaps I had been mistaken. I was about to check the other rooms when a man's voice said, "How many more of these things?" Boots stomped on the hallway flagstones, heading my way.

Hide.

I ran and dived behind the sofa at the far end of the room, only to bump into another person hiding there.

Bella?

"What the . . ." What was she doing there?

"Shh." She shook her head at me in an exasperated way that reminded me of Jade as a teenager. "Will you *please* go back to bed," she hissed.

"What are you up to?" I whispered. I was trying to reconcile two images in my head, the Bella of last night with her hunched shoulders and the mousy voice, and the one before me now, dressed all in black, poised like a jaguar about to pounce, her head tilted to pick up the slightest sound.

Who is this Bella in black with leather gloves on?

"I saw you sneaking around last night. What were you doing?" I asked.

She opened her palm to show me a bunch of shiny new keys. Her eyes blazed at me. "Don't get in my way."

She heard something and ducked lower, waving me to do the same.

"Come on, lads, let's speed this up. I really want to get out of here," said Franklin.

I heard a *click*, and my curiosity couldn't be quelled. I peered over the top of the sofa. The men were standing in front of the paneled wall at the far end of the drawing room—the one nearest to us—as it swung open.

A secret door to the vaults.

Bella dragged me down and my elbow hit the parquet floor, a painful tingle racing up my arm. She glared at me.

"That's the vault door?" I mouthed. My heart hammered in my ears.

She tutted and, after a moment, stood up. "Stay here."

Panic flooded me. "What are you doing?" I searched the room for Franklin and the other men, but they were gone, and the secret door had reverted to a paneled wall.

"Didn't you hear the elevator? They are all the way down there now." Without waiting for an answer, she ran to the panel. Her fingertips traced the opening for the switch.

I was about to join her when a whirling of cogs and a clanking of metal came from the opening, and Bella darted back behind the sofa.

"What did Arthur see in you?" she said, glaring at me as the men reappeared.

The second they left the room, she hurtled back toward the hidden door before it could close again. It was risky, as their footsteps could still be heard in the hallway.

I admired her speed and agility, and it had been a long time since I'd appreciated someone's skill quite as much. The last person had been Arthur. But Bella wasn't the only one who could be fast when she wanted to be.

As she started to close the secret door behind her, I shot across the room and stuck my foot out to catch it.

It was time to uncover what Arthur had really wanted me to find in the vaults.

35

"Always watch your back."

—Arthur Crockleford

Behind the secret door was a small hallway, and beyond that, Bella stood on a metal platform. I joined her and she closed a flimsy-looking bar behind us. She didn't look surprised that I'd followed her.

"You need to be faster than that," she said, pressing a red button. The platform shuddered to life.

The elevator shaft was made of bare brick walls, small wall lights illuminating the way, and the farther we descended the colder it became. I studied Bella. She was so different from the timid woman who'd been at dinner last night, almost folding in on herself next to Giles's stark strength. Now she stood tall and strong on the wavering platform—emitting a smooth, controlled confidence. It was a bit like looking at a younger version of myself. I longed to be that person again, and maybe it wasn't too late after all.

"I mean it—don't get in my way. This has been a *year* in the planning." She sighed. "Arthur told me to help you, but after meeting you I decided not to bother."

"Thanks. How kind." I gritted my teeth.

"No offense or anything," said Bella. "You just look a bit old for this game."

"I'm also experienced," I snapped back.

The elevator jolted and my grip on the rail tightened. I didn't feel as old as I looked, and I didn't care how Bella saw me—I was back in the game; Arthur had made sure of that.

"A little sensitive, I see," Bella muttered.

"The real you is such a charmer," I replied.

The elevator stopped and I stepped onto a brick floor before Bella could insult me again. I was going to get what I came for. The "item of immense value" Arthur mentioned in his letter.

We were in a wine cellar–like basement. The air around us smelled of musty earth mixed with new wood, which probably came from the plywood crates I'd seen the men move out of the manor.

"Who are you really?" I asked Bella. I looked back up the elevator shaft at the closed door and wondered how long we had before Franklin and the men came back. I couldn't decide if I needed to hide from Franklin or call to him for help.

"Who I am is none of your business. Didn't Arthur tell you anything?" She pressed the button to send the elevator back up to the top. "If you're caught, you could get us both killed." Bella listened for the men as the elevator stopped at the drawing room level. "I bet Frank is happy the electricity is back on," she said. "I just needed it to go out for a while to keep everyone distracted."

"You killed the electricity. How? Why?" Presumably she'd done something around that time to trip a fuse somewhere.

"I overheard my charming boyfriend on the phone and knew my time was running out. I needed to look around without everyone in the manor drinking all night. I also wondered if the electricity was out, the paneled door might open. It didn't, so I'm on to plan B. It's not hard to overload this old system. I just plugged in a few things on a timer in an empty room. They all went on and the lights went off." I realized I hadn't seen Bella when we were all walking to the dining room last night. She didn't elaborate further and walked away. "Can you hurry up?" She beckoned me over.

I didn't move. It was clear I couldn't trust anyone—if Bella could hide who she truly was, they all could.

"If I was going to kill you, I wouldn't have sent you the note and I would have bumped you off when I cut the electricity last night, and no one would've known a thing about it." Bella walked past Vaults One and Two, which were opposite each other, and stopped a little farther down outside Vault Four. She put a key in a lock and turned it. "As you're here now, you can be useful."

"You wrote 'LEAVE NOW'?" I asked, not moving.

"It was crude, I know, but I was trying to keep my promise to Arthur and help you out."

"And how did you do that?"

"By trying to get you out of a situation you didn't understand, of course." Bella seemed satisfied with her logic and I didn't press her further. I was more interested in finding out where the "item of immense value" was.

I passed an open vault to my right with a "1" over the door and I looked inside, my curiosity getting the better of me. There were three crates left, and on the tops I could just make out photographs of what must have been the contents. The small crate closest to the door was labeled with four photographs showing cuneiform tablets of different shapes and sizes. I knew those items; they were in the back of Arthur's journal. I was pulled toward them. They were the kind of objects that Arthur and I both cherished—antiquities of a long-forgotten time, precious artifacts.

I reached into the box and pulled out what seemed to be a large rock the size of my hand wrapped in protective cloth. It was a terracotta-colored clay tablet engraved with triangular, wedge-like symbols. Cuneiform script was first developed by Sumerian scribes in what is now modern-day Iraq—it's the earliest known writing system. The tablets were mainly used for bookkeeping or something similar, although there have been cuneiform tablets depicting astronomical calculations. I knew they shouldn't be hidden away in a vault—they should be in a museum in Iraq or with experts in that field. Arthur would've thought the same. But something in the way the tablet felt in my hand didn't seem right. I needed a closer look.

"What are you doing?" Bella whispered from somewhere down the hall.

I compared the tablet to the photograph on top of the box until I found its likeness. But it wasn't the same one; the color and text were ever so slightly off.

"They're fake," I whispered to myself. "And Arthur knew."

In Arthur's journal entries, red dots had marked each of the pictures of furniture upstairs, as well as these tablets. A red dot must mean the item had been replaced or wasn't authentic. Perhaps a tourist wouldn't be able to tell, but an expert would. The thrill of uncovering the truth tingled through me. I was reaching in to retrieve another tablet when Bella pulled me away.

"Stop. I need to see—" As I was hauled from the room, I noticed a small pile of Polaroid photographs discarded in the corner.

Before I could reach for them Bella said, "We don't have time for that." She dragged me toward the last steel door at the end of the corridor, marked with a four. This was Vault 4 and it was open. "After you."

I hesitated in the doorway, looking back toward the vault I'd just been pulled out of. The original tablets must be pretty special, I thought, for someone to go to the trouble of forging them.

Bella nudged me. "They'll be back soon, and we need to be hidden in here when they do."

I followed her into the domed, brick-walled room filled with boxes, eager to know if there were more fake tablets inside or real items from the missing Copthorn Manor Collection.

I looked at the keys in Bella's hand. "You stole his keys when the lights went out?"

Bella closed the door behind us, and the clanking of metal sounded as the elevator lowered Franklin and his men down into the cellar. "No,

I'm far more organized than that. I broke into his office last week, made copies, and then returned his set, him none the wiser."

Vault 4 had dry, stale air and the heavy steel door was old but sturdy.

"How can you be so sure Franklin won't come into this vault?" I asked.

"He's emptying Vaults One and Two, the ones several criminal entities kept their stolen art and antiques in. He has no need to walk farther down the corridor to this vault."

From what I've seen, someone has replaced the original ones that Arthur took photos of.

I wasn't going to tell Bella because I'd no idea who she really was.

Bella continued, "Arthur knew that after Lord M's death those criminal entities, or 'individuals,' as Franklin calls them, wouldn't trust the change of management. No one likes change, do they?" I could see by the glint in her eye that Bella admired Arthur. "This room here was the private room of Lord Metcalf before his illness. Of course, he wasn't actually a lord. He was an East London real estate agent at one point."

"It was all a facade?"

"It was." I barely caught the next words, spoken under her breath. "All of life is." Something passed over her face. Was it sadness or regret?

"And what happened when he became ill?" I asked.

"Amy heard he was on the way out and decided to come home to look after her poor ailing father. Although, she was incredibly bad at it, as he seemed to deteriorate quickly and became bed-bound." Bella sounded insincere.

I understood what she was getting at. "And let me guess. All the silver picture frames went missing first. Then the furniture, then the paintings, and on and on."

"Good. You're smarter than you look," said Bella.

"And the only person around who could tell a fake from a forgery . . ." It was all beginning to make sense now.

Bella finished my sentence. "Was Arthur. I imagine Arthur wasn't happy with what he saw going on here and decided to write it all down. I believe that on his last visit he told old Lord Metcalf about his logbook. You don't happen to know where that record is, do you? It would hold a lot of powerful information." Her eyes sparkled at me.

Does she know we have them?

"I don't," I lied.

Bella didn't look convinced.

We heard the clanking of metal as the elevator hit the ground, and Bella placed her finger to her lips. She reached for the light switch by the door, plunging us into darkness.

"Now you just have to find the *original* artifacts for me," she whispered, and pulled out a small, slim flashlight from her pocket, placing it between her teeth.

One by one, she quietly opened boxes, her frown growing deeper with the sight of the contents. Plucking the flashlight from her mouth, she said, "These are just documents, photos, and junk. Don't know why they'd be with the artifacts."

Men's voices got louder. I stepped away from the door and pressed myself against the wall.

"Do you want to tell me what you're searching for?" I asked, but Bella was too busy digging through boxes. "Why did Arthur ask you to help me?"

She moved to the other side of the room and tried to open another box. It wouldn't budge. I hurried over to her, but she didn't want help and pulled away. The box clattered on the floor.

"Who's there?" one of the men called from the corridor outside the room. "I'm armed if you're wanting a fight."

Bella switched her flashlight off.

I froze. *What will happen if we're found?*

He tried the handle, but the door was locked. I hadn't seen Bella lock it again, and it made me understand just how well trained she was. Just as I'd once been.

A large crash came from the corridor. "You bloody idiot," screeched Franklin.

The man walked away.

I breathed deeply, trying to stop my hands from shaking.

"You're a private investigator hunting down stolen antiques and art," I whispered. "Like Arthur?"

She laughed without making a sound and adjusted her black leather gloves. "Sometimes my path crossed with Arthur's, and sometimes we held the same objective. When we did . . . it's like that saying, my enemy's enemy is my friend." She noticed something behind me and directed her flashlight at a box. "This is it."

Carefully, quietly, she heaved a moving box down from the second shelf onto the brick floor and opened the lid.

The box was filled with shredded paper, and Bella rummaged around in it like a grab bag at the village fair until her fingers closed around a velvet pouch at the bottom. As she opened it, I could see her eyes light up even through the darkness.

"How much do you know about these artifacts?" she asked.

If someone had asked me that question a few days ago I would've searched my memory for what Arthur had once taught me. But having spent last night memorizing the first journal, I knew I was looking at cuneiform tablets and other artifacts from Iran and Iraq. Archaeology was Arthur's passion—and it had once been mine.

"I know quite a bit, but first, how about you tell me a few things?"

"Arthur seemed to think you knew everything. Is this one real or not?" Bella held out a roundish terra-cotta stone that was the size of a small book with lines and dashes on it.

That's when I knew what was going on in the other vault. "In the vault Franklin is emptying, there was a box with photographs of tablets exactly like these ones." I held open my palm.

"Yes," said Bella.

"Those are forgeries and the real ones are stored here," I guessed.

"I know, it's *so* clever. You've got to give it to the Metcalfs." Bella pulled out a few more tablets.

Arthur's words came back to me. *"The workshop never had direct contact with the big forgery boss they manufacture for. It was only when someone turned up at Asim's father's house asking about a bird. The clever boy took a photograph of the man and ran back to the workshop to take the Martin Brothers for us."*

I looked down at the cuneiform tablet in my hand. It was so similar to the ones Asim used to replicate. Unless you were an expert or had something to compare it to, I could see how easy it would be to sell a fake. "These pieces are from Mesopotamia—modern-day Iraq—the site of the world's earliest civilizations." I turned the clay tablet over. "These could be dated between 2000 BC and 500 BC. Arthur loved these items and it stemmed all the way back to his days as an archaeologist." In the Middle East in the early 2000s, there was a lot of looting of Iran and Iraq with little protection of cultural heritage. That was almost impossible today. "How did these get to the UK? What will you do with these?" My grip tightened on the tablet in my palm. I was quite sure it was real and priceless.

Bella smiled. "This is one of those times when Arthur and I were on the same side. We both believe in cultural repatriation. Arthur told me these are from Irisagrig, a lost ancient city. The city's existence became known only when some tablets mentioning it were seized at the Jordanian border in 2003, while thousands more surfaced in international antiquities markets . . . and now here."

"In 2003," I echoed. The year after Arthur and I fell out. "Why didn't he just repatriate these himself?"

"He was in Lord M's pocket and had to do his bidding." Bella started to rummage in the box again.

"How?"

Bella didn't answer; she was too engrossed in her search.

After a moment she said, "Are these the real ones that Arthur wrote to me about? Can you verify them?"

"They look a lot realer than the ones in Vault One," I said. It was thrilling to use all the knowledge I'd learned over the years once again.

Bella pulled out a thin folding backpack. "That's good enough for me. You probably have an eye for these things, like Arthur did." She started putting the various-sized velvet pouches filled with artifacts inside along with some paper to cushion them.

"Stop, you can't do that! They're delicate and so, so rare. We need to tell the police or someone." My pulse picked up.

"Why would I do that? I probably wouldn't get a reward if I did. And don't worry, I've been doing this a long time. Breaking something would cost me money." Bella felt around the base of the box until she was satisfied she had everything in her huge, bulging backpack. "Look, Giles thinks I'm stupid." She beamed at me. "It's my very best trick. But I remember everything. Giles is involved in everything here and I don't need to be associated with it when this is all discovered."

I must have looked confused, as she continued, "This 'bank' holds people's collateral—gold bars, gems, expensive art and antiques. Anything that criminals can trade for instead of money. Money is traceable and these things . . . not so much. Some are kept here. When a deal is done, sometimes they move the item, and sometimes it's kept in the 'bank,' moved between rooms or to another bank in Scotland or somewhere else. That's what these 'pick up or withdraw' antique weekend events are for. They don't like opening the vaults often, so they organize withdrawals for all their 'clients' at once. Make a party of it, get Arthur to verify it's all in order—no fakes."

I watched as she looked in a few other containers and pulled out a number of velvety jewelry boxes, opening one to reveal a diamond necklace, then shoved them into her pocket.

"What are you doing?" I demanded.

She smiled sweetly. "When in Rome . . ."

"Then you're just another common thief." I tried to grab the necklace, but she'd already hidden it away.

She glared at me. "These were stolen a long time before I got here and their owners have probably already had the insurance payout." She looked at the tablet in my hand.

I closed my fingers around it, and within seconds I was staring down the barrel of a small, black gun.

"Give it here, if you please," she said.

My heart thundered but I clung onto the tablet.

"I could've killed you at any moment. But where would the fun be in that? If you really are going to take over Arthur's business as Franklin says—"

She was cut off by boots on the brick floor. "It's time to leave." She was now next to the door, pulling on a black balaclava. "You should look at those documents. One of them is a picture of you. I imagine that's what Arthur wanted you to retrieve." She opened the door and looked out. "Sorry about this, but I can't have you slowing me down."

Bella left the room, locking the door behind her.

I was trapped and alone.

36

Bella

Despite her best efforts, Bella liked Freya Lockwood. She could see that below the surface there was intelligence and courage, the two things that Bella greatly admired—along with self-made wealth. She'd liked her enough, in the end, to do as Arthur had asked. Freya was surprisingly alert for someone pushing fifty. Bella had been very careful no one saw her—she was an expert at that—but Freya had followed her all the way to the vault. When Freya had arrived behind the sofa, Bella had discovered how nice it was to be challenged on one's own assumptions for once—life could be very dull when you know almost everything.

It hadn't been hard to get out of the vault cellar. Frank and those men didn't care enough to check who was watching or even following them. They just wanted out of the manor and Bella knew that feeling well. It was time to go somewhere hot, and the bag full of goodies she was now carrying would do her nicely for a few months. When she returned the antiquities to Iraq it would swing the karma balance back in her favor. Every so often that was important; it's best when you don't *always* wallow in the black markets. Arthur had taught her that.

She crossed the main hall and peeked between the window curtains as the men loaded the last of the plywood crates, and she clearly heard the word "tea." It didn't matter if a moving man was taking a piano to a new owner or removing stolen art and antiques to another secret location—they always wanted tea and cookies as a reward.

"You can take your tea to go," said Franklin as he walked past the window where Bella was hiding.

"We don't drink and drive, mate," one of the men barked.

Bella watched and waited. After fifteen minutes the men climbed back into the van and drove away. Amy ran out the front door shouting at the van speeding away, then stormed over to Franklin. Next, Carole hurried out from her cottage and across the front of the manor. She was probably looking for Freya. Her stomach twisted a little at the thought of Freya locked in the vault, but she wasn't clear why. She told herself it was all part of the world she lived in and she had to look out for herself.

Time was running out—someone might easily spot her standing there. While they were all distracted, she rushed back through the kitchen, out of the broken door, and to Giles's Audi, where she'd stored her suitcase. It was a massive relief to be nearing the end of her time with Giles. He was broken beyond repair and needed putting down.

Almost a year ago Arthur had told her about some rare cuneiform tablets in one of the "banks." It hadn't taken her long to devise a plan to get them. She'd expected to befriend Amy and get an invite to one of their parties, but then she'd met Giles one drunken night and . . . well . . . she always did have terrible taste in men. Within a week she had seen what a challenge it would be to stay his girlfriend, but she wasn't going to go back. She spent as little time as possible with him, actively encouraging his affairs, while still learning as much as she could about his family and Copthorn Manor.

It took every bit of her willpower not to poison his drink about twenty times a day. It was sort of fun playing meek and demure though, knowing a gun was within reach if he ever thought of turning on her the way he had with his previous girlfriend. Bella had gotten that girl out of the house and far away as soon as she knew she was going to need Giles to get the stolen artifacts.

The trunk clicked open, and she glanced over at Giles's cottage. No sign he was awake. She'd slipped him some sleeping pills like she always did, but it sometimes took an elephant amount to knock him out.

A black car with tinted windows came speeding down the drive, swerving around potholes on its way to her. It stopped in the shadow of the wooded tunnel and the trunk of the car opened automatically. She didn't wait for her feelings about Freya to get in the way of her objective. She ran over and carefully placed the bag of cuneiform tablets inside the trunk and tapped twice to let the driver know he could go. It was a job well done; Arthur would have been proud of her.

37

"The answers are inside us if we trust what we have learned."
—Arthur Crockleford

Freya

I tried the vault door handle over and over, but the door wouldn't budge.

Bella had locked me inside.

"Bella?" I beat my fists on the door. "Hello?" I didn't care who heard me; I needed to get out of here. I turned the light back on. My hands were bright red and stinging but I was too mad to care. "Franklin?"

Was this all a trick to get me out of the way? Bella had sent the "LEAVE NOW" note and when we didn't leave perhaps this was her next option.

I checked the curved walls and reached for the ceiling with my fingertips. . . .

Is this to be my tomb?

Panic tightened my throat and hammered through my veins.

How long would the air last in here? Was there any ventilation?

Will I suffocate to death?

I couldn't see a vent. The entire room was like a castle dungeon. I reached into my pocket and pulled out my phone only to realize it wasn't my phone. The phone I was holding was Amy's. I tried to make an emergency call.

No signal.

I banged on the door again, my voice strained. "Bella, let me out of here!" I waited and listened.

Nothing.

I sat on the nearest box and tried to do those deep-breathing exercises they teach you in yoga.

Breathe in, count to four, and breathe out.

It didn't work, and it might use up air faster. I gripped my shaking hands together and pressed my thumb into my scar.

Jade!

I pounded on the cold metal door until my knuckles were raw.

Jade!

Despair crept over me. I would never see my daughter or Carole again. I had failed. Just when I thought I was close to uncovering the "item of immense value" Arthur had sent me to find—just when I was getting closer to finding Arthur's killer—I'd been stopped dead in my tracks.

Carole knows I wanted to find the vaults. She'll miss me and go for help, won't she? Then I remembered both Giles and Amy were waiting to get into the vaults at 10 a.m. But there had been some sort of decoy on Franklin's part so that he could get into the vaults without them being present.

I searched the walls for another way out.

Bella, why?

I crumpled to the floor and placed my head in my hands. How was I going to get out of this? Everyone here knew Arthur, maybe wanted him dead. But I didn't know all their motivations yet and there was no way to prove if any of them had been at the antiques shop the night he died.

Arthur had sent me on a pointless mission, and one that would end in my own death.

A question niggled at the edges of my consciousness—if I believed

Arthur had told Bella to help me get into the vault, there had to be a reason. The whole basement was full of items that could have been retrieved. Why this vault? Antiquities were Arthur's passion, but I didn't believe he ever dealt in those stolen items. He had always been determined to return cultural items to their rightful place. That was the main reason he took every Middle Eastern job he was offered. If he wanted *me* to find the cuneiform tablets, then why tell Bella where they were?

There had to be something else in the vault he wanted me to see, and he knew Bella was already in place to help me get here.

What did Bella say about the boxes? A photo of me?

I lifted the lid of the first large filing box Bella had looked in. It was filled with old folders with a name on each one. None had my name on them. I looked inside the folders and found only paperwork, old bank statements and company information.

Confusion and frustration overwhelmed me, and tears threatened. I looked around at the boxes. Was Arthur killed because he knew these stolen antiques were hidden here? In photographing and describing the items in the manor and in the vaults, he'd made it so the antiques could be traced. I was quite sure, having once been a hunter myself, there would be a lot of people keen to get their hands on a log of stolen and misappropriated art, antiques, and antiquities. No one from the black market would want their items traced. It would not be inconceivable for one of Franklin's "individuals" to kill for it. I knew of a few instances when those sorts of people had killed for less.

I couldn't just sit around waiting for the air to run out. I needed a distraction.

What did Bella see in these?

I opened the next box and the next—they were all the same.

The last box made me stop—on the front was scribbled: "Workshop of A. A. M. Egypt."

A. A. M. was the Egyptian forgeries workshop owned by Asim's family and where he had worked. Inside the box were two black drawstring bags. The first one was heavy, and when I moved it there was a sound like plates bashing together. I opened it to find a large ziplock bag. I caught sight of jagged feathers.

It couldn't be, could it? Not here, not after all this time.

I unzipped the bag and reached inside, my hand shaking as if a deadly viper were coiled up in the corner of the bag. But I had to make sure I was wrong.

My fingers closed around a cold shard of stoneware.

It was half a talon.

A very distinctive talon.

One from *the* Martin Brothers bird.

The very tip was covered in a reddish rust colored substance—it was Asim's blood. I knew it was.

Bile rose up my throat. The room seemed to move like a ship at sea until I realized it was me swaying, and I grabbed the shelf to steady myself.

My breathing was fast and uncontrollable. I threw the broken talon back in the ziplock bag and pulled the drawstring tightly shut.

Giles wanted the broken Martin Brothers bird from Cairo.

I hesitated to open the next bag, but it couldn't be worse than seeing the broken bird. The other bag was far lighter—perhaps empty.

Inside was fabric of some sort. Even before I took out the whole ziplock bag I knew what I was about to uncover, and my stomach churned again.

It was a scarf. Not just any scarf. It was my scarf and it was in the same box as the broken Martin Brothers bird. It looked exactly like the one I'd bought at the Cairo airport to cover my head when necessary. I had thought I'd lost it when I ran from the restaurant that day.

Cairo and Copthorn Manor were tied together by Asim's death. Arthur knew it and that's why he sent me here.

I turned the bag over and saw that the same dark brown stain was on the scarf. Had my scarf fallen in Asim's blood as I'd leaned down to check whether he was breathing? I couldn't remember.

I shoved the scarf back into the bag and the memory of that day along with it.

I ran my hand along the sides of the box, double-checking if there was anything else inside the box and ran my hand along the sides. My nail caught the corner of something. I felt around and found there were some cards tucked into the side of the box.

I picked them up and turned them toward the light.

I was holding three black-and-white photographs that curled at the corners with age. The first one was of a young man with a beard and a cap pulled low, walking down a back alley, his hands covered in dark liquid.

I turned to the next photograph.

It's me.

I could barely recognize myself. The photo was taken in Cairo as I entered the café to meet Asim. Arthur was in front of me, though the photograph showed only his back. The third photograph was me fleeing the café, the horror in my eyes clearly visible. Who had taken these photographs?

It was clear there had been someone else in Cairo, watching the café; did they see who killed Asim? Did they kill Asim?

Arthur's letter slowly began to make perfect sense. I retrieved it from my pocket and read it again.

Freya, I know how hard things have been for you. I'm deeply sorry and I have found a way for you to get back to the career that you were made for. But for this to happen you must first finish what I started. It has taken me over twenty years to find an item of immense value. I have been told its location, but it seems I will not be able to retrieve it. Get it back, Freya, and you will have your life and your career back. I'm sorry I cannot be clearer; I have been betrayed and can't risk this letter being discovered. Tell no one. There is no one left to trust. Hunt the clues and you'll find a reservation. I implore *you to attend, but be careful. My betrayer will be following your every move.*

I always wanted to tell you the truth about Cairo, but I needed you out of the antique hunting game back then, and now it seems fate has decided that I won't get the chance to set it right. You need to see the truth. I hope that in learning what really happened, you'll forgive the choice I had to make.

For your first clue—a bird in the box is more important than two in the hand.

All my love,
Arthur

Arthur had not only been hunting stolen antiques; he had been hunting the broken Martin Brothers bird and my bloodstained scarf. But what would these things mean to Lord Metcalf?

Understanding twisted like a knife inside me. *Blackmail.*

It all fit together now. Shame crashed into me at the same time as realization. Arthur had made it almost impossible for me to continue antique hunting. He had told me that he was wrong: I didn't "have what it took," no one would hire me after Cairo. He crushed my dreams because Metcalf had all the evidence he needed to frame *me* for Asim's murder. Arthur sent me away so that I wouldn't be involved in the blackmail and was therefore forced to work for Metcalf. He had taken on all responsibility for what happened in Cairo. He sent me away as an act of love, not hate. I had been wrong about everything, and Arthur had let me believe it.

My eyes stung.

I scrubbed the guilt away.

Stay focused.

I considered all I'd learned while I was down there. I stopped at the empty box Bella had found the original cuneiform tablets in and I knew what had happened.

"I'm so sorry, Arthur," I whispered. "I was so very, very wrong. How can I ask for your forgiveness when you're no longer with us?"

I needed to tell Carole what I'd discovered, apologize for our argument last night and for misunderstanding Arthur. I needed her to comfort me and tell me I'd made the only choices available to me—but that wasn't the truth. I sank to the floor and placed my forehead on my knees, closing my eyes to shut away the past, scrunching my palm tightly around the scar. Ever so slowly, to my horror, pictures of a different life blazed through my mind. One where I had truly trusted Arthur had nothing to do with Asim's death and I'd fought to find out who'd killed him. A life where I'd been determined to keep the career I adored and honored the memory of the man I'd loved by continuing to repatriate items of cultural importance. A life that I wasn't scared to live for fear that someone I loved would leave me.

I couldn't get back the last twenty years, and although running into James's arms might have been a mistake, I had my beautiful, fearless daughter as a result. Now that Jade was grown and relied on me less and less, it was time to live for me.

I breathed in again, this time gathering all the energy I could—I wasn't going to die in a vault. My daughter needed a mother, my aunt needed me, and I needed my life back. I had found so many answers inside the vault, but they were useless until I could find a way out.

I cupped my face to the window in the vault door. "Hello?" I called one last time, banging my fists on the vault. "Help me."

It became clear that no one was coming. Franklin had probably left with the moving van and he was the only one with the code and the key to get into the vault. I was alone. And my darling aunt could be up above me with a murderer.

38

Carole

Carole stood at the cottage door, worrying for Freya. She watched Franklin closing up the van and shooing the men into the cab. Just as the engine started, Amy came hurtling out of the manor's front door screaming at Franklin, "Stop the van! Stop the van!"

The van's tires spun on the drive and it sped away toward the tunnel of trees.

When the van didn't stop, Amy turned on Franklin.

Franklin shuddered as Amy stormed over, but his eyes gleefully watched the van getting away. Carole wondered if she should go and help him, but she was deeply concerned for her niece's safety.

Where's Freya?

A sickening dread twisted in her. She wasn't going to lose Freya! Carole grabbed her coat and strode toward the manor.

Amy and Franklin were arguing under their breath.

"Did Freya verify the antiques?" Amy spat at Franklin. Her stance was fierce, hands on hips, a hint of worry etched on her forehead.

212

"I'm so sorry to interrupt your tiff, but have you seen my niece?" Carole asked them.

Amy glared at her. The act of being the charming hostess had faded away in the bright morning light.

"No, not since last night," replied Franklin, backing away toward his car. "She wasn't in the manor."

That gave Carole an idea. If Freya wasn't in the manor, it was possible she had gone to look for the folly. She seemed to be making a habit of leaving Carole out of her adventures at the moment, but, she thought worriedly, it might also have something to do with their argument last night.

"Where's Phil?" she asked Amy.

Amy threw her hand toward some trees to the left of the manor, on the opposite side from the cottages. "My father gave him the gardener's cottage, but he's never in when I go over there. I reckon my father employed him as some sort of bodyguard, as he doesn't seem to do much gardening." She glared at Franklin. "And I don't see why I can't fire him, whatever my dead father's wishes were."

"I'm just following instructions." Franklin edged farther away. "I think I'll go and pack." But he was heading in the direction of his car.

"No, you won't." Amy grabbed his arm. "We have estate issues to discuss." She almost dragged Franklin toward the front door of the manor.

Carole could have tried to save Franklin, but she'd never really liked solicitors and they seemed to be able to slink their way out of any situation.

If he needs saving, I'll save him later.

At the moment, she had a more pressing problem. *Freya, what have you gotten yourself into? Couldn't wait for me to slap on some lippy. Did you have to go running off?*

She hurried in the direction Amy had pointed and it took her another couple of minutes to find a path that led into some trees. She expected to find a chocolate box cottage, but the gardener's house was more like a ramshackle bungalow that hardly looked habitable. Carole strode up to the once bright red front door, now faded and peeling, and knocked hard.

"Phil, are you in there?" she called through the letterbox. "I have an emergency."

There was no answer.

"Hello?"

"All right, I'm coming," replied a sleepy voice from inside.

Carole got on her knees and placed her eye to the letterbox. "Well, I can't see you coming, darling!"

Within moments Phil hurried toward the front door, wrapping a towel around his waist—she admired his gym-fit body. It didn't occur to her that, as it was 6:30 a.m., he might've been asleep.

"Can't you put some clothes on and look presentable? You'll make a lady blush."

Carole was still on her knees when the door opened. To anyone else, this might've been a precarious position to be found in. But Carole was not most people. She lifted her hand up as a queen would to a minion. "I'm not as sprightly as I once was. Help me up, darling. Please."

Phil sighed and pulled her up. "What are you doing here?"

"Freya's gone missing around here somewhere." She threw her head at the manor. "And I need someone who knows the area well—knows where the folly is."

"What?" Phil didn't wait for an answer and ran back down the corridor, throwing on jeans and a T-shirt. He picked up his phone and sent a text. "Let's go look for her before people wake up." He tugged on some welly boots. "Why are you both still here?"

Carole ignored the question, which was her usual response to hearing anything she didn't want to. It had served her well in life. She gave him one of her fanciful looks. "You're a darling for helping me." Without waiting for him, she hurried back down the path to save her niece. Even though she had no idea where her niece was or how she might save her.

Phil jogged up next to her. "After this we need to have a chat. Now, please, go back to my cottage and wait there. And I will find your niece."

"I never wait for a man, darling, it's not in my nature," Carole replied, picking up her pace to prove the point. "I believe that Freya is searching for either the vaults or the folly. Are you going to tell me where the folly is? You are the gardener after all."

Phil shook his head. "No, you need to keep out of this."

"Right." Carole was getting more anxious. "If you won't tell me where the folly is then perhaps you can show me where the vaults are. I have a feeling you know a lot about this manor."

When Phil stopped at the end of the path, looking as if he was going to turn around, Carole knew she was going to have to press her point. "I'm going to level with you. My darling Arthur is gone and my niece is now all I have left in the world. I'm begging you to help me. Arthur told Franklin that Freya would be a verifier of the antiques here. He was trying to get her back into a career she once loved and now she is in mortal danger. I won't stop. I will do this with or without your help."

Carole knew that she had taken a risk by opening up to Phil, but something in her bones told her he was not a murderer. Carole assumed cold, hard killers did not have lovely, smoky eyes. Phil was, however, hiding something, and he definitely knew where the folly was—she would get that out of him later.

There was no more time for talking. Carole marched toward the manor, hoping Phil would follow, and if he did it would mean he knew exactly where the vaults were. If he didn't, she would find Freya one way or another, even if that meant taking on every last guest at Copthorn Manor herself—including Arthur's murderer.

39

"Nostalgia is the bittersweet acceptance of all we were and what we'll never be again."

—Arthur Crockleford

Freya

I sat on the floor, staring at the two black drawstring bags and three black-and-white photographs. The scarf would have incriminated me in Asim's death, and Arthur had saved me from that.

Sickening guilt swirled in my stomach. I knew that if I didn't find a way to push that aside I was never going to uncover what happened to Arthur. I distracted myself by running through what I'd uncovered. Arthur had spent twenty years trying to find these items, knowing that they could be used for blackmail. The search had tied him to the criminal world—all because I'd been stupid enough to drop a scarf. I believed Lord Metcalf, on his deathbed, must have told Arthur exactly where the items were and then gave Arthur the keys.

But why, after so long, would he have just handed the keys over?

Last night Amy had asked the table if anyone knew where the journals were. She'd said her father believed they were to be returned to him. It was clear to me now that Arthur had made a deal with Lord Metcalf on his deathbed. The items of blackmail for the journals—journals that

216

would have gotten Lord Metcalf into a lot of trouble if placed in police hands.

But Arthur didn't give the journals to Lord Metcalf—he left them for me to find.

Arthur was being blackmailed, so he couldn't tell anyone about the stolen antiques and antiquities he was seeing. Therefore, he'd started writing it all down and hunting the "item of immense value"—my scarf—that bound him to the underbelly of the antiques world. He was waiting for the day he could free both of us from the blackmailer's hold and set everything right.

I looked again at the photograph of the bearded figure with the cap leaving the café. This had to be the person who murdered Asim. I took it over to the light on the wall. The man's face was mainly covered, so I studied the other details in the image.

What else can I see?

I took in a sharp breath. His right hand was clenched and wrapped in what could have been a napkin from the cafe. It was darkened by blood. Asim's blood? Or had the man hurt himself? I tilted the photograph closer to the light. At the edge of the bandage was a small glint of gold. I strained my eyes. It was a signet ring. I searched the partially hidden face of the man again. . . . If I aged those eyes by twenty years . . . if the beard was removed. . . . I covered the beard with my finger.

Giles Metcalf.

I looked over at the vault door.

Giles killed Asim and he's now somewhere upstairs with my aunt.

I wiped away the tears that were threatening to spill down my face.

I've been so blind.

I listened for voices or footsteps. No one was there. I knew that for the moment, I had to bury the past just as I had learned to do over the decades. There would be time to sit and consider how wrong I'd been about Arthur, but that time was not now.

I had to get out of there and make sure Giles paid for killing Asim. Had he also killed Arthur? It seemed likely. I needed to make sure my aunt was safe.

I put the photograph of myself in my coat pocket and my fingers brushed something cold and metal, then closed around the two bobby pins I had tucked into my pocket the night before.

Could I remember how to use them again?

I slung the two drawstring bags over my shoulder. The pieces of broken Martin Brothers bird clinked together—everything had started with that bird. I unbent the bobby pins, straightening one and bending the other in a right angle. I inserted them into the lock, thanking all the gods that the door was old and the Vault 4 lock had not been changed. Presumably, Lord Metcalf had decided constructing the new entrance was sufficient, that the first line of defense was the strongest.

I tried to visualize the barrel and the pins as I manipulated the bobby pins.

It didn't work.

"Ahh." I slammed my fist against the door. "Arthur shouldn't have placed so much faith in me." I rested my forehead onto the cold metal for a moment, then called again. "Is anyone there?" I called.

Silence.

I went back to the lock, this time closing my eyes. I tried again, allowing myself to remember exactly how Arthur had taught me.

In discovering the truth about Arthur and the blackmail plot I had allowed my anger and pain to soften, slightly. Now, memories of my past life and all that Arthur had shown me came streaming into the space that had created. It had started with a table full of locks. "There are two ways to open a locked door. Break it down or pick the lock," he had said. "Let's start with the latter."

I'd thought it would be a fast lesson. It wasn't. Day after day passed with my hands growing tired from working the locks with bobby pins. My eyes stung from studying the written instructions Arthur had given me. I memorized the different types of locks, the different tools needed to unlock them. I spent every quiet moment in the shop practicing, and eventually it paid off. By the time we needed to pick the lock of a

St. Lucian vacation home high in the rainforest, I was as fast as any professional.

Letting those memories in again seemed to refresh all of that long-suppressed knowledge and instinct. I allowed who I had been then to merge with the person I now was.

The pin found the barrel.

Click!

40

"We only ever see what we want to see."

—Arthur Crockleford

Giles

Giles searched the drawing room's paneled wall—exactly where Franklin had said it opened. If he couldn't find the opening to the vaults, he would use an ax.

That gardener will probably have one.

Giles didn't know *exactly* what Phil did, but he wasn't who he said he was, that was for sure.

His phone buzzed.

No Caller ID.

"Hello?"

"You're messing with things you don't understand."

Giles gave an indulgent smile. "I understand more than you ever will." He really needed an ax. "I saw you at Arthur's funeral."

"I needed to be there," said the caller. "I followed those women and I saw you doing the same. Although they made you, didn't they? You're crap at your job, always have been."

"This isn't just a job; it's family!" spat Giles. "And I'm here to get what's mine."

220

"Don't be stupid." The words were hissed with pure venom. "No one is going to let you walk away with the only reason you've been kept under control for most of your life. You're a liability."

"I have killed over and over for this family, but I won't be ordered about anymore." He kicked the paneled wall once, then twice. It felt good to let off some steam. He'd been on his best behavior for far too long.

"You can't be left for a minute without creating chaos. Now old Metcalf is dead. There are big plans for Copthorn Manor and you're not part of them."

"What?" Giles sputtered. "No one else can do what I do."

"Actually, I can."

Behind him, a breeze rushed in from the opening of the drawing room door.

Giles turned around to see a hooded figure holding a phone in one hand and, in the other, a gun fitted with a silencer. He didn't understand what he was seeing.

"You don't need to do this," he said desperately.

"No. I want to." They squeezed the trigger.

41

"The right answers come only with asking the right questions."
—Arthur Crockleford

Freya

Iran back down the cellar corridor toward the elevator, adrenaline pumping through my veins. I'd discovered what Arthur sent me here to find. Giles was a murderer and I had to get my aunt away from the manor and give the bird to the police as evidence. The hunter I used to be had been born again—*I remembered how to pick a lock.* I pressed the button and waited impatiently for the elevator.

At the top, I searched for a handle to open the secret door.

There wasn't one.

My fingers traced the side of the door. Nothing. I moved to the far right and found a small, red button.

Was that a mumble of voices?

The door popped open and relief washed over me. I was free.

I shoved it open wide, shielding my eyes from the early morning sun streaming through the drawing room windows.

What is that on the floor?

I let my eyes focus and shuddered at the sight. Phil was leaning over someone. I stepped closer.

222

"Stay back," he demanded.

I kept walking. At my feet was Giles, blood pooling under his head. His unseeing stare was just like Asim's had been.

Dead.

My head hammered.

"A clear shot to the temple. A professional," said Phil, standing and motioning me to leave. "We need to get out of here. It's not safe." He guided me to the French door.

"Giles is dead," I said to myself. "It wasn't the justice I had wanted." I couldn't quite make sense of it all, but one thing was clear: he wasn't the only killer at Copthorn Manor.

"Darling?" Carole's voice snapped me out of my thoughts. "I'm here to rescue you, darling." Carole was about to come in through the set of doors at the far end.

"We need to get her out of here—she can't see that," I told Phil, nodding in the direction of Giles. I knew that sort of image never leaves a person.

"Stay where you are," he called to Carole as we hurried toward her.

We all stood on the patio outside the drawing room. Giles had gotten what was coming to him but I felt no pleasure in it, just an overwhelming sense of sadness. I believed Giles killed Asim because he found out that Asim was going to give the bird back to us, and therefore his father. Asim would've also given us the photograph he had taken of the head of the forgery ring when that person had gone to Asim's family home demanding the return of the Martin Brothers bird that his son had given them to copy. It must have been a photograph of Mark Metcalf. If Arthur and I had had all of that information, we could have made the connection between the Egyptian forgeries workshop and Lord Metcalf, who was commissioning fake antiquities made to sell in Europe.

It must have been clear from my expression that something was very wrong as Carole placed a hand on my arm. "What's the matter?"

"Giles Metcalf has been murdered," said Phil, in a very matter-of-fact manner.

Carole stepped away from Phil. "Why? How? Is that why you told me to check around the front while you went around this way? You murdered him."

"No! I don't kill people; I try to stop people *before* they kill. Unfortunately, by the time I arrived, the killer had fled." He looked at Carole. "Did they leave via the front?"

She shook her head.

"I thought I saw someone in a black hoodie leaving the room as I arrived," said Phil.

"Bella was wearing a black hoodie when she locked me in the vault. It could have been her—she isn't who we thought she was," I said.

"We need to leave," said Phil again.

I wasn't going anywhere with Phil. I had no idea who he was.

"We are going home," I said. I went to leave but Carole didn't move.

"Darling." Carole grabbed me and pulled me into a bear hug. "I'm so glad I was here to help you." She squeezed me tightly. "Especially when there was a gunman on the loose and you were stuck in a vault."

"You didn't rescue me from the vault or the gunman," I replied. "I rescued myself." A rush of pride in my own abilities swept through me.

"I've told you before, never to let the truth get in the way of a good story. The Women's Institute of Little Meddington is going to just *love* this one, darling. I'm a hero!" replied Carole.

"And what am I?" asked Phil.

"That has yet to be decided, darling," she replied.

"I'll call it in, but you have to come with me." There was a strange edge to his voice, like he was very used to giving orders. He tilted his head slightly to see what I was carrying.

"No, I don't think we will," I told him. "How did you know I would be in the drawing room?"

"The lovely Bella sent me a little text just moments ago saying you were there," said Carole. "We were about to search the woods for you. It is strange, as I didn't even give her my number. She told me we might need to find Franklin Smith. But Mr. Dashing over here thought he could find you himself." She nudged me. "If he turns out to be a good-un, then, you know."

I rolled my eyes at her insinuation. "I don't think there is anything 'lovely' about Bella by the way." Then I lowered my voice. "I have what Arthur sent me here for and it's not at all what we think—"

"I'm not going to ask again." Phil crossed his arms.

"Do you know, leaving aside Giles's death, I don't think I have ever had such a thrilling adventure before nine a.m." Carole paused. "I mean, outside of the bedroom—"

"Oh, please *stop*, I don't think I can take any more of this," I said. I turned to Phil. "Thank you for coming to help, but we really can't just be walking off with someone we don't know. Not after what has just happened to Giles."

Phil frowned at me. "This isn't a game. Arthur was murdered for what he knew, Giles has just been killed, and you two are swanning around like you're at a garden party."

The word "murdered" had my attention. "How do you know Arthur was murdered?"

"How about we talk about what you were doing with Bella and what you have with you?" He pointed to the bags.

I shifted away from him.

He put his hands up. "Calm down. I only need *one* of those bags—I just want the bird."

The hairs on the back of my neck prickled. "How did you know that's what I'm holding?" I asked, tightening my grip on the drawstrings.

"This is not the place to discuss it. If you want to know about Arthur's murder, then follow me." He checked his watch. "We don't have much time. There is a folly Arthur and I used to meet at out of the view of the guests." His eyes flicked toward the manor. "I'm quite sure that no one knows about it, and it has been set up as a place to run to if things kick off. And you need to know where it is—things are on a knife's edge here after what has just happened to Giles. I gave Arthur my word."

"A folly?" said Carole. "You lied about it yesterday and now you want us to go there with you?"

"Arthur asked me to keep an eye out for you both, and if anything went 'sideways' to reveal myself to you," Phil explained. "I've had you both checked out and it seems now is the time to explain the relationship between Arthur and me. Then perhaps you will tell me where his books are."

The journals. I caught Carole's eye.

"I thought it might be nicer to talk about this over a cup of tea. But we can sit on a damp log if that's your preference?"

Carole seemed to relax at the mention of tea. "Tea is exactly what we need; we haven't even had breakfast. I do hope you have real milk?"

"Yes, but I'm not sure anyone will be getting breakfast this morning," said Phil, striding down the path.

"We have to find out what he knows," whispered Carole. "If he gets any funny ideas, I've got a penknife in my pocket."

I looked at the manor, where an armed killer was walking about inside. Arthur had been right when he'd said to trust no one, but we were out of options.

It was time to find out what Phil knew about Arthur.

42

"Sometimes an antique shows its true value only when you understand its history."

—Arthur Crockleford

As we followed Phil deeper into the woods I slowed my pace until he was out of earshot.

"This might not be the best idea," I whispered to Carole. "I don't trust him."

"You can be *so* dramatic. He offered tea, and murderers don't offer tea, do they, darling?" Carole tutted at me. "Giles never offered us tea."

I leaned toward her. "They do if they mean to poison it."

She brushed down her red-and-orange quilted smoking jacket. "Arthur told Phil to look out for us."

Another secret plot of Arthur's. But maybe he truly was trying to protect us. After what I'd uncovered down in the vault, I had begun to see Arthur in a new light. He'd been blackmailed into criminal activity, but to even the scales of justice, he'd tried to find a way to fix it. What he did, he did it to protect me, and it filled me with shame when I thought of the hatred I'd carried with me for so long. I remembered the code in the journal and filled Carole in. I explained that the antiques in the vaults were the same as the ones pictured in the journal, that the red dots Arthur placed next to items meant the items had been swapped for fakes.

"Oh, my darling Arthur was simply fabulous."

227

For the first time in twenty years, I agreed with her. "I'm so very sorry about our argument last night. I know now how wrong I was."

She rubbed my arm. "Don't think of it again."

I paused, thinking about Franklin and the van. I wanted to know where all those plywood crates had been sent and what exactly was inside.

"Where do you think Bella is now?" asked Carole.

"I'm not sure. But Bella isn't who we thought she was." The image of her putting the cuneiform tablets into her backpack came back to me. "She knew exactly what she was doing—where to get Franklin's key from his office and the real time that he would be opening the vault door." I told her the rest of what I'd learned about Bella in the vault.

"She does seem to be marvelously clever." Carole pulled her hair out of her bun and shook her mane.

"She locked me in a vault!"

Carole shrugged. "In the full knowledge that you would get out of there eventually, darling."

I was about to argue further when Phil called, "We're here." He stopped in front of a large bush and pulled it aside, and I saw that it was covering another slip of a path.

We followed him down a steep bank overflowing with brambles and branches. More than once Carole's long smoking jacket got entangled and I stopped to free her. By the time the path flattened out, the smell of the damp lake reeds washed over me. Murky lake water rippled under the overhanging trees.

"The folly." Phil pointed.

A towering turret rose out of the undergrowth in front of us, complete with a battlement and a studded arched door. A murder of crows perched on top of crumbling stone walls that were covered in moss and ivy.

"Oh, that's a wonderful example of a folly, if ever I saw one," said Carole.

Phil pushed open a broken wooden door that was splintering at the edges.

"What is this place used for?" I asked Phil, remembering Arthur's entry in the journal.

IMPORTANT—Copthorn Manor Old English Folly—built by the original owner, the Cravens, in 1903. Took quite some time to find, but it's the best place for overseeing events.

Phil didn't answer me. Instead, he walked inside and turned on the lights. The black interior was transformed in the warm glow.

I found it suspicious that Phil was now being so amenable.

"I was trying to keep you out of things, but considering you have just had an encounter with a killer I thought it best to help."

I stepped over the folly's threshold and into the once frivolous, now deteriorating, stone building. The whole of the ground floor consisted of one square room. The ceiling soared upward. At the back of the room was a new pine staircase leading to the second floor. Large, glazed windows overlooked the lake. The morning sun glistened on green water. Through a glass door opposite us, I could just make out a jetty.

Phil saw me looking around. "It was in quite a state when we found it." He turned on an electric heater that faced two old sofas, then lit the camping stove on a modern pine coffee table and filled a kettle with bottled water. "Some years back, Arthur was visiting Mark Metcalf when he found a map of a folly and realized that the ailing Metcalf probably never ventured that far from the manor. If we could clean it up a bit, while still keeping it hidden, we would have a place to observe what was going on when these 'retreat' weekends took place." Phil motioned to the sofa opposite him.

Even with the heater on, the room had the musty smell of an uninhabited building. I sat down, and the sofa cushions were damp to the touch.

"You put electricity in here?" I asked.

Phil nodded. "Arthur was insistent that we needed somewhere out of the way and I knew. . ." He paused, a deep frown crossing his brow—he was weighing up how much he would divulge. "People can have deep

pockets when it's needed. Mark Metcalf was away a lot and Arthur offered to look in on the place from time to time. He hired an electrician
to connect this up. It wasn't until last year that I got the job of gardener."

Carole was standing at the glass door that led to the jetty, watching
the sun. "I need to stop you there." She turned to Phil. "First, I think you
must tell me exactly who you are and how you came to know Arthur."

Before answering, Phil went to the arched front door and locked it,
but left the key in the door. He knew what he was doing—it seemed like
he was keeping us safe without it looking like he was keeping us prisoner.
He'd done this before.

"You're right. Although I'm still not clear why you're here."

"Arthur wanted us here," Carole replied.

Phil studied us. "I'm terribly sorry about what happened to Arthur.
He must have become careless, or . . ."

"Or what?" I asked.

"Do you get the feeling there are too many coincidences?" Phil asked.

I crossed my arms. "What's your theory?"

"I believe Arthur planned all of this." Phil was watching me for an
answer.

I wondered if Phil fully grasped just how meticulously Arthur had
planned this weekend. Instead, I said, "Bella told me Vault Four was the
personal vault of Lord Metcalf. Arthur wanted me to get into that vault,
which is why he sent us here." Saying it out loud made me understand
something I hadn't seen clearly before. It was Lord Metcalf who had been
blackmailing Arthur into being his verifier for over twenty years.

Phil nodded. "That's right. Mark Metcalf believed the locations of
these 'bank vaults' were kept secret from his children, Amy and Giles.
But we know Amy discovered the vaults when she returned to the manor
to look after her dying father. Slowly Mark Metcalf began to let her
run the 'retreat' weekends where criminal 'individuals' would trade art,
antiques, diamonds . . . you get the idea. In return for . . . well, anything
from the black market, from guns to hit men."

"You say 'Mark Metcalf' as if you know he wasn't a real peer of the realm," I said.

"He is not. He just liked the idea of being a 'lord' and no one ever checked." Phil walked under the wooden staircase and pulled up a flagstone. A box was hidden underneath. He retrieved a letter and handed it to me. "Arthur sent me this."

Carole hurried over to join me on the sofa. "That's Arthur's handwriting," she said.

Dear P,

I'm sorry I didn't have the time to explain on the phone just now. I worry they're listening, but I've been betrayed and now it's only a matter of time. I have arranged as much as I could—set up C. M. retreat as normal. I will be sending help in the form of Freya Lockwood—she will get to the bottom of it and retrieve the proof you need. Please do what you can to help her. Please be careful.

It has been a pleasure, dear sir, to work with you over the years.

Arthur Crockleford

I could see Carole's eyes welling up. I took her hand in mine.

"Dear sir," Carole murmured. "He used to say that a lot."

"He did." Phil dipped his head. "He used it when I met him for the first time in Cairo."

Cairo. There was that city again, over and over since Arthur died. Everything kept going back to Cairo and what had happened there. On my lap was the bird that had started the whole sorry affair. "You still need to tell us who you are, and who you really work for. And what were you doing in Cairo?" I picked up the envelope from the coffee table. It was addressed, in Arthur's handwriting, to the FBI Art Crime Team. "This was sent to you?"

"Yes. I'm police." He showed us his badge, but I'd never seen one before and I'd no idea if it was real. He frowned when we didn't seem convinced. "We're thorough with our background checks and I already know everything I need to know about both of you. I also know that Arthur never forgave himself for what he put you through in Cairo. He never knew they were watching or that they would use the tragic death of your ex-boyfriend to blackmail him into helping them."

I held up my hand. "I'm sorry. What were you doing in Cairo? I don't remember seeing you there."

He shrugged. "You were just always so focused on the hunting. I don't think that you ever considered where Arthur got his information from. Arthur was one of the very best at tracking down an object. He knew everyone and therefore could always find out if a robbery was a petty thief looking to buy some more drugs or an organized heist."

Carole nodded in satisfaction. "What you're saying is that Arthur wasn't dodgy as my niece believes; he was working with the FBI all along." Pride shone in Carole's voice.

"I'm so sorry, Carole," I said. The weight of knowing what Arthur had done to try and protect me shuddered over me.

"We had just started working together when Mark Metcalf contacted Arthur to find his stolen Martin Brothers bird," Phil continued. "Later, when Asim told you he had seen the Martin Brothers bird at his family's forgeries workshop in Egypt and that he had a photograph of the head of the British forgery ring, which had been importing fakes for quite some time, we couldn't miss the opportunity. We offered Asim money and a new life if he could help us bring them down. Unfortunately, someone got to him first."

I leaned forward on the sofa. Perhaps Arthur hadn't trusted Phil enough yet to introduce us at that point.

"And the Martin Brothers bird and the photograph Asim had said he had taken were never recovered," Phil said. "We knew that the pieces of the bird were collected. We didn't know by who."

I gripped the bags on my lap. It sounded like Phil had no idea about my scarf. A lump built in my throat. I couldn't form the words to tell him the truth—it was my own carelessness in dropping the scarf that had lost me my career and forced Arthur to move into the black market of the antiques underworld.

"I want to be clear," I said. "Arthur never murdered anyone or touched the bird. When we arrived at the rendezvous spot to meet Asim, he was already dead, and the bird was already broken. I want to know who picked up the pieces in Cairo and placed them in here." I held up the bag.

"I don't know the answer to that." He studied the bag. "When I got there I found only Asim. No pottery pieces. No sign of the photograph. Back then the most important thing to Arthur was getting you out of Cairo. Once you were gone, Arthur willingly entered the darker world of the antiques trade with Metcalf, and at the same time, he became my informant."

"How do you think this broken bird found its way into Metcalf's vault?"

"Metcalf must've had you both followed by one of his lackeys and had it collected," replied Phil.

"And that lackey wasn't you?" I wanted to see his reaction.

"Not me."

I paused. "It just seems strange to me that I wouldn't have noticed you in Cairo. I would've remembered you."

"I can be quite discreet." The corner of his mouth curled into a smile. "And I remember you."

My cheeks reddened under his gaze.

Carole coughed, and I didn't dare look at her.

The kettle started to whistle loudly, and steam flowed toward the ceiling.

"Arthur protected you all those years ago and he has asked me to do the same now," said Phil. "I'm going to have to insist you both go home."

"That's not . . ." I cleared my throat, my resolve hardening. "That's not what Arthur wanted, and I'm not the person I once was."

A knock came at the folly door.

43

"We all make mistakes; it's what we do afterward that matters."
—Arthur Crockleford

A s Phil unlocked the door, I took a deep breath and composed myself.

Who is it?

"This is my partner, Clare," said Phil.

Clare inclined her head at us. Dressed in tight black jeans and a maroon turtleneck sweater, she seemed like an entirely different person from last night, just like Bella. It made perfect sense; she'd never seemed much like a housekeeper.

Phil returned to the sofa and poured boiling water into four camping mugs. I wondered why I hadn't noticed before that there were four cups laid out.

"If they pack their bags, I can follow them home to make sure they're safe." Clare's accent was different from Phil's, but she was also American. "I've called in the death of Giles Metcalf to the office and I am awaiting instruction."

I shook my head. "Arthur wanted us here and we're not leaving until I find out who killed him." I remembered that Phil had sounded like he knew the answer. "It's time you told us who that was."

"I stated that he *was* murdered, not that I knew who'd done it. If I had uncovered that, then I would've called our friends in the local police force and had them arrested," said Phil, handing Clare a cup of tea.

"You Brits drink a *lot* of tea," said Clare, sniffing the mug.

"It's British fuel, darling. Get it down and you'll be ready to take on the day," Carole said. "Giles came to our cottage last night saying he wanted to find something of his father's in the vaults and he wanted to have it 'before anyone else.'"

"I believe it was the broken Martin Brothers bird. My guess is that Giles was also being blackmailed by his father," I said, opening the drawstring bag and picking out the picture of the bearded man in the alley. "I believe this is Giles Metcalf leaving the café where Asim was killed." I pointed to the bandaged hand and the signet ring. "He is still wearing this ring and he has a jagged scar on his right hand which could be the wound under that bandage."

Phil looked at the photo and nodded. "It is a young Giles Metcalf. Arthur never told me about Giles. I think he only recently found out Giles was Asim's killer and where the bird was stored."

"We think Lord Metcalf told Arthur everything a week before he died," said Carole.

"That would account for Arthur's strange behavior," Phil replied. "Sending me the letter. Arranging this weekend estate valuation like one of the withdrawal retreats when it is actually very different from that. There would normally be tens of people here."

I considered the bags on my lap. If there had been things in the vault that could be used to blackmail Arthur . . . maybe there was still black-mail material in there. "Perhaps Mark Metcalf didn't entirely trust his son and daughter. He didn't leave the vault keys with them—he gave them to Arthur. There are a lot of boxes down there filled with paper-work. Vault Four was Mark Metcalf's personal vault. What if he didn't just trade in stolen art and antiques—but in information?"

Phil seemed pleased, and a flutter of pride made me smile a little. He walked over to a backpack that was slumped by the door, retrieved a brown folder, and handed it to me. It was a detailed account of my life, and on the front was the insignia of the FBI's Art Crime Team. I showed the page to Carole.

"I'm an FBI special agent from the FBI Art Crime Team. And that over there"—he tilted his head toward the manor—"is a bank of sorts that has been set up for the international criminal underworld to trade in art, antiques, antiquities, and, as you have now correctly surmised, most probably, items and information used in blackmail. They have some American items we are interested in, and Arthur always kept us in the loop."

This confirmed what Bella had told me in the vault.

"But why would criminals want to keep antiques?" said Carole.

"Because you can move these objects more easily than moving cash or bank transfers. A Picasso sketch can be placed in a suitcase, and you can tell anyone who asks that it's a print. Arthur was used by middlemen to verify and authenticate the items, so everyone knew they were getting what was being traded. He used a color code to keep track. A few months back he said he was placing them all in a book, a sort of guide to what was going on."

I knew that if Arthur had wanted Phil or the FBI to have the journals, then he could have sent them over directly. He hadn't done that; he had sent them to me.

Clare continued, "Art crime is intertwined with all other criminal activity—human trafficking, arms trading, drug dealing . . . they're all one. Hundreds of thousands of stolen or forged pieces are seized every year and taken off the market, but it's still a drop in the ocean." She blew on her tea. "We're tracking some individuals that are moving items around."

"So that's why you let the moving truck go," said Carole.

"And the car last night," Clare replied. "We need to track where it all goes. You two snooping around might've made people suspicious and check for trackers."

"We don't snoop!" Carole and I said in unison.

Clare ignored us. "Giles was here to collect the Martin Brothers bird and was killed before he could enter the vault."

I hesitated, then held out the bag to Phil. "You said you wanted one of the bags I was carrying. I presume you want what Giles was looking for. The broken Martin Brothers bird. It was used to kill my friend Asim. And the picture places Giles at the scene." I took a steadying breath. "Arthur told Giles the bird was here. He needed us all to be together this weekend so that I'd see the truth—I believe that Giles killed Asim before we could retrieve the Martin Brothers bird. Mark Metcalf had employed Arthur to track down the stolen bird—but he probably wasn't a man who trusted people easily, so I imagine he had Arthur and me followed, taking photos as well. After Giles had killed Asim, whoever was following us collected the pieces of the bird and gave them back to Mark Metcalf along with the photo of Giles at the crime scene. From that moment on, Giles was under his father's thumb."

Phil reached out and took the bag, opening it and pulling out the ziplock bag. I turned away. I couldn't see it again.

Carole reached over and rubbed my leg. "It's all right."

Phil relaxed back onto the sofa. "Very clever. But I'm not only here for this. Did Arthur leave his journals with you?"

"No, but as my niece is a master at digging up the truth, I'm sure we'll hand them over if she finds them," said Carole, rising from the sofa and checking her watch. "Now, this was all excellent fun, but we really must get to breakfast. My stomach won't wait any longer."

Phil frowned at Clare, and I knew they were debating whether we were free to go.

"I was in my twenties when I was in Cairo with Arthur, and maybe back then I might have needed some protection. But now . . ." I went to stand next to Carole. "*We* are grown women and can do as we please."

"You could damage this case with your snooping around," said Clare. "It's safer to remove you."

I wasn't going to ask how she would remove us.

"That word, 'snooping,' again!" Carole almost shrieked. "*We* are the ones solving all these crimes. Thank you very much, darling."

"I've just given you something quite valuable there." I looked at the bag in Phil's hand. "I expect that I will see justice for Asim. Giles had a large cut on his hand—I believe this was done when he drove the stoneware into Asim's head. I would imagine both men's blood is on those pieces. Along with the photo it's quite convincing."

Clare shook her head. "Giles is dead. It was a long time ago in a foreign country. There's nothing that can be done."

I breathed deeply. I had solved Asim's murder just as Arthur had intended me to and retrieved my scarf and the photos that had been used to blackmail Arthur. I supposed my scarf might also have been used to blackmail me if someone had wanted to try; that must have been why Arthur wanted me to locate it so badly. Now it was time to find out who had killed him—and who had just murdered Giles.

Phil handed the bag to Clare. "Fine, you can stay. But I'm coming with you. There is still someone with a gun around here, and I don't want any more deaths on my watch."

I remembered Amy's phone in my pocket. I pulled it out. "If you are who you say, can you unlock this?"

"I can try," said Clare. "Whose is it?"

"It's Amy's. I think there might be something on there that could help us. . . . I just don't know what."

Clare and Phil exchanged a smile. "I'll work on this right away," Clare said.

Satisfied with what we'd learned from Phil and Clare, Carole and I left the folly, Phil on our heels. I had a feeling he was going to stay that way, but I wasn't leaving just yet. I had a murderer to find, and the answers were in the manor.

44

"Always be prepared for the tides to change."

—Arthur Crockleford

C arole, Phil, and I walked through the manor's front door and into the main hall.

It was 9 a.m. and I was already exhausted. My mind was spinning with what Phil had said. My gut told me he probably *was* from the FBI Art Crime Team, but I wondered where the Scotland Yard Art and Antiques Unit was in all this. I was still unclear of Arthur's motives in giving the journals to me rather than to Phil. Surely, they would be better off in the hands of the FBI?

I couldn't help but stare at the drawing room, knowing Giles's body lay behind the locked doors. "What about that?"

"It's under control." But Phil looked worried.

I could hear voices drifting down the corridor. There was a rumble of laughter.

The small dining room was exactly the way we'd left it the previous night; dirty plates with their knives and forks crossed, empty wineglasses stained with the dregs of pinot noir, and the candles burnt down to stubs. I might have found out Clare was undercover, but she still needed to look like she was a housekeeper, didn't she?

On the sideboard there were several jars filled with cereal, along with two large cartons of milk. The sharp, warm smell of freshly made coffee filled the room. Amy and Franklin were standing next to the cafetière talking, but stopped abruptly when we entered.

Carole headed for the chair she'd sat in last night and I took a seat next to her. Phil remained standing near the door.

"Someone has locked up the drawing room," said Amy. "Which one of you was it?"

None of us spoke.

"Amy has graciously put out some things for breakfast," said Franklin, breaking the silence. "Why don't you help yourself."

A shiver went down my spine. I was taken aback by Franklin's lightness of manner until I remembered he probably had no idea Giles was lying dead in the drawing room. I had to shut the thought of it from my mind and tell myself that Giles was a murderer—he had killed Asim over twenty years ago when he could've been only in his early twenties himself.

Still, Franklin looked overly confident. Something was very wrong.

"I thought I saw someone else in the manor when we were heading out for our walk. Is there anyone else staying here?" I asked.

Amy shook her head. "It's just us."

I wasn't hungry and I was considering telling Carole that Phil was right—we should leave. I was convinced there was someone else here as well as Franklin and Amy. I had no idea where Bella had gone after locking me in the vault. Perhaps on her way out she'd killed Giles for all she'd had to put up with? But my gut said it wasn't her.

"Is there any tea?" asked Carole. "Because I think it's best we talk about Arthur's double life over tea, don't you?"

I glared at her. That was the last thing I thought we should be doing.

"Did Arthur have a double life?" asked Franklin. "How interesting."

Amy strode toward the door. "It's not interesting in the slightest and I've no intention of listening to such rubbish. I need to find Clare."

"Did I hear my name?" Clare swept into the room, now changed into a floral dress and clogs. "I'm sorry, I overslept. Give me a minute and I'll have all this cleared up." She stacked some plates into her arms and hurried out.

"We need a teapot," called Amy, rushing after her.

Carole, Phil, Franklin, and I settled down at the table. Moments later there was a squeak of a floorboard somewhere above us, followed by a thud. I glanced at Carole, but it didn't look as if she had heard.

Was that Amy? Clare? Or someone else?

I wasn't going to wait for Phil to stop me. "I'm going to use the bathroom," I mumbled as I left the room as quickly as possible. Phil made a move to stand, but I placed my hand on his shoulder. "I'll be fine. Stay with Carole."

I didn't want anyone else to get hurt.

~

I sped down the corridor, back toward the hallway, and then turned right to the grand staircase, following the way I'd gone the night before. The lights were on, and for the first time I could clearly see the area. On the ground floor there were a few reproductions of old masters, and as I looked up there were lighter areas on the maroon wallpaper where other paintings used to hang.

I climbed the stairs carefully. At the top, I paused and listened. I could hear the guests in the dining room, but nothing else. I hurried along the hallway toward Amy's room. If it was Amy, then surely she would be there.

In the daylight the extent of the manor's deterioration was evident; the carpets were worn and indented by the chair legs or chest frames that had once rested on them. And the wallpaper was peeling in places. The air was bone-chillingly cold.

I tried the door I thought was the one from last night, but on opening it I saw that it was an abandoned room. Bare floorboards, no curtains, no furniture. I tried the next door down.

The door opened a crack—enough for someone to get through, but something was in the way, something heavy. I remembered that Amy had barricaded herself in the room last night after Giles had confronted her with the fire poker.

"Hello?" I whispered through the opening. "Amy, are you there?"

Silence.

"Amy's not in the kitchen. Is she in there?" I jumped and turned to see Phil behind me.

"Don't sneak up on me."

"I'm checking that you're all right." He put his eye to the crack.

"Sneaking up on someone does not make them feel safe, just so we're clear." I tried to open the door further but it hit against something on the other side.

"Amy?" I stuck my head through the gap but all I could see was a chest of drawers. I glanced back at Phil. "It's a small gap—could Amy fit through there?" I gave the door a shove with my shoulder to make more room, which was not as easy as it looked in the movies. My shoulder blazed with pain.

"Shall I have a go?"

I didn't budge. "I don't think a man should be breaking into a woman's bedroom, do you?"

"I think we are past the point of worrying how this might look, when something far darker could have happened. Perhaps someone is intent on taking down the Metcalf family one by one," replied Phil.

I agreed it was a possibility. "Perhaps one of those 'individuals' Franklin keeps mentioning found out their antiques have been replaced with fakes?" Even as I said it, I wasn't sure it was the truth.

I stepped away from the door and Phil shoved it open enough to enter the room. I held my breath and followed him. A large chest had been placed up against the door, and the bedroom was dark and stale.

I noticed Phil had pulled on some black leather gloves as he drew the curtains. I found the light switch and clicked it on. There were clothes scattered on the floor, and all the drawers were open. What had someone been looking for?

"Don't touch anything in here," Phil said. "You need to go back into the corridor."

"What's wrong?" I followed his line of sight. On the old Persian rug was a black hoodie with a stain of deep crimson blood on one sleeve. "Is that . . ." I whispered, not wanting to hear my suspicions out loud.

"I wouldn't like to speculate, but if it's what I think it is then someone has been badly injured or . . ." Phil pulled out his phone and tapped away. "I'm going to get Clare up here to take a look around the property, take photos, samples." He nodded at the carpet.

"Or it's Giles's blood and Amy is the killer," I said, scanning the room again. "And we have no idea where Bella is! None of this makes sense. Do you think someone forced their way in here?"

Phil shrugged. "I don't like guessing."

Footsteps came from down the hall and Clare walked in.

"I don't have long. The kitchen is a total mess." She lifted a large black bag that could have been a doctor's case.

"You weren't seen?" asked Phil, motioning her over to the rug.

"They're all in the dining room." Clare knelt on the rug and examined the hoodie. "This doesn't look good, does it?"

Phil shook his head. "Take as many photos as you can, a swab, and then we'll all leave."

"I'll be all right if you want to go ahead." Clare got out a large camera and started taking pictures. "We're going to have to report this."

"I think we'll keep a lid on it until this afternoon and then we'll shut the place down."

I was confused. "Amy told me the house was being closed up this afternoon. Is that what you mean?"

Clare put down her camera in surprise. "You're going to be the star of the show according to the program, and we've never had a program like that before. We assumed Arthur was trying to tell us something."

He was trying to tell me *something.*

I didn't know what she meant about me being the star of the show, but I was filled with a sinking dread as I left the room.

This weekend was very far from over.

I returned to the dining room, where I found Carole quietly sipping tea. I desperately wanted to tell her about the hoodie, but I didn't want to worry her.

"Are you quite all right?" she asked, touching my arm.

Franklin raised an eyebrow.

I smiled my best smile. "I'm perfectly fine." I tried to calm myself or at least tried to *look* calm. But really, I wanted to yell that there was a killer here. *Someone had killed Giles and then perhaps left their bloodstained hoodie in Amy's room. Or Amy was hurt. Or Amy killed her brother . . .*

"Franklin, do you know where Amy is?" I asked.

"I'm afraid not. Didn't she say she was getting a teapot?" He looked unsure.

"That is what she said," replied Carole. "But when she didn't come back, Phil kindly went to get it for me, and she was nowhere to be found so he went upstairs to look."

As if on cue, Phil walked into the room. "No sign of Amy," he said.

"We should get packing." I jerked my head to the side to indicate we should leave.

"Arthur insisted on sticking to the program—there's to be a talk," said Franklin. "I'm so looking forward to what you're going to enlighten us on, Freya. I'd love to know what each and every item in the manor is worth. It's necessary for the inventory of the Metcalf estate. At twelve o'clock, right?" He pulled up his sleeve to check the time. On Franklin's left wrist was a Rolex Daytona with its white-gold case and brown alligator strap—it was in almost perfect condition. My eyes did what they always seem to do when an item of excellence is displayed—I fixated on every last detail, the quality of the gold and gleam of its newness. The last time I had seen Franklin's watch, back in his office in Little Meddington, it was a cheap and fake Rolex. The original one he was now wearing was a beautiful and expensive piece. How could he afford a watch worth between twenty and thirty thousand pounds? He saw me staring and pulled down his cuff. It was clear Franklin was up to something.

"Talk?" Phil barked at him. "There's not going to be any *talk*. It was Arthur having . . . a laugh. And there won't be any antiques fair either."

"Of course, no one needs to attend any antiques fair," said Franklin. His mouth twitched ever so slightly.

The insistence by both men that no one should go to the antiques fair began to harden my resolve to go.

It was true that the program had said there was going to be a talk, but I hadn't expected *I* was to be the one to give it. Yet I couldn't ignore that the clues I'd found in the program had pointed us toward the vault and the forgeries. There could be something else Arthur wanted us to find out at the fair and the talk.

"There is an antiques fair up the road," I said, looking at Carole. "Instead of packing up, how about a trip to the fair? You do love a good snoop around the stalls."

"I do, don't I?" said Carole, looking at me with a glint in her eye. She knew exactly what I was hinting at. "I think it's a fabulous idea. Let's finish breakfast and get on our way."

Franklin shook his head but didn't protest.

I knew it was a slightly preposterous thing to do, going to an antiques fair in the middle of a murder investigation, but time *was* running out and we were no closer to finding Arthur's killer.

I was more convinced than ever that answers we needed could be found in everything Arthur had planned for the weekend.

45

"To find the best deal at an antiques fair always turn left, because everyone else always turns right."

—Arthur Crockleford

The stalls at the antiques fair were arranged in long rows down the length of a large field. Carole and I waited in the line of fellow antiques enthusiasts. The dew on the grass had already started to seep through my sneakers, dampening my socks.

"Arthur would've been tutting by now," said Carole, looking just as impatient. "He never liked to stand in line for anything. Though of course he never complained."

I laughed at the lie. "Of course, Arthur never complained about lines."

Fonder memories of Arthur were easier to retrieve now that I had uncovered most of the truth about that day in Cairo. My emotions bounced between relief that I had been wrong all along and guilt for being wrong for so long. Arthur had done so much for me.

It was time to really clear the air with my aunt. "I was desperately wrong about Arthur. I'm so sorry." Tears threatened. "You tried to tell me. . . . I never listened." I hung my head.

Carole reached over and put her arm around me. "I know you're shaken by your discovery in the vault. You couldn't have known without Arthur telling you. I didn't know the full extent of it but I always knew

Arthur loved you like a granddaughter. The journals are his way of making it right, and in return we're going to catch his killer, aren't we?" Her eyes locked on mine and she lowered her voice. "Giles's *murder* is distressing! But he turned out to be most unsavory, so we are trying to push away our feelings over his demise and concentrate on the mission—"

I tried to smile. "We are."

I'm going to find Arthur's killer and start repaying the huge debt I owe him.

We edged our way toward the front. The coins for the entrance fee were now sweaty in my palm.

"I still don't understand why Arthur would send us here," I said, looking around the stalls. "What could we possibly learn?"

In the car journey to the fair, I'd told Carole what I had seen in Amy's bedroom and my suspicions about what could have happened. We'd come to an agreement that Arthur was probably killed for what he had written down in the journals, and Giles hadn't seemed interested in those. Giles wanted the Martin Brothers bird, and Arthur had helped him as much as he could—therefore, we had decided to believe Giles was unlikely to be Arthur's killer. That left Franklin, Amy, and Bella as suspects.

We reached the front of the line and handed over our money, then entered through the gate. Carole made a beeline for the coffee truck, which was also drawing in visitors with wafts of bacon.

As we stood in yet another line of people, my mind began to run through what we knew. "Giles steals the Martin Brothers bird from his father, Mark Metcalf—an international criminal."

"And blackmailer," Carole added.

"And somehow Giles gets his father's forgery contacts in Egypt and takes the bird to the workshop there. He was probably hoping to give the fake back to his father and keep or sell on the original. But Giles isn't the sharpest knife in the block, and he not only shows his face to Asim but tells Asim about the family connection to Mark Metcalf and Copthorn Manor. Metcalf discovers the bird has been stolen, so he hires

Arthur to hunt down the bird, promising that if he finds it then he will pay Arthur's debts for the shop. Somewhere along the line, Metcalf realizes that his own son is the thief, follows Giles to Cairo, and goes to Asim's family home to ask if they have the bird. Asim takes a photograph of him. If Metcalf sent Arthur and me to find the bird, I think it is also possible he sent others to follow us—perhaps that someone else took those black-and-white photos of us at the café and collected the broken pieces of the bird."

"Ah yes, the photographs," said Carole. "Or Mark took the pictures and retrieved the broken bird himself. We also know Phil was in Cairo at the same time."

"Mark Metcalf didn't seem like someone who got his hands dirty. We know Giles got to Asim before we did and killed him to stop Asim from telling Arthur what he knew. We never found the photo Asim said he had, so we can assume Giles probably took that."

"Or whoever was following Giles took it," said Carole.

I waited for the image of Asim lying on the kitchen floor to overpower me. But it didn't come. Had the answers I'd found earlier this morning and what had really happened in Cairo softened the sharpness of those memories? I rubbed my face and tried to focus on the clues in front of me and not the past.

"There is one thing that's been bugging me, darling," Carole said. "Harry said he saw Arthur with a Martin Brothers bird the day before he died—he didn't say it was broken. So where is *that* Martin Brothers bird? We have to assume it's a different bird from the broken one that was in Vault Four."

"True. And the image Harry pointed at was not the same bird as the Cairo one. Everything has to come back to that night. If we find out who took the second bird, we know who was with Arthur the night before he died and who might have killed him."

We frowned at each other. It was still confusing. I could really do with some coffee to wake my brain up.

"We know Giles was here for the bird, Bella was here for a robbery, Phil is here undercover watching the manor's goings-on, Amy—" Carole stopped, surprise opening her mouth. "Is right over there."

I spun around. Amy was standing beside one of the furniture stalls, handing over money to a man I didn't recognize, likely a vendor. He gave her a few pieces of paper in return.

"What's she doing here?" asked Carole.

I knew exactly what she was doing there. "The contents of Vaults One and Two were copies. Amy probably believes the 'individuals' who own the antiques that were stored in Metcalf's vaults won't be able to authenticate those items. But I never saw any furniture from the Copthorn Manor Collection down there. I think that's because the originals were sold and she didn't replace them. She's here buying bad reproductions." I pointed to two men unloading a couple of chairs from the back of one van and placing them into another van. "To the unsuspecting eye, those chairs could pass as Chippendale—see the ball-and-claw feet? I believe Amy is taking over her father's business, and it might have been Amy that sold the original Copthorn Manor Collection and replaced a few of the furniture pieces in the main reception areas with reproductions while her father was bed-bound."

"But why?" asked Carole.

"I think Amy probably offered Franklin money, and a very expensive watch, to either hand over the keys or to let Amy into Vaults Three and Four. I found out that the antiquities in Vault Two were fakes—Vault Three could be the same. Perhaps she bought herself some time to replace anything that might be missing from there," I replied.

"Amy is covering her or her father's tracks and Franklin is helping her."

"That he is," said Phil, coming to stand next to Carole. "We had a tip-off that Amy had made arrangements to meet some dealers here." He smiled at Carole. "Let me get the coffee."

"Well, I would, darling, but my niece here thinks that you might spike it!" Carole stepped up to the vendor and ordered three coffees.

I looked Phil dead in the eye. "Still being our shadow?"

He smiled. "Your aunt doesn't seem bothered by my presence. And to be clear, I don't spike ladies' drinks."

I shrugged as if I didn't care. "I've no idea what you do."

"I've told you; Arthur wanted me to keep an eye on you two, but it seems I can't even have a good night's sleep without you getting locked up in a vault."

I didn't know how to reply and felt uncomfortably warm under Phil's gaze. I refocused my attention on Amy, now barking orders at the moving men.

Carole returned with the coffees and handed them out. She beamed at Phil. "Our Freya is just *so* good at digging things up." She flicked her hair back. "Wasn't it marvelous what she uncovered while you were sleeping?"

"It wasn't our intention to enter the vault . . . and it shouldn't have been yours." Phil raised his eyebrow at me, obviously expecting to be challenged, so I bit my tongue.

Coffees in hand, we strolled down a lane of stalls, pretending to scan the items on display while watching Amy.

"I was into art as a kid," said Phil, looking at a pencil drawing of a dog. I must have appeared shocked because he continued, "My mother worked at the Charleston Museum, and I spent a lot of time there, wandering the halls, imagining how different my life would've been in the past." I turned to Phil and realized I knew nothing about him. He told me his mother had been an art critic in Mexico, where she had grown up, and had fallen in love with his father, who owned a farm outside of Charleston, during a chance meeting on one of her business trips to America. They were married and she got a job at the museum in the city shortly after.

"My father was curator at the British Museum and my mother was an art restorer," I said. "I spent a lot of time in museums as well. They feel like a haven to me now."

Phil smiled and his eyes caught mine. "I couldn't agree more. I'm sorry for what you went through at such a young age, and for what happened to your boyfriend."

"Thank you. It's a strange thing, but knowing who killed Asim and why has started to make me accept the loss a bit more. I don't know if that makes sense?"

"It does."

I looked back toward Carole, who was now in deep conversation with a stallholder. We stopped at a booth overloaded with copper kettles and pans. I picked one up and frowned at the price tag. "This is very overpriced." I put it back down. "Do you know why Giles was so fixated on the Martin Brothers bird? Did he really need the money from selling the original?"

"All I can tell you is what Arthur told me," Phil said. "Giles was very good at stealing things; he liked the thrill of it, and his father liked to collect. Giles's mother loved Martin Brothers Wally birds so in his teenage years Giles stole one for her. After she died, Lord Metcalf locked it away in a cabinet behind his desk. Giles said the bird got to see everything that went on in that office. It got to overhear every plan and every deal. Clients always ended up talking about the Martin Brothers bird. Always using such cruel words. Always debating its value. Apparently, Metcalf didn't care about it either way. He just cared about what it was worth and what he could trade it for, but Giles's mother loved it, and Metcalf kept it for her sake. Some years after her death, he set about finding a buyer, and Giles, it seems, set about trying to save it. As we know, it all went terribly wrong that day in Cairo, and those events haunted those who were there."

The world became very quiet, the hustle of the fair drowned out by my sorrow and regret.

Carole caught up with us. "Well, don't you two lovebirds . . ." She registered the expression on my face. "What's wrong?" She turned on Phil. "What have you said to upset my darling niece?"

"No, don't give me that wild look of yours," said Phil. "I was only telling your niece what she asked to hear. We were talking about Cairo."

"He was, and Giles and the Martin Brothers bird. It's all quite clear now. . . ." I took a gulp of my coffee and Phil did the same.

"Well, then." Carole patted my arm. "Arthur must have known Amy would come to the fair. I suspect it's one of her regular trading places."

I agreed. "Here and at auction." I was glad that we were back to discussing Arthur's clues and not the painful past.

We reached the end of the row of stalls.

"I don't suppose you're going to tell me where you found Arthur's journals and where you've hidden them?" Phil's voice was low and soft.

"I don't suppose I am, no." I smiled at him.

"I do hope if you uncover any proof of wrongdoing you will give me a call." He handed me a card with only a mobile number on it, and I slipped it in my pocket without Carole seeing.

"If I have the journals and if I read anything . . . unsavory, I might call," I replied.

Phil nodded.

"Now, you two, no more of your cooing. We have to get back to the manor and find something that points us toward Arthur's killer," said Carole.

I agreed and we all headed for the parking lot. Bit by bit small pieces of the puzzle were beginning to make sense. For the first time I really did have Carole's "deep-in-my-bones knowing." And I was sure we were closing in on Arthur's murderer.

46

"A sleeper is an item no one recognizes apart from the most experienced in the room. You have to be always on the lookout."

—Arthur Crockleford

Back at our Copthorn Manor's cottage, I hurried upstairs. All the talk of the journals had put me on edge. Before we'd left, I'd arranged everything very carefully so I could check if things had been moved, and sure enough, I could see now that clothes had been lifted and replaced. Someone had searched our vacation cottage when we were out.

I walked across the small hallway and knocked on Carole's door. She opened it, looking flushed.

"I've a funny feeling my room's been searched," she whispered, like someone was also hiding behind the curtains.

"The only two people we didn't see at the fair were Clare and Franklin. Phil asked about the journals, so I wouldn't put it past him to have Clare search the cottage."

"Or perhaps Amy had Franklin search for her?" suggested Carole.

"The other option is that someone else arrived at the manor last night and is still here. Perhaps they killed Giles and searched our cottage for the journals?"

Carole nodded. "Where *are* the journals?"

"I put them in the trunk of your car before we left. I thought it would be better if they were locked away and with us," I said.

"Good thinking. We're going to have to find a safer place to hide them in the future," said Carole. "I'm going for a nap."

"Absolutely, get some rest."

The idea of someone rummaging through Carole's things had shaken her and I was annoyed at myself for not thinking about what she'd been through: Arthur's death and the belief that it wasn't an accident, the letter, and the invite to the manor. A lot had gone on over the past week and I would have to make sure that Carole took it easy.

My phone buzzed in my pocket.

No Caller ID.

"Hello?" I waved at Carole and walked downstairs, thinking it could be Jade calling from abroad. The anticipation of hearing her voice reminded me of how much I missed her.

"Freya?"

It was James. I instantly thought there must be something wrong if he was calling again so soon.

"Is Jade all right?"

"This isn't about Jade," he snapped. "Everyone's fine apart from you. We've been trying to get hold of you, but your phone's always off."

I didn't have time for one of James's lectures on how I should be acting. Instead of placating him as I used to, I changed the subject. "What do you want?"

"There's no need to be so abrupt. Where are your manners?" He waited for me to apologize, but I didn't. He huffed. "We now have multiple offers. The house is going to sealed bids on Friday and then it'll be sold. Three months, that's all you have. No dragging your feet, do you hear?"

To my surprise, I wasn't flooded with panic. "I look forward to hearing from the real estate agent. I must go. I have things to do."

"What is wrong with you today? Don't be so bloody stupid. You don't *do* any—"

I hung up. The phone started buzzing again immediately, and I sent it to voicemail.

Selling the house and moving on was no longer the most fearful event I could imagine—in the last twenty-four hours I had freed myself from a vault, uncovered Asim's killer, encountered Giles's body, and survived a murderer on the loose, at least, so far. I looked through the window toward the manor—I had bigger things to worry about right now than the London house, and James no longer had the power to make me feel small and insignificant.

A knock on the door shook me from my thoughts. I went to the entrance and saw Clare through the glass. She gave a quick, impatient wave and glanced around, as if she was concerned about being seen. I opened the door, and she hurried in, closing the curtain over the door.

"What's wrong?" I asked. Her face was pale. I wondered if she really had searched our cottage while we were out.

"I needed you to see this." Her voice was hushed. In her hand was Amy's phone. "Phil is terrified you're going to ruin the case, so he didn't want you to see this, but I'm thinking you might be the one to help. I really don't think you're safe here anymore."

Bella's note "LEAVE NOW" flashed into my mind.

"What's going on?"

"I unlocked the phone. Are you *sure* it belongs to Amy?"

"I'm sorry?" I had never considered that the phone belonged to anyone but Amy. "If the phone isn't hers then... well, I don't think anyone else was in the kitchen last night. Last night a car arrived in the storm. Carole and I saw it leaving—or we saw it drive away and stopping at the gate...."

"Yes, I heard a car last night as well. I ran to the front door and saw Amy and someone else loading four large paintings into a black Volvo." Clare held out the phone. "Do you know these phone numbers?"

I scrolled through the phones' message log. None of the numbers had names. Last night's message was now fully visible. "The person who owned this phone received this message when the electricity was cut last night." We've run out of time. Do IT NOW. Time to search the cottages for the journals.

If this message was from Amy to the owner of the phone, then she was working with whoever owned this phone. And they were here last night.

I read some more messages.

Dated Tuesday, May 14.

Arthur knows about the vault and what's inside.

I opened the calendar on my phone. The fourteenth of May was three days after Mark Metcalf died. "That message confirms what Carole and I suspected. That Arthur was told about the vault and what was in it."

I kept scrolling. There were messages about dates and times of meetings.

Then I saw: Arthur arranged the dates for the meeting, and the time the vault will be open is 10 a.m. Move the last of the stuff before then. I think there is only one copy of the books. Can't be sure.

The next message to catch my eye made me shiver. It was dated Sunday, May 19, at 9:42 p.m. If he won't hand over the books, I'll sort it.

I rechecked the dates of the messages. "That message was sent the evening Arthur died."

"This is what I really wanted to show you." Clare clicked through some other messages and pointed at one. "This one is from Monday at one twelve a.m. the night Arthur died, but it doesn't make any sense. It reads '120908.'"

I took the phone. The text made my stomach flip-flop. It was the shortest message, but it gave me a very clear idea of what was going on. I turned off the phone and handed it back to Clare. "I'm going to do the talk."

I pulled out my phone and sent Phil a message.

Just then Amy's lost phone started to ring. The number was unknown.

"Do we answer?" I asked.

Clare nodded and accepted the call but didn't say anything. I bent toward the phone.

No one spoke.

It didn't matter. I had a pretty good suspicion of who the phone belonged to.

~

Once Clare left, I woke Carole and filled her in.

"We thought the phone belonged to Amy, and it *was* what Amy was looking for, but now I don't think it was hers. When they discovered it was lost, Amy went to look for it. That's why the car stopped for so long at the gates last night. Clare told me she saw Amy load paintings into a car. That's probably because Amy didn't want expensive paintings included in the inventory of the estate that therefore the tax man might know about." I held out my hand to Carole and helped her to stand.

"I've messaged Phil to meet us at the manor. We will need his help."

Carole's eyes widened. "Have you swapped numbers with him, darling? I can't wait to tell Jade I found her mother the most dashing man in the middle of a murder investigation. Sometimes, I absolutely outdo myself with all my multitasking."

"It's not like that."

"Well, it's not like that at the *moment*, but I am very sure you won't be able to keep your hands off that toned body for long!" She clapped her hands together with glee.

"Please stop. I'm over forty, not eighteen." I stepped back out into the corridor.

"You're never too old for a jolly good time," Carole called after me.

I put my hands up in defeat—I was never going to win the argument. Changing the subject, I said, "Grab your coat. We need to get to the manor and prepare our trap." I walked toward the cottage door.

"A trap! That's exactly what we need. But first, are you going to tell me what happened the night Arthur died?" asked Carole.

"I'm going to do better than that. I'm going to prove who killed Arthur."

47

"There are always more tricks to teach an old dog."

—Arthur Crockleford

Carole

Carole strode across the drive toward the manor. She wished Arthur were here to see what they'd been up to. But today was not the day to be morose. Today she was going to accomplish what he'd asked her to do.

I'm going to put those dancing shoes on again, Arthur.

Freya hurried ahead of her; she normally wouldn't have been so slow, but on seeing Phil waiting outside the manor Carole had made up an excuse about needing lipstick. She wanted them to be alone together. By the time she caught up to them, they were both a little bashful and Carole knew she was on the right track.

"Clare tells me you both think the phone isn't Amy's?" he asked.

"Arthur put in the program that there was to be a talk this afternoon," said Freya, "but we know that can't be the case as Amy would probably have closed up the house by then. When Clare showed me the phone it gave me a clue as to who murdered Arthur and Giles. I need your help to prove I'm right," said Freya.

"Clare wasn't authorized to show you the phone." He held up a hand to stop Freya and Carole protesting. "Even though you found it."

"That's true. I need you to do something for me and then I'll tell you both everything." Freya smiled at Phil. "It will get us the proof we need, and I can't do it without you." Which Carole knew was a lie as Freya was more than capable of catching Arthur's killer on her own.

Phil shook his head, then sighed and looked at Freya with something in his eyes. Admiration. She blushed again. "What do you need?" he asked.

Carole knew there was definitely a spark of something there, and she intended to fan it. Freya did need a bit of fun. Not a boyfriend or anything—no one needs one of them to hold them back. A . . . what was the modern term for these things? Oh yes, a friend with benefits. Carole had seen him topless, so she already knew that the goods were worth having.

Freya was trying to remain businesslike. "I presume you have the phone numbers of all the guests here? Can you send a round-robin and say the talk will be going ahead at noon and that you've found a phone? Say you'll bring it with you." Freya checked her watch and said to Carole, "That gives us an hour to pack and give the cottage a good cleaning. We don't need the wrong type of people knowing we were here when they come looking for their real antiques."

"Do you really think whoever owns the phone will come and collect it?" asked Carole. "How would they get the message if we have their phone?"

"I'm quite sure someone will tell them," Freya replied.

"I'll send a message after I check the drawing room is still secure," Phil replied, making his way into the manor.

"One last thing." Freya reached out to stop him leaving. Her hand gripped his arm. He spun around, bringing them face-to-face. There was an electric second that filled Carole with utter glee before Freya snapped her hand away and stepped back. "Um . . . sorry, I . . . You need to stop the moving truck that was here this morning."

Phil shook his head. "We want to track it and get the full picture of the operation."

"It's not the antiques inside I want. It's the person driving it."

"Those moving men?" Phil looked bemused. "They're just hands for hire."

"I imagine the moving men won't be driving the truck for much longer, not if Bella has anything to do with it," said Freya.

Carole was quite sure Freya was going to make Bella pay for locking her in the vault.

"I will have someone discreetly check who is driving the van. Now, if you will both excuse me, I need to make sure the drawing room is secure." Phil sped inside the manor.

"Where will you hold your talk?" asked Carole.

"In the main hall, I guess. Let's try and set it up."

The first thing Carole saw on entering the main hall was Phil in the doorway to the drawing room. The door was wide open.

"What's he doing?" Carole asked Freya. "I thought no one was meant to go in there."

"Why haven't the police arrived yet?" Freya whispered to Carole.

Phil overheard. "I was told not to inform the local police until after the van had left the country. Clare would call it in as soon as we could, and the room had not been disturbed." Phil was pale. "But now . . ."

"What's wrong?" asked Freya, walking over to the open door. "Let me see."

She pushed past Phil, and Carole followed. "I don't see anything," said Carole.

"Exactly." Worry was etched on Phil's brow as he sent another text on his phone.

"That is the oddest thing I have ever heard of," said Carole. "Are you saying that Giles isn't dead; that he just got up and walked away?"

"He was dead." Phil frowned. "Someone must have moved the body while we were at the fair."

Freya hurried to where Giles had fallen. "There's only a slight blood-stain here. That's quite a cleanup job. He was a big man—it would probably take two people to move him."

Carole raised a questioning eyebrow at Phil. She thought she trusted him, but then, she had always been a sucker for a pretty face and a nice body.

"This is all most odd. . . ." Freya's voice was distant—as if she was lost in her thoughts.

"Giles's killer must still be here, and they moved the body to cover their tracks and in the process the arm of their sweatshirt became covered in blood."

Freya was shaking her head. Now she too looked awfully pale. "Maybe getting everyone together for a talk is too risky."

But Carole was not about to stop now. If Freya thought holding the talk and luring everyone back into the manor would enable them to catch Arthur's killer, then they were going to have that talk. The show must go on.

"Everything we've done has been to catch Arthur's killer," she said firmly. "We're following Arthur's plan, no matter what. He spent a very long time stalking his prey and now we are going to finish the job he wanted us to do and that's the end of the matter." Carole put her hands on her hips.

Freya nodded slowly like she knew something Carole didn't. "I need to look for something in the dining room. Can you arrange some chairs in the hall for the talk?" she asked.

Carole got that deep-in-her-bones knowing—Freya was well on her way to catching a killer or two.

48

"Sometimes it's the smallest detail that gives a fake away."

—Arthur Crockleford

Freya

I walked into the main hall at Copthorn Manor, the house that only yesterday I had been hesitant to enter. Back then I had been on the edge of something I didn't understand. Now, though, I saw what Arthur wanted me to see. Now I understood the past and had hope for the future.

A lump formed in my throat and I turned to the window facing the lake. The storm had bent the reeds circling the edge of the lake and I noticed a lone duck bobbing on the murky water. The sun was heading toward full strength and the breeze had picked up. A strong gust made the grasses ripple. The storm that had battered Copthorn Manor and the vacation cottages last night was over, and the rolling days of spring had returned.

The front door was open and the sun lit the flagstones. We had turned the main entrance hall into a lecture theater as well as we could, gathering chairs from the dining room and placing them in a semicircle facing the fire. There was a fire poker on hand if I needed it, but I was hoping to catch Arthur's murderer off guard. I'd set up a flip chart found in the kitchen storeroom hoping the guests would believe I truly was going to give a talk. I couldn't have them turning on their heels before we'd had a chance to get things out in the open.

"All good?" asked Carole, carrying a tray of teacups and saucers. "Have you got one of those old stone things for the talk?" She nodded at the cuneiform tablet on the table by the fireplace.

"Yes, I remembered that I'd placed one in the drawstring bag with my old scarf, so that will have to do. This is the original tablet I kept from Bella. The fake ones are in Franklin's van—I'm quite sure Bella will hijack that van at some point. I think it would be in keeping for her to get both the original ones *and* the fake ones."

"What a woman she is! Darling, this is all going marvelously well." Carole set the tray down on another small table, then walked around the chairs in the main hall. "Where shall I sit? I suppose that I should be by the front door to stop anyone running away?"

"I think we will leave that to Phil."

"So do I," said Phil, pulling a chair back against the wall by the front door. "Clare is discreetly placed outside as you asked. Are you going to tell me what's going on?"

"As long as she's totally hidden. It might spook my guests to see her lurking about. I'm hoping everyone takes the bait."

Both Phil and Carole looked at me in surprise. "Now, you know I'm not a fan of you keeping secrets," Carole said. "I think you're going to need to tell me what's going on first. I do like to be in the know." She settled herself on a seat by the window and rested her chin on her hand.

"I'm going to tell everyone together. It's the way Arthur wanted it to happen. This"—I gestured around the room—"was all Arthur's doing."

She sighed and checked her watch. "You'd think people would be on time."

Franklin arrived first and sat next to Carole.

A car pulled up and a door slammed. Amy strode in wearing an expensive-looking jacket and sunglasses and walked straight over to me.

"You've no authority here, Freya Lockwood. What's going on?" she said, her cheeks reddening. "This is my house and you're standing there looking like the Lady of Copthorn Manor."

I gave her my sweetest smile. "I'm just following the program that was sent with the invitation."

She huffed and turned to Phil. "I got your message. Where's my phone?" Before Phil could come up with an answer, her eyes caught the cuneiform tablet resting on its velvet pouch on the table.

I picked it up for safekeeping.

Amy glared at me. "If you have that, then . . . Wait, where's Bella?" she demanded. "Is she here?"

I didn't reply.

Her fists clenched. "Bella's a double-crossing . . ." She stopped herself and regained her composure. "When my business here is done and the house closed, I'll find her."

"What business could be so important that it would stop you hunting down someone who wronged you?" I asked, knowing Amy had no chance of catching up with Bella, not the "new Bella" I'd met in the vault.

"It's nothing to do with you," she replied.

"If you would sit down, Amy." I gestured to a nearby chair. "It's what Arthur would have wanted."

Amy scoffed at the mention of Arthur but did as she was asked.

"Is this going to take long? I have a busy diary." Franklin drummed his fingers on the arm of his chair.

I stood in front of the fireplace and watched Carole, Franklin, Phil, and Amy settle down for the talk.

"Thank you all for coming," I began. "I understand you don't normally have a talk at these . . . meetings, but then, I also know that normally there are a number of 'individuals' at these weekend events."

Franklin shuffled in his seat at the mention of the "individuals."

"This weekend is an anomaly, isn't it?" I went on. "Considering the owner, Lord Metcalf, has been dead for over two weeks and no one is here to trade. No, everyone is here to get something, which was Arthur's plan all along. I knew from the very beginning that Arthur wanted me to attend this weekend to find a murderer. He said so in his letter. A letter he could've sent to me or given to Carole or his executor. But instead he left it at the village tearoom, knowing Carole and I would end up there if we went to Franklin's office. Arthur had planned everything because he knew he was being watched. He knew he had been betrayed."

Franklin looked worried and tried to catch Amy's eye. Phil scanned each of them one by one. Carole sat with a smile on her face watching it all unfold.

"Arthur lured you all here," I continued. "He offered Giles the chance of retrieving the Martin Brothers bird. A way for Franklin to settle the Metcalf estate quickly. Although perhaps he didn't know quite how much you like making deals on the side, Franklin." I nodded at his watch.

Franklin glared at me.

Carole shuffled forward in her seat.

"For Bella it was the lure of the original cuneiform tablets." I saw Amy bristle at the mention of Bella's name. "Yes, you didn't know who Bella really was, did you, Amy? She lured your brother into a relationship and then got all the information she needed, feeding it back to Arthur."

Amy squeezed the arm of the dining chair. "This is none of your business."

I had no intention of stopping. I was over being told what I could and could not say. Carole was right, this was actually quite fun. "Bella was with your brother to find out what she could about the 'banks'—how to get in and out of them. She played you, and you weren't even strong enough to go and sort her out."

Amy shuddered with rage. "My brother was a stupid fool."

"'Was' is a word in the past tense. Do you know something we do not?" I asked.

Amy didn't look in any way remorseful. Her eyes flickered toward the lake, and I understood why I hadn't noticed the ducks before. The reeds normally hid the banks of the water.

"Do you know, I've never seen the reeds on the lake bent like that," I said. "It almost looks like something has been dragged through them."

Amy sprang to her feet. "Your games are over. Hand over my phone and leave my house. You're no longer welcome here."

I turned to Franklin. "When you entered the vault, did you know something was wrong? Did you see that the items inside the boxes didn't match the photographs on top of them? Is that why you took all the pictures off the tops and threw them in the corner?"

Franklin pulled his cuff down over his Rolex. "I don't understand what this has to do with you? You shouldn't even be here."

"Amy gave you a lucrative way out, didn't she? You're both hoping no one realizes the items in the boxes are fakes."

Franklin went a paler shade of white. "This has nothing to do with me. I didn't kill anyone. I'm leaving. My business here is concluded."

"Hand me the phone and see yourselves out," Amy snarled.

I smiled at Carole; everything was coming together. I pulled out the lost phone and felt for the photograph in my pocket, the one I'd just collected from the drawer in the dining room. It wasn't the same as the one I had seen last night but it was good enough.

I dialed the most recent number on the call log.

A muffled phone started to ring.

49

"Sometimes your instinct is all you have, Freya. To act on your
instincts takes absolute faith in yourself."

—Arthur Crockleford

Everyone in the hall looked around except one person. Amy caught
my eye, fury etched into her mouth, and I knew I was right.

"Aren't you going to answer your phone?" I asked.

"I've got two phones. What of it?" She reached into her purse to
silence the phone, then relaxed back in her chair, trying to look casual.

I've proved my first point; now for the next one.

"That is a plausible explanation ... except it's strange that you would
be messaging with yourself, isn't it?" I studied the cuneiform tablet in
my hand and then placed it gently down on the table in the center of the
room. The only sound was the stoneware touching the mahogany table.
Questioning eyes rested on me.

I turned to my aunt to explain. "Around a year ago Amy, knowing her
father's health had deteriorated and the family business was in trouble,
returned to the family home. She might have sold the Copthorn Manor
furniture collection and the family silver, but the photographs inside
the silver frames were placed in a drawer in the dining room. Last night
she saw me looking at one and got worried. That didn't make sense at the
time because I was only looking at a photo of her father in his office and
a Martin Brothers bird. About half an hour ago I went back for another

268

look in daylight and discovered their charred remains in the fireplace. However, I searched the drawer again and found another one which had been tucked away at the back. This photograph showed just what an exceptional collection this old house used to hold and some people who used to live here." I looked at Amy. "Arthur saw what was happening here, didn't he?"

"Enough!" spat Amy, heading for the door.

Phil blocked her way. "My friend hasn't finished. Please sit down." There was something in the way he held himself, his feet firmly planted on the flagstone floor with his shoulders squared, that gave Amy pause.

"There were some beautiful examples of Gillows and Chippendale furniture along with a lot of British and European masters. . . ."

"There was no money left—something had to be done," said Amy.

Franklin frowned, and I said, "That's not true, is it, Franklin? When Arthur came to visit Lord Mark Metcalf, he was asked to be an executor, wasn't he?"

Franklin hung his head.

I continued, "It didn't sit right with me that Arthur came into your office and started booking moving vans and telling everyone what would happen this weekend. Until I realized he must have had some authority. Lord Metcalf loved his collection and he believed that it was still intact. He didn't care that most of it had been probably acquired on the black market or stolen by Giles. He probably wanted his treasures sold to other collectors who would appreciate them—but when Arthur arrived here he saw the truth of the situation. Arthur took the deal Lord Metcalf offered—make sure the collection and the other items stored in the vault went to the right homes, and in return he freed Arthur from his service, telling him where the items of blackmail were so that when the vault was opened, Arthur could retrieve them. Perhaps Arthur guessed the items in the vaults had also been switched out and thought that by having Franklin send them without Amy knowing, those 'individuals' would also discover the truth and come after any Metcalfs."

I wasn't going to mention the journals' role in the negotiation.

Tires rumbled down the drive outside, and then a car door slammed shut.

It's time.

Phil took a few steps toward the front door.

I put up my hand. "If you could stay with us for a moment and wait for them to arrive."

He nodded, but stayed by the door.

"That better be Bella you have lured back here. I have a bone to pick with her," said Amy, shifting to the edge of her seat.

"It was these messages that gave some of it away." I faced the front door and called, "Come on in."

The sound of footsteps echoed on the stone steps, along with the skittering of paws.

Then Harry walked into the main hall, Harley beside him on a lead.

"What's going on? Where's the phone?" The meek and feeble Harry from Arthur's funeral reception was gone.

Harley started barking as soon as he saw Carole. "Harley! Oh, my darling boy!" Harry let go of the lead and Carole flung herself at the delighted Harley, who greeted her with a bottom-wiggling tail wag as she enveloped him in a bear hug.

Amy glared at Harry. "I said I would deal with it. Leave."

"Shut up," snapped Harry. "I need my phone. You said the gardener had it."

I turned to Carole to explain. "I saw one text and it all began to make sense. The text was just six numbers: 120908."

Carole gasped.

Phil shook his head. "I don't understand. What does that mean?"

"Those numbers are the alarm code from the shop. I imagine Harry got the code off Arthur at some point and texted it to his mother on the night of the murder, perhaps in case something went wrong."

"What?" screeched Franklin at Harry. "You swore you didn't know it. Wait, they're related?"

Harry shrugged. "Back in your box, fool."

"He couldn't let anyone know he had the code as it would have shown he could've entered the shop at any time." I held up the phone. "The messages on here are between Amy and Harry." I met Harry's eye and then looked at the photograph in my hand. "This is a family photo. There is a little boy on Amy's lap no more than two years old, but the eyes are very much Harry's." I showed the picture to the room. "I imagine you searched the shop, and once you didn't find the books there you offered to dog sit Harley hoping to find them at my aunt's house," I said.

Harry didn't reply.

I wasn't going to stop until I had said it all out loud, as Arthur had wanted me to. "Once I realized who the other number belonged to, I began to see everything clearly. Amy would've been worried about Arthur being close to her father, especially when she'd planned to sell the collection on her return. It made sense that she would place someone close to Arthur to watch him." I stared at Harry. "Of course, you used a different last name—your father's?—to avoid Arthur discovering who you truly were. Did you see Arthur writing the books, or did Amy find out when she overheard Arthur and her father talk that day?"

No one answered me.

"Either way, Harry was in a position to find those books. It was your insistence that you saw a Martin Brothers bird, however, that was your biggest mistake." I cocked my head at him. "Did you hear your mother talk about a very valuable Martin Brothers bird in Vault Four and think it would be a good item to place in Arthur's hands to insist his death was a burglary? You couldn't have known what that bird meant to me. And you didn't know the bird in Vault Four was a broken one."

"Shut up." Harry stepped toward me. "Or I'll shut you up."

I was getting under his skin. "At the beginning, I thought there were two birds, but there was only ever one. A broken one that Giles killed Asim with, and the pieces were then used by Lord Metcalf as an item of blackmail to keep his son in line. I imagine it was Amy who was sent to follow us in Cairo?" I turned to Amy.

"Giles was a mama's boy who couldn't keep it together after she died," said Amy.

"He was a liability," said Harry.

"And that's why you killed him and dumped his body in the lake?" I asked. "And you staged the shop to look like Arthur fell down the stairs by accident."

With lightning speed, Harry pulled out a gun with what I presumed was a silencer on the end. A small smile of pride touched the corners of his lips.

"All Arthur had to do was tell me where the journals were. Then he starts smashing things. . . ." He backed toward the front door.

Clare ran in and froze when she saw the gun. Then Phil withdrew his gun. "FBI. Put the gun down!"

"You've been told," said Amy, pulling out a gun of her own and pointing it at me. "You can't prove any of this." She held the weapon with both hands and widened her stance. She had done this before.

I dove toward Carole and pulled her behind her chair.

"It's time," Amy said to Harry. "Anyone here going to stop us?"

"Yes," said Phil.

Harry raised his gun. The *pop* of the silencer sent Phil crumpling to the floor.

Clare ran toward him. Cold, blood-draining dread crashed into me. *Is he dead?*

Some hurried toward the door, others toward Phil.

The moments that followed were a blur of panic. Carole and I hurtled toward Phil to help Clare.

I looked around but Amy and Harry were nowhere to be seen.

Silence.

Is he breathing?

Phil coughed and everyone breathed in relief. "Bulletproof vest," he murmured. "Still hurts like hell." He rested his head back on the floor.

Not long after, the sound of car tires screeching on the driveway echoed in the hall.

"Amy and Harry are getting away," said Carole.

"Phone the local police," said Phil, trying to stand.

"So, it was Harry in the car last night?" asked Carole.

"I believe it was." I helped Phil to the nearest chair. "After I found the phone, I remembered a dog barking in the distance when I called out for Amy."

Harley was probably in Harry's car, but I thought it best not to emphasize in front of Carole that the dog had been driven around Suffolk on a stormy night by a murderer.

"I assume Harry must have gone into the kitchen to find his mother, he scared her, and that's why we heard her scream. In the darkness he lost his phone. I imagine Amy had stored the paintings—the ones Clare saw loaded into a car—near the kitchen, which is why she was uneasy that evening: not sitting to eat, following Clare around to make sure Clare didn't see what she was doing. Leaving by the broken back door, Amy quickly loaded the car with the paintings and decided to search our cottage for the journals while we were all distracted. After Harry had driven off, he discovered his phone was missing, but by that point I'd already picked it up."

Carole rose and, without a word, enfolded me in a bear hug. "I knew you would get to the bottom of it all. Thank you, my darling girl, thank you. We must get back home. And *gosh*, Harley has been looked after by Arthur's murderer, and he will need *so* much therapy to get over it."

We both turned to where Harley was sitting and staring adoringly at Carole, his tail thumping on the carpet.

50

"Always be ready for the next grand adventure."

—Arthur Crockleford

Carole

Carole placed a steaming cup of tea in Freya's hands and settled down into the director's chair next to her. May was one of her very favorite months and Freya was her favorite person. She was glad Freya was home for a while.

Carole firmly believed painful things needed to be faced with your shoulders straight and your lungs full of air, but it was equally important to allow your heart to break—that showed true courage.

Arthur had promised her that he would make things right. He'd come back from Cairo a shadow of himself, and it had taken Carole a lot of pestering to get a sliver of information out of him—it was clear he hadn't told her everything. He had certainly never said he was being blackmailed with Freya's scarf.

Freya had been young and impulsive and keeping her out of it had seemed like the right decision. Carole just hadn't realized how much influence James had over her niece until Freya was married and pregnant.

There are seasons in life, and back then Freya had entered one that needed to be embraced.

Carole loved her grandniece, Jade. She was a firecracker, but she was grown, and now it was Freya's time to shine.

"What a weekend we've had," said Carole.

"Are you going to tell me how much you knew about Copthorn Manor?" Freya munched on a chocolate-chip cookie. "How much Arthur told you?"

The afternoon sun warmed Carole's cheeks and she closed her eyes, lifting her chin. Freya was always so full of questions, but Carole had no intention of divulging all she knew—where would be the fun in that? It was clear there were more adventures to come, and at her age she wanted to embrace each moment. She would make herself important to each hunting trip—she felt like after a few weeks to rest and recuperate she might mention a cruise.

"Do you think those criminal 'individuals' who had their original antiques swapped for fakes will catch up with Amy and Harry?" asked Carole. "I do hope so."

"I'm sure they will sooner or later. Phil told me he was still acting as the gardener when the police showed up to dredge the lake. They found Giles. It would've taken both Amy and Harry to get him into the lake, and I'm still not sure which of them actually pulled the trigger. There is a hope that forensics will tie the bloodstained sweatshirt to Amy or retrieve the bullets."

Carole nodded. "Well, that's that, then. Let's go check on the chickens." She reached over and squeezed Freya's hand. "When the London house sells, you can stay here for as long as you like, until you decide what to do next. There's always the shop Arthur left us."

"I've been thinking about the shop. It's a big space: perhaps we could also sell some books? And we could do coffee. . . ."

Carole shook her head. She couldn't think about such things yet. She changed the subject. "Have you heard from FBI Phil?"

"Only regarding work," replied Freya.

Carole winked at her. She didn't believe for one moment that it was about work.

To prove her point Freya pulled out her phone and showed Carole a text from Phil. *If you ever want to get back to hunting, give me a call.*

"That Phil, he's quite handsome, don't you think?" Carole raised an eyebrow at Freya.

"I see what you're doing. Phil's a good connection, that's all. He sent me a contact in an art-and-antique insurance firm, Scotland Yard Art and Antiques Unit, and so on. I have some thinking to do." Freya breathed deeply and Carole copied her, inhaling the apple-blossom scented air.

She watched Freya rise and walk down the garden toward the rolling hills and grazing cattle. It wouldn't be long before Freya was back to hunting—it was what she had always been happiest doing, and now there was nothing stopping her.

Dew seeped into Carole's sneakers and she looked down at the overgrown lawn at her feet. An unexpected wave of grief at Arthur's passing came hurtling over her.

"Arthur, you old rogue," said Carole. "The grass is getting long. What will I do without you?" She allowed a tear to form and flow down her cheek while Freya crouched to collect some wild poppies that had grown through the rewilded lawn. "I wish you were here to see how well she's done."

Carole wiped her face and decided to get out her mid-century Royal Copenhagen vase for the flowers Freya was collecting. She was old enough to remember her mother buying it brand-new in a shop while on vacation in Denmark. It would be Freya's one day and Carole knew how much Freya would treasure it—it was a family heirloom now.

Harley sauntered toward her, carrying his favorite ball. "Let's put the kettle on and get you a bone. I know you're still deeply traumatized after I left you with Harry the murderer, but I shall do whatever it takes to make it up to you." Harley dropped the ball and barked for her to throw it.

Carole threw it in Freya's direction.

"Arthur, I'll miss you more than you can imagine, but thank you for bringing her home, even if it's just for a while. I'm not sure you would like the changes she has been talking about for the shop, but we can't be stuck in the past, can we? That never did anyone any good."

51

"At the end of the day, it's our actions that define us."

—Arthur Crockleford

Bella

Bella stood on the deck of the Stena Line ferry and watched England fade into the fog. Wind whipped at her, and she held on to the railing. By the time land was out of sight, she knew she was free—free from that murderous family and their controlling ways. Below her was a van filled with items to sell or return that would keep her going for quite some time.

It was a shame about Arthur. As always, he'd been right. Freya, it turned out, really did know her stuff and was a bit of a hound dog when it came to getting to the bottom of things. Bella had no doubt Freya had realized who Harry really was.

Bella had seen Harry with his mother at a party in London last winter but had kept her distance. There was something wrong about him—he was like his uncle Giles but with brains, a dangerous combination. On her first night at Copthorn Manor, Giles had mentioned that his nephew Harry had helped to carry Arthur's coffin, which "was a stupid thing for Amy to allow him to do." Bella had put the pieces together.

She pulled her scarf around her, a beautiful vintage Hermès she had found lying around somewhere, and buttoned up her coat. The Hook of Holland would take another six hours to get to, and by then she would have convinced the drivers of the van to hand over the keys or perhaps slipped them something. Either way she would be disembarking in the Netherlands with everything she needed to start again. Bella was well practiced at fresh starts.

Leaving the deck, she retreated inside to find the bar and have a celebratory glass of champagne. She settled on a bar stool looking out at the sea and the darkening sky, the motion of the boat reminding her of the next adventure Arthur had planned. By the time she had finished her glass she'd decided to keep her word and help Freya out a little.

Inside Bella's handbag was a new phone, and she dialed one of the many numbers she had memorized. "Hello, it's Susan Jones here. I was wondering if you needed another expert for your antiques cruise in the autumn?" She'd enjoyed perfecting her posh, upper-middle-class accent. "Wonderful, I'll send you her details."

Satisfied, Bella pulled out her cabin key and went to change into something more suitable. Perhaps she would choose a blond wig this time.

Those van drivers don't know what's about to hit them.

She smiled to herself. She really did like her job.

52

"Every time an antique passes through our hands, we become part of its story."

—Arthur Crockleford

Freya

Crockleford Antiques Shop was bathed in late-afternoon light when I placed my keys in the front door and opened it. I could have been sixteen again, but I wasn't, and I didn't want to be. I punched in the newly updated alarm code, pulled back the curtains, and switched on the lights. A cloud of dust engulfed me and I hooked the door open to let in some fresh air.

Carole and I had gone to Arthur's grave together. I'd left her arranging the flowers, knowing she liked to have a cry on her own.

I stood in the middle of the shop and wondered where to start. It had been four months since Copthorn Manor, a month since my home was sold and I'd squeezed all my possessions into Carole's spare bedroom, and three days since I decided to open the shop again.

The shop, once the gateway to my love of antiques and antiquities, was now my future. My path was now as clear as the blue skies above the rolling Dedham Vale fields. Arthur had done what he'd promised and given me a way back into a world I'd desperately missed. He knew that in directing me to retrieve my bloodstained scarf he was also drawing me back into the hunt. It was why he'd left me the journals, instead of giving them to the FBI. Each step I'd taken into my past had allowed me to walk simultaneously toward a new life.

Clever, Arthur.

Arthur was in every object I saw before me. He had handpicked each antique, mainly because he liked it himself, and he wanted to be surrounded by things he admired. I walked over to the grand mahogany desk and pulled out the George IV library chair—the casters were well-oiled and moved easily—and settled down on the red leather cushion. Running my hands down the carved arms, I relaxed into the cane back. Arthur had loved this chair and I could see why. It was probably out of fashion, but as Arthur would say, "We buy an antique because we love it, love its history, its story. We want it in our home, so to hell with what the fashionistas think."

A breeze swept in and picked up even more dust. I opened the first drawer of the desk and flicked through the papers inside. Fond memories of Arthur trickled in, and I didn't crush them with anger as I once would have. This shop had been my favorite haven from the world, at a time when a newly delivered auction catalogue brought with it the excitement of a treasure waiting to be discovered.

"Oh, Arthur, you placed so much faith in me to finish what you started," I whispered to the walls. "If only you were here to see there was a sort of justice for Asim. And there will be justice for you too. I wish you were here to talk it all through with me."

I stood and ran my fingers along the dust-covered bookshelf behind the desk. It made me remember the last journal—the empty journal.

"Why an empty one?" I asked the deserted shop.

But I knew in my heart what Arthur was telling me. He was giving me a blank page to write my own guide. He was telling me to hunt again.

A lump built in my throat and my eyes stung. I breathed deeply, pushing down the guilt.

Your journals are called the Antique Hunter's Guide. But my hunting hasn't been as straightforward—your guide led me on quite an adventure.

I picked up the two reproduction vases on the central table and carried them into the kitchen. Harry's first mistake had been thinking that no one would notice he'd swapped them. Arthur had broken the original ones on purpose, hoping that Carole would realize.

"Thank you," I murmured. "I'm so sorry I didn't get to say that in person. Thank you for all you taught me and for protecting me."

"Hello?"

I jumped. A delivery man was standing in the doorway.

"Are you open?" he asked.

"Um." I didn't know what to say. Carole wouldn't hear about opening the shop just yet. "I'm afraid not. I'm just checking in on the place."

"Are you Freya Lockwood?"

"I am."

"I have this for you." He handed me an envelope. "You'll need to sign for it." I signed, and as he turned to leave, he pointed at two brass Art Nouveau candlesticks on the far shelf. "They look pricey, but I bet my wife would love them on her dinner table."

"When we're open again, I'll let the post office know, and I'll give you a good price on them. They look more expensive than they are," I said reassuringly, knowing that they weren't an item of any note.

"Excellent, but we'll let my wife think that they're worth a fortune." He smiled warmly back at me, then left.

I opened the envelope and pulled out two tickets and a letter.

Dear Ms. Lockwood,

You have been recommended to us as an expert for the antiques cruise to Jordan . . .

"Your legacy wasn't what I expected, Arthur." *Is this the same cruise Bella mentioned?* "Never going to leave it to chance, were you?" I laughed.

The dust caught in the back of my throat and I went into the kitchen to find a glass of water and a cloth and polish. Back in the shop, I opened the first cabinet and picked up a frosted-glass flower, recognizing it at once as a small Lalique anemone sculpture. I sprayed a little polish on the cloth, and the shop filled with a sweet, musky scent that had always brought back memories of my teenage years.

Carole swished through the shop door. "Oh, you're cleaning?" Her silk tiered dress caught the breeze and lifted outward. She pulled it into submission and looked inside the cabinet. "Wonderful idea. I'll help."

That was how we spent the day, and the next one—putting everything in order. By the fourth day my desire to return treasured items to their rightful owners had been reignited. I knew it was time to start hunting again. It was what I was always meant to do.

ACKNOWLEDGMENTS

For over ten years I have dreamt of walking into my local bookshop and seeing my book on a shelf. Without the people mentioned below I would never have been able to do so.

To my agent, Hannah Todd, your never-ending enthusiasm, encouragement, humor and industry knowledge have made this journey everything I hoped it would be. And thank you to the whole "powerhouse" team at Madeline Milburn Literary, TV and Film Agency, Maddy, Giles, Liane-Louise, Georgina, Valentina, Amanda and Hannah Ladds.

To my amazing editors Natalie Hallak at Atria and Sarah St. Pierre at Simon & Schuster Canada along with Francesca Pathak at Pan Macmillan in the UK. Thank you all so much for your faith in this book and in me. I'm so very grateful for your guidance, vision, and warmth. This book was most definitely a team effort and it's the best team!

A huge thank you to the wider team at Atria: Lindsay Sagnette, Elizabeth Hitti, Dayna Johnson, Gena Lanzi, Laywan Kwan, Annette

Sweeney, Yvonne Taylor, Stephanie Evans, Paige Lytle, Shelby Pumphrey, Lacee Burr, Nicole Bond. And at Simon & Schuster Canada: Mackenzie Croft and Cayley Pimentel—thank you all for getting this book into the hands of readers.

Sophia Bennett, Caroline Green, Karen Ball, Becca Langton, Sophie McKenzie, Tamsyn Murray and Holly Domney, thank you for guiding this book in the right direction from the very beginning. Roisin Heycock, Nicola Penfold, Lui Sit, Ali Penny, Tania Tay, Annette Caseley, Catherine Whitmore, everyone in the Furies Writing Club—thank you for all the laughter and support. Ali Clack, for our Dedham Boathouse coffees throughout the seasons that have kept me sane, kept me writing, and kept me laughing—and for being my only beta reader. Jessa Maxwell, thank you for answering all my panicked author messages in the middle of the night when I hadn't checked the time before pressing send—I'm thrilled we turned to crime at the same time! Clare Flaxen, I don't think I would have even started writing this book without your faith in me.

To Nanny Frances who nurtured my love of reading and knows what this publication means to me. My sisters, Sam, Tanya, Tasha, and Kirsty and brother Tom. My childhood friends Virginie, Kat, Katy, and Lizzy who have all been with me every step of the way. John Wainwright for all your support and who checked random antiques facts in this book—if something is incorrect it is down to me! Mike and Magda Lawrence for your friendship. . . and the office space!

To my husband, Billy, for your everlasting faith in me and my writing. To my children Aria and Leo, when you hold this book in your hands, I want you to know that dreams can come true—dream big! To Jane Peters for being our very own M C Beaton expert and an honorary family member.

The marvelous Aunt Carole character in this book was inspired by the truly extraordinary ex-Bond girl, Carole Ashby—you are like an aunt to me and thank you for filling my childhood with stardust.

My parents, Judith Miller and Martin Miller, never got to see this book in print but they inspired every page and every character. My childhood was filled with antiques and books, and I am forever grateful. My mother helped me so much with the antiques in this series—we had such fun deciding which ones we could put in—it is a time I will always treasure. I am exceptionally proud of what they both achieved and I will miss them both, always.

To you, dear reader, thank you for reading.

ABOUT THE AUTHOR

Cara started working life in publishing as an editorial assistant for her mother, Judith Miller, on the *Miller's Antiques Price Guide* and as a researcher for the *Antique Hunter's Guide to Europe* and then went into hospitality and events. After she had children, she decided to follow her long-held dream of becoming an author and took time out to concentrate full-time on her writing.

Cara lives in a medieval cottage in Dedham Vale, Suffolk with her family.

Visit her at www.clmillerauthor.com.